GOING HOME AGAIN

HOWARD WALDROP

ST. MARTIN'S PRESS ❧ NEW YORK

For the people who waved good-bye in Austin
and the people who said, "Oh. It's you."
when I pulled into the Northwest:
Dave and Hali, John and Eileen
and Rhonda (thanks for the 5lb tub
of peanut butter).

Library of Congress Cataloging-in-Publication Data

Waldrop, Howard.
    Going home again / Howard Waldrop.
        p.   cm.
    Includes bibliographical references.
    ISBN 0-312-18589-8
    I. Title.
    PS3573.A4228G65   1998
98-13555   813'.54—dc21
                                                   CIP

First published in Australia by Eidolon Publications

First U.S. Edition: July 1998

10 9 8 7 6 5 4 3 2 1

Table of Contents

Some Varieties of Approach Toward an Introduction to the Fiction of Howard Waldrop, or . . . Three Shots of Sour Mash and a Beer Back

Lucius Shepard

In addressing the problem of how to introduce the fiction of Howard Waldrop, one seeks a non-traditional opening, something on the order, say, of a cross between "God so loved the world he gave his only begotten son . . ." and "Sumbitch, that little sucker's alive!", statements that alternately speak to the quality of Howard's unique talent, and to his equally unique style of career-building, which causes him to produce his wonderful stories at a rate approaching that of an oyster's manufacture of a pearl, a strategy that earns him slightly more per annum than the aforementioned mollusc.

No, no, no! Much too formal. And too pompous by half. How about something along the lines of a quasi-fiction . . .

Cornbread Jesus, every twitch of his bulging biceps causing Aryan Nation tattoos to quiver like agitated spiders, strolled up to the equally muscular Jerome "Mighty Boo Ya" Labonte in the yard on Jerome's first day in the joint and held out a sheaf of manuscript paper.

"Fuck's that?" said Jerome, curling his hands into fists like black cannonballs.

"That, fish, is Howard Waldrop's unwritten prison story, 'The Chattahoochie Mysterians', as channeled by my special friend Kiki. Read it, and you just might qualify to survive in my walls."

Bemused, and not in the least afraid, Jerome accepted the manuscript, sat down in the shade created by the presence of an

Afro-American convict even larger than he, and began reading. Before long he was smiling. Soon after that he was laughing.

"Thass some dope shit, man!", Jerome told Cornbread Jesus on returning the story. "Specially the part 'bout the Japanese movie star bitch. Y'know, where she gets stuck in the warden's escape pod with the incubus Bill Clinton. I'm down with that motherfucker."

Nah, that's not it, either. That's just good old-fashioned bullshit. Hmmm. Lemme see. What about something personal . . .

The first time I met Howard Waldrop I was coming down from acid, standing outside Eileen Gunn-and-John Berry's place in Seattle. Some time earlier I'd entered the house, but blurts of high-pitched laughter and disconnected conversation, tangled skeins of light, and a peculiar ochre stain that appeared to be spreading through the air proved too much of an assault on my senses, and I retreated to the comforting solidity of a gray car parked beneath a smallish tree that displayed no tendency whatsoever to converse or laugh. I leaned against it, happily sipping on a 40-ouncer, and engaged in a whimsical appreciation of the exterior of the Gunn-Berry manse, picturing demented faces poking out every window, arms waving like those of victims in a fire, and watching the roof as it billowed gently with the rhythm of a sleeping man's breath.

Mosquitoes, their crimson eyes aglitter, fangs like scimitars, orbited me and sang.

Several minutes after I had taken up my stand, a solitary tight-faced woman wearing an ankle-length dress approached from the west, spotted me lurking in tree-shadow, and crossed the street to avoid harassment or worse.

A police siren corkscrewed through the distance, heightening the moment for us both.

I considered trying once again to enter the house, but decided against it.

Eventually the front door opened and several individuals descended the stairs and came toward me. There was something grimly purposeful and posse-like about their approach, the way they fanned out across the lawn, half a dozen surly female deputies preceded by their sheriff, a shortish, solidly constructed man with brown hair and a wide, thin mouth. That was the first thing I noticed about Howard—that his mouth was (or appeared to be) extremely wide and thin. It put me in mind of an illustration in one of my childhood dinosaur books that was intended to portray the earliest forerunner of the amphibians. Howard's mouth had the exact same slightly goofy, straight-line-gone-crookety flatness of attitude that Whateversaurus-it-was had exhibited. And his stare, essaying, regarding, as if measuring me by a standard based on number-of-bites-it-takes-to-consume, but friendly, you know . . . Well, it kind of reminded me of that old illustration, too. Maybe, I thought, this was because Howard spent so much time in waders, with cold bright water rushing between his legs in an eternal perfect flush toward Mother Mystery's Tiger-striped Mountain, Oso, and the Fortress of Imperiled Philosophies . . . maybe because of this he had achieved some sort of oneness with the amphibian class.

We didn't speak long. Unused to conversation after twelve hours at warp 16, I was reduced to blithering. I'm quite sure that Howard said to himself, "Damn, this man's on drugs. Gonna be no talking to him." And so let himself be called away to some more rewarding exchange.

It was not until years later I realized that his handshake had indelibly impressed onto my palm the emblem of the Red Indian Montpeliers, thus weaving my fate inextricably into the great design of that mystic brotherhood about whose terrible rituals and eccentric goals I am forbidden by oath to speak.

Well, I'm not too sure where that's going. More blithering, no doubt. Perhaps something cryptically metaphorical would be better . . .

Waldrop, a man to whom truth has the alchemical valence of a red goat dressed in a Chicago Bulls sweatshirt sitting on a hillside, watching a burning city, moves like a technicolored shadow through the literary underclass of science fiction, either its first saint or its most relevant madman.

. . . or I guess I could whip up a little academic souffle:

The post-modernist gloss of obscure plottery that imbues Waldrop's ouvre with its cultist appeal; the matter-of-fact eccentricity of his characters, so redolent of—yet at the same time so philosophically distinct from—the anti-fictions of Robbe-Grillet; the logical dissonances expressive of the incomprehensible theories of Jacques Lacan: these all serve to mask the energies of an in-the-grain American moralist.

Somehow I don't believe Howard would appreciate this sort of thing. As an antidote, let's try a tabloid approach:

BABY JESUS DOLLS SPEAK SCI-FI WRITER'S NAME

(Calexico, California). Shortly before ten p.m. yesterday evening, the entire display of Talking Baby Jesus dolls in the window of the Calexico Walmart began as one to pronounce the name of award-winning science-fiction writer Howard Waldrop. The dolls, designed as elements of a Christmas Madonna-and-Child set, were manufactured by Yaweh Toys, a division of minister Jerry Falwell's GodSpeaksThruMe Corporation. They had been programmed to say, "Ma-Ma", but hundreds who filed by the display testified that the dolls were actually saying, "How-wah, Wah-drop".

When interviewed, Falwell suggested that a computer chip defect might be responsible, but did not rule out the possibility of Satanic influence.

"Considering the proliferation of godless fantasies by men like Waldrop," Falwell said, "something of this sort was bound to happen."

Then, of course, there's the cinematic:

Howard Waldrop is . . .

TROUTMASTER

But Can He Tame the
Gilled Monster of the
Stillaguamish . . .

Maybe a testimonial to Howard's compassion and heroism:

> "It was purely horrible. The man was covered with frogs! You
> couldn't even see him no more. Just this big pile of frogs hoppin'
> up and down, slitherin' and squirmin'. We was all backed up
> against that ol' Frosty Root Beer sign they left rustin' out back
> the drive-in. I was terrifed, and some of the women was down on
> their knees and hollerin' to Jesus. I don't know what would have
> happened Howard hadn't come along. He just walks up to the
> frogs and tells 'em to get their asses gone, and off they go . . . all
> except this teeny feller what's got hisself crushed beneath all the
> rest of 'em. Wellsir, Howard he don't hesitate an instant. He
> picks the sucker up in one hand, and then, real careful, like he's
> trying to fan a spark into a flame, he puts his mouth to that
> frog's mouth and goes to breathin' life back into its pulpy little
> lungs."

Honesty, I suppose, is always an option:

> There could scarcely be two more different writers than Howard
> and I. His lovingly meticulous approach toward the craft we
> both espouse is diametrically opposed to my passionate sloppiness.
> The results of our approaches, too, are markedly dissimilar. Yet
> I find myself turning time and again to his stories to experience
> the pleasure those differences provide.

Accurate, but hey, that's full-on boring, right? A slight enlargement of
the truth always makes for a more entertaining option:

> Waldrop's claim of being a man of humble means has lately
> been exposed as a fraud by the *Washington Post*. In an above-the-
> fold front page article the *Post* reveals that Waldrop, under the
> name of Dinshah P. Ghadiali, is the genius behind the best-
> selling love manual, "Your Thing, My Thing", hailed as a
> breakthrough by sex researchers around the world. Waldrop's
> inventive and foolproof techniques for maximizing the female
> orgasm (among them, the oftimes fatal method that he has labeled
> The Mandarin Gentleman) should make him an object of
> affection, if not one of veneration, to the women of Australia.

As you can plainly see, I have no gift for this. Introductions are best left, I should think, to professional introducers, those who pass their professional lives in contemplating such niceties of presentation. If it were up to me alone, I would simply say, "Hey, you oughta read this guy Waldrop? Pretty great". But that, albeit entirely in character, would not satisfy the requirements of the form.

So, having failed to create a proper intro, I'll plagiarize one. Some years ago in Honduras I was privileged to spend the evening at a performance by one of those tiny circuses that travel the length of the Caribbean littoral. The ringmaster, a shabby, bearlike man who looked to have tossed back more than a few shots of something strengthening, gave forth with a stentorian patter as we filed in, words I found memorable, and while they do not comment directly on the contents of this book, I feel they reflect upon its essence:

WELCOME, LADIES AND GENTLEMEN, TO THE CIRCO MARAIMBOMBO! WELCOME ALL! TONIGHT YOU WILL WITNESS THE MARTIAL ARTS WIZARDRY OF BILLY JACK COCHISE, MASTER OF THE KNIVES! THE BEAUTIFUL ALVINA WILL INITIATE YOU INTO THE MYSTERIES OF THE EAST, POPO THE CLOWN WILL CAUSE YOU TO WEEP WITH LAUGHTER! FREDO THE KING OF THE BEES WILL FIRST TERRIFY YOU, THEN CAUSE YOU TO QUESTION THE NATURE OF THE UNIVERSE ITSELF! AND LASTLY, LAS CHICAS DEL ORO, THOSE PERFECT CHILDREN OF THE AIR, WILL PERFORM AN EXOTIC DANCE! HURRY NOW, LADIES AND GENTLEMAN! ONLY THREE LEMPIRA! JUST THREE! FORGET YOUR FINANCIAL WORRIES, YOUR LOVER'S LATEST COMPLAINT! SET ASIDE ALL THE DEEP CONCERNS THAT SHADOW YOUR LIFE! PARK YOUR EXPECTATIONS AT THE DOOR AND PREPARE TO BE AMAZED!

Introduction

A lot has happened since we talked last (*Night of the Cooters*, 1991).

For one thing, I used to come to you from Texas. Now I'm coming to you from my rented shack in Oso, Washington, where I moved months ago.

After I donated all my books and papers to the Special Collections Library at Texas A&M University (because they'd been asking for 20 years . . .), went to Mississippi and Arkansas to see all my relatives *that* way, I drove 2,418 miles—awash to the gunwales with fishing gear, the manuscripts I'd be working on the rest of my life, and enough clothes to keep me decent and warm—in Chad Oliver's old 1985 Toyota wagon.

Chad's death was as big a reason as anything—it was like losing another Dad. (A nurse at one of the hospitals asked me if I were his son; "The one they don't talk about," I said.) I was going to move somewhere with trout, long before Chad's final illness; I'd had maps spread out all over the place for years.

See, Austin used to be the best and only place to live in Texas. I gave it 21 years. It used to be like a great small town; now it's just another jerkwater big city on the make. After a boom and a bust, they're looking for another boom to fix it all again. The city council there might as well be the L.A. Prosecutor's Office; they've screwed every pooch put before them for 16 years now.

So, essentially, I've gone from (theoretically) fishing while I look at pods of okra to (rhetorically) fishing while I look at pods of orca.

And, as the Beatles say, my life has changed in Oso many ways.

Oso has a general store, two part-time shake mills, a couple of nursery/antique stores and about 50 perpetual yard sales. It's the kind of place where guys drive to the store on their riding-mowers.

Why here? The river's open year-round. In the past it had one of the greatest salmon and steelhead runs in the Northwest (no longer, but signs look good for a comeback). And the North Fork of the Stillaguamish here is fly-fishing only for eight months of the year.

Is it Oz?

Sometimes it isn't even *Kansas*. Like, you couldn't fish for about a hundred days last year this side of the Cascades because of floods, mud, high water. When it's good, it's good; when it's bad, it's as bad as a bad Italian '60s SF movie. I'm a few miles from two other watersheds and, if worse comes to worse, I'll even fish in a lake.

Of course, it would be a lot better if I had a lot of money.

Which brings us to this book.

This is nine squeals against the void which is the world. It's the best stuff I've published since *Night of the Cooters*. It's pretty much the *only* stuff I've done since then, as a lot of the time you're not seeing has been spent on two novels, *I, John Mandeville* (twenty six years and still counting) and *The Moon World* (eight years and still counting).

This is *not* the way to make lots of money.

You'll also notice the stories in this book have afterwords (rather than introductions like my other three collections). Whether going from stories that need intros to ones that need afterwords is progress or devolution, I don't know. The stories stand alone, of course (all stories have to, or they're not stories; as I tell all the Clarion students, if it ain't on the page, you ain't got squat). I tell you the same things in the afterwords I used to in the intros: something about the writing, what process led to it—if *I* know—stuff I've come across in research; you know, writer stuff.

A couple of them I'd like you to jump into cold (smartie-farties will of course read the afterwords first) to see if you're as confused as some readers were on their initial appearances. You're on your own with the original, "Scientifiction", but then again, so was *I*.

This is the second try at this intro. The first one got so bitter even I had to quit.

There's a lot to be bitter about out there, but let's try to keep this short and bitter-sweet.

You absolutely cannot make a living writing short stories, even in SF and fantasy where there are five or six or seven magazines and God's own number of original and theme anthologies (great, if the theme is more than a gimmick *and* you've been wanting to do a story on the subject for years). Ergo, you have to write: a) novels; b) tv or movies; or c) comic books to make any kind of decent living (not that I even need a decent one) at it. I've done all three, some successfully, some not, but let that go. I'm essentially a short story writer, so I'll never make a living, so I don't live . . .

If you've got what it takes to do ten series novel tie-ins on something that shouldn't be a novelette in the first place, fire away. If you like committee work, join the PTA or write a movie and try to get it produced. If you're a third, fourth or fifth generation fanboy who grew up reading *nothing* but fourth, third or second generation comic-book writers, be my guest. (Although some individual novels, the movies *Matinee* and *Ed Wood*, and the *Watchmen* comic books—now more than a decade past— gave me some hope.)

George R. R. Martin, who's been doing movies and tv for 10 years but who has now gone back to writing Real Live Books again, is always going at me about muffed chances. Disney once took their comic books back from Gladstone, and were going to publish them themselves. I got the bibles—character designs, setting, background specs, etc.—for their line. And, as George said, "What did you do? You could use Mickey, Goofy, Donald, Daisy, Gyro Gearloose . . . What did you want to do? A team up of Bucky Bug—Disney never had a character called Bucky Bug!—and Horace Horsecollar!" (Steve Utley and I once wondered whether we could bring back DC's Rex, the Wonder Dog and Bobo, Chimp Detective. Don't laugh.)

But that's neither here nor there. ("Then where is it?" as Bogart said.) What I'm saying is, I'll keep writing this stuff as long as editors keep buying it and readers keep reading it. (All 6,435 of you, as it seems to indicate on the Final Royalty Statement on one of my *paperback* collections . . .)

I pretty much know what I'm doing by now (I just don't know how to do it, most times). But the stories, contrary to the popular notion, have gotten harder, not easier to do as time goes on. The last two or three of these have been like pulling teeth. I wouldn't have worked as hard digging a damn ditch as I did writing them.

That's because (he said, music up, stepping into the muted spotlight)

I pretty much refuse to take the easy way out *and* (nod of head, eyes down) I think you people should have to do between 40 and 50 percent of the work when you read a story. You got to, in Robert Mitchum's immortal words, bring *something* to the party. Even if it's incomprehension (you have to at least care to have not liked a story).

There, that wasn't so bad, was it? It's a hell of a lot better than that first one, which by the time I got to this point had already gone on for eight or ten more pages, carping and whining about the place of the indigent writer in American literature.

I've just finished Gore Vidal's *Palimpsest: A Memoir* (not as nasty as I wanted it to be by a long shot, but refreshingly candid about what he had to do to pay off a monster—in 1950—$9,000 mortgage on a mansion). Go pick up a copy of *Death in the Fifth Position*, by Edgar Box.

So what's a swell guy like me to do? Well, finish, *I, John Mandeville* and *The Moon World* (not that anybody over here in American publishing is excited about the prospect). Then I'll become a "hot property", you bet. Meanwhile I have to write stories to get the money to get the time to write novels . . .

One of the questions most frequently asked by people who should know better, and those who don't, is "What made you become a writer?"

There are the usual long answers, like: in my case, I didn't, I thought I was going to be an artist (there are stacks of old fanzines with art and covers, some good, some bad, some not even indifferent that testify to *that*, till some time around 1964 I realized I could write a little better than I could draw); and that the publication of the late Lin Carter's *The Wizard of Lemuria* (I can write better than *that!*) was the impetus for buckling down and *really* writing, though it took four years before I made any money—$35 Big Dollars!—at it; etc. etc.

Or, the short answer, always true: writing chooses you.

Or, in my case again: my doom was sealed long 'bout grandfather time, 1952, first grade. I'd been reading since age four, comic strips etc., no mean feat in 1950. (Now, because of *Sesame Street* and *Electric Company* and *Scholastic Rock*—shows produced when America was about as smart as it was ever going to get—any kid over three who can't read is a *yutz*.) Anyway, since I could already read—and do some math, which I hated, and which is what first grade was all about in those days—I got to help other kids, and when I got through with that, Mrs. Howard let me read.

Pantego Elementary School was six grades, six rooms, a cafeteria and the principal's office. Each grade had its own library in a bookcase. I went through the first grade one. Then I got to go to Mrs. Eddings' second grade one and read all *those*. Then Mrs. Johnson's third grade one— coming in while they were all out at recess; kids more than three feet high! gah!—and read all *those*. Then Mrs. Stewart's fourth grade library bookcase. I reached in and picked up a book: *The How and Why Club vol. 4*, or, to be precise (and what follows is due to the excellent sleuthing of Ms. Sally Shelton, paleontologist extraordinaire, who has the only copy I've ever seen other than a busted up one—missing the front stuff—I found in a Half-Price Books twenty years ago for 10¢), *The Scientific Living Series: The How and Why Club vol. 4*. Copyright © 1939 the L.W. Singer Company Syracuse Chicago Dallas. The authors are George Willard Frazier, Helen Dolman, Francis Shoemaker and Katherine Van Nuy. The illustrator is Guy Brown Wiser. (L.W. Singer no longer exists. It wasn't subsumed by another publisher. The copyright, if renewed, would have expired last year. It's strange, because such a backward place as Texas was then would buy almost *any* textbook, as long as it was cheap.)

I opened it, flipped through. Sections on bread mold, identifying birds, what causes an eclipse. Then I turned the page, and to the chapter "Jack Finds Some Fossils", (Shelton again: "How We Know Plants and Animals of Long Ago: Jack Finds Some Fossils".) It runs from page 128 to page 147. Jack visits a sheepherder to deliver some mail while visiting his uncle's ranch out west. Pictures of the sheepherder's wagon, Jack, the fossils of some bones. Then I turned to page 133, and saw, in shades of grey and pea-soup green, a sauropod.

The illustration was showing how big a brontosaurus (screw *apatasaur*) was. That's not what I saw. I saw a dinosaur standing behind a barn. I wanted one. It was but a short step (the next year) to Roy Chapman Andrews, *Unknown Island* on tv, *King Kong* (released in 1952), on to *The Enormous Egg*, later *Plutonia* by I. A. Obruchev, and so on and so forth.

I'm convinced that's what did it.

From the second I saw that illustration, my life was *this* one.

So it's Guy Brown Wiser's fault. He's probably dead and forgotten somewhere, too, like everybody who's led kids into lives of SF Fame and Glory.

Whew. I'm sitting here fairly drenched in nostalgia. It's a Monday. I've just written you people a story, and an afterword to it. It's raining and miserable, but it might bring some steelhead up the river, I've got $4.80 in the bank (I carried around a royalty check for a week for $1.92 because, till some more money came, I didn't have gas to get the 15 miles to the bank).

But what the hell, I should be used to it by now, after 28 years at it. Nine tries, then, against the roaring void.

Your pal,
Howard
Oso Washington
October 14, 1996

P.S.: As I say in one of the afterwords, life is still a song. (Sometimes it's a good one; sometimes it's "Doggie in the Window" or "(Everybody Get Down Tonight) Everybody Wang-Chung Tonight"; once or twice a century, it's "Good Vibrations" or "Eaten by the Monster of Love.") This collection coming out from St. Martin's Press is one good sign (after its limited wonderful edition from Eidolon Press of Perth, Australia); people beginning to pay me on time for my short stories is another.

And I caught and released a 14″ sea-run cutthroat yesterday whose back was as blue-green as the Indian Ocean.

And, except for the four days a couple of months ago when I, literally, lived on salmonberries picked off the riverbank, my career is taking off like a skyrocket.

The one in "The Marching Morons" . . .

—Sept 22, 1997

You *Could* Go Home Again

The Joint is Jumpin'

They had slipped their moorings at Ichinomaya, Japan in the early evening of September 15, 1940, amid the euphoric shouts of well-wishers, fresh from the Tokyo Olympics that had just ended.

Wolfe hadn't noticed the crowds. He'd arrived late, a couple of new shirts (specially tailored—the Japanese weren't used to six-foot-six men buying off their racks, and he'd had to get the address of a British men's shop from someone at the American Embassy) in one hand, his old suitcase and bulging, torn briefcase in the other, holding his coat, hooked by one thumb over his left shoulder. He'd barely made it; the boarding platform was being unbolted at the bottom as he ran up to it.

He'd been shown to his stateroom; felt a lurch as they got underway. Then he'd folded down the couch that made into an upper and lower berth, and had sprawled across the lower one and had slept for a little more than an hour.

He awoke near sunset. The bell in the dining salon was ringing. He was disoriented. Then memories of the last two weeks had come back to him; the Olympics, the crowds, being a giant once more (as he used to feel in America before the operation and the weight loss) in a world of Lilliputian Japanese.

He put on his robe, found the Gentlemen's washroom for his set of cabins, showered, then shaved, something he'd forgotten to do during the last two days of *bon voyage* parties.

He went back to his stateroom, made up the couch and changed for dinner. Then he laid his things out on the desk while sitting on the folding, backless stool which fit under it. (Wolfe was glad of that: he'd usually had to take the backs off chairs in the old days—his body had been so tall and thick, chairs had seemed like toys that cramped him, making him feel like a golliwog in some circus act.)

He went to the reading and writing room just after dinner (he'd had double portions of everything) and dashed off a postcard or two, which he knew he would forget about if he didn't do it then. He could have put them in the pneumatic tube that took them straight to the mailroom, but decided to take them there himself tomorrow. Instead, he read over the passenger list.

It was the usual kind for a trip going back to Europe and America from the Orient the long way, going west. Wolfe had traveled every possible way in his life: luxury liners, tramp steamers, ferries, airplanes, coal barges, buses, a thousand different trains, cars (after that National Parks thing—six thousand miles in twelve days with two guys that led up to the illness that almost killed him two years ago—he'd sworn never to ride in any automobile but a taxi cab again), bicycles, hay wagons, once even roller-skating for two miles with some kids when he lived in Brooklyn.

There were the usual two dozen nationalities on the manifest—lots of Americans, Brits, Frenchmen, Indians, Syrians, Swedes, Germans, a Russian or two (probably White), some Brazilians and Argentines, an Italian count, and several Japanese.

In all, there were 320 passengers and a crew of 142 on the first leg of this trip. Several would be leaving in India, more no doubt getting on there, going on to Egypt, then up to Italy, and the rest of the European stops.

As he read the list, a man with sergeant's chevrons on his R.A.F. uniform came into the writing salon, nodded, sat down and began scribbling on a small pad.

Wolfe heard music in the air. They must have cleared away the last of the dishes from the evening meal, the stewards would have pulled back the tables, and the band begun to play in the main salon. He finished the postcard in his (since the operation) much smaller and more controlled loopy scrawl. He looked at his watch. It had been an hour since he'd eaten. Time had a way of getting away from him lately.

He stood, nodded to the R.A.F. man, who gave him back a strange smile. The man was heavily tanned, though blondish; his eyes stood out like bright blue marbles in a brown statue. It reminded him of the face of one of the stone angels that used to stand on the porch of his father's shop in Asheville.

Wolfe checked his own reflection in the corridor mirror—brown suit, buff vest, white shirt. Thinning on top (he turned his head far to the left, smoothed the bit of hair that always stood at right angles over the scar from the brain operation), cheeks now a little sunken in a long wide face (three teeth removed, and seventy-five pounds of lost weight), eyes too big and bright. He pulled on the knot of his black tie with its Harvard Club tie tack, grimaced to make sure there was no food on his teeth, and went back to the main salon.

He eased his way through the few couples who stood talking at the doorway of the ballroom. Art Deco metal palms arched to each side of the opening, forming a heart-shaped portal in a glassine wall.

It was smoky inside. Candles were lit on the tables; waiters went back and forth between the chairs and the dimly-lit bar on the right side. Wolfe made his way toward it, where other men traveling alone, and a few women, stood watching the band.

Bars were always something Wolfe had liked in the old days.

The band—clarinet, banjo, violin, cornet, drums, bass and piano— were on a small raised platform. The unused piano looked dull and grey from the bar area. Probably the light, thought Wolfe. The band was in evening wear. They played "Marie" but, as no one was singing, it sounded thin. A spot for dancing had been cleared; no one was taking advantage of that, either.

"Bourbon and Coca-Cola," said Wolfe to the barman. That was one thing about a trip like this. Everyone was first-class: there were no passenger divisions, no one-deck-for-you-Mr-Average-Guy, the other for the Hoity-Toity. That was one reason Wolfe had chosen to travel this way.

He got his drink, turned, and leaned against the aluminum bar with his right elbow. He saw, with some discomfort, two women looking at him, talking back and forth. He knew, without a second glance, that they were asking each other whether that could be *him*; no, he's tall but too thin-looking, and much older than his photos. (The one on the jacket of his newest book had been taken two years ago, before the operation. Not that he didn't look bad enough then, he just looked differently, and worse, now.) Wolfe focused his attention toward the front of the salon. He'd had plenty of shipboard flings in his time. (The great love of his life, so they told him in those fuzzy first days at Johns Hopkins, had started on the *Berengaria* in 1926. To him it was only a skewed memory. When he had seen the woman, Aline, for the first time during his recovery, he had been puzzled. This woman—twenty years older than me, hard of hearing, hair going grey—was the love of my life?) But in the last two years, some memories had come back. (Wolfe sometimes viewed himself as standing on the far northern shore of Canada, looking out to sea, and occasionally an iceberg, heavy with remembrance and emotion, would drift toward him from the North Pole of Time, crash into him, immersing him in a flood of scents, thoughts, visions, from a past usually as closed off to him as if he were locked in a vault with no key.) He recalled some of the affair with Aline; the memories were fragmentary. He remembered fights as often as lovemaking, jealousy of her theater friends as well as the quiet afternoons in Paris hotels, an attempt of hers at what he first thought of as suicide, which wasn't.

Now, he was on his way to Germany to see another woman.

As he turned toward the band, Wolfe saw a huge light-skinned black man with a pencil-thin mustache sitting at a table near the front, deep in conversation with two other Negroes.

It was then that Wolfe realized how unobservant he had become. The last thing he would have thought was that the T. W. Waller on the passenger list was Fats.

Wolfe had seen him many times before. He dimly remembered trips to Harlem in the late twenties when he had still been an English instructor at Washington Square College. They'd gone to Connie's Club, where Waller was playing to packed houses. He'd had quite a following among the jazz-mad students. One night Wolfe had been surprised to hear Waller on the radio, singing some novelty tune. Then suddenly, he had been everywhere. While Wolfe had been struggling to be a playwright, Waller had three or four reviews or musicals running in the late twenties—and unlike other songwriters and composers, Fats had been right there every night playing the piano for the shows.

Wolfe had seen both movies Waller had made in the thirties. He lit another cigarette, signaled for another drink. The band finished its number, "Nagasaki", a corny tribute to the land they'd just left.

The bandleader—surprisingly, the banjo player—stepped up to the star-webbed microphone (there were loudspeaker boxes at the rear of the salon so people there could hear as well as those up front) and said, "Thank you, thank you," to polite applause. "We're the Band in the Stars, and we'll be with you for the whole voyage. But enough about us—" the drummer hit his tom-tom *thump!* "Tonight, we're honored— we really are—gee whiz!—to have a special appearance, a special guest, one of your fellow passengers—I think he'll be with us to France—" There was a yell from the audience "England!" "—England, but he says he needs some sleep, so, tonight only, he'll be sitting in—er, ladies and gentlemen, the Band in the Stars, and the *Ticonderoga* are proud—well, here he is, the one, the only, Mister Fats Waller!"

Some people were taken aback—there were gasps and oohs—as the huge man stood up at his table. Waller was dressed in a black pin-striped double-breasted suit with a black vest, white shirt and a flamingo-pink tie, wide as a normal person's leg. He waved to the crowd. He would have seemed incredibly round, except that he was so tall, he seemed only plump. He walked to the grey piano—like all huge men he had a smooth grace about him, not as if he were moving in slow motion, just that thin people moved too fast; his motions reminded Wolfe of Oliver Hardy's.

"Thank you, thank you," he said, pulling out the piano bench. "I never played on an al-loomin-eum piano before. Let's see—" he ran his fingers over the keys, "—my, my, that's sweet. I see it's tuned in the key of R. Well—" *Blang!* he hit the keys. "Here I am, one night only, 'cause gee I'm tired." The man at the table with him brought him a full gin bottle and a glass and set them on the piano. "Oh, suddenly I ain't so tired any more!" He took a drink straight from the bottle. "Wow! That's the stuff. Now I feel like I can play till we hit an iceberg!"

The passengers laughed.

"All right. Here I am, Mrs. Waller's Harmful Little Armful, Mr. Fats himself. Let's go. One two three—" he pointed at the band, who had no idea what was coming, so waited. He broke into a medium stride measure, his left hand covering ten keys between notes, his right way down at the other end, and he began "The Joint is Jumpin'", and the Band in the Stars jumped in right behind him.

As he sang, Fats noticed a great big galoot watching him from the bar with his eyes all bugged out.

The audience roared when they finished the song. Fats drank more gin and leaned back, making tiddling noises with his fingers on the keys.

"Ain't this band sharp?" he asked the audience. "Dressed like that, you'd think the only song they knew was 'Penguins on Parade', wouldn't you? And me as the walrus. Haha."

Then he struck up "I Can't Give You Anything But Love", and the bandleader and he did *sotto voce* repartee over it, making fun of the lyrics, themselves, the passengers. It was totally unrehearsed, so it worked.

"Like working with Charlie McCarthy," said Fats, when it was over. "'Cept he always brings that guy Bergen along. I don't know why he don't split up the act. We knows who's got all the talent in that team, don't we?

"I worked with everybody," said Fats. "'Bout the only two I ain't performed with is Donald Duck and Goofy, and I hear tell Disney's trying to book me with them three weeks at the Apollo next year!"

There was laughter and more applause.

"Next thing you know, ol' Fats will be selling U.S. shares and singing on the floor of the Stock Exchange with Ferdinand the Bull! That'd be a tough act to follow, wouldn't it?"

He took a drink. "Well, we gonna hafta do it sooner or later before drunks start yelling for it, so we might as well give Hoagy his two cents now."

Then they did "Stardust" and the cornet man took a surprisingly good solo, for somebody in a ship's band.

"Most beautiful music *this* side of the Monongahela!" said Waller as they ended the song. "I can say that without fear of obloquy."

They went into a medley of five of Fats' songs, the band shifting tempo and lyrics with him as soon as they heard a few notes; these guys, they shouldn't just be playing here.

When Waller looked up again, wiping the sweat from his mustache, reaching for the bottle, he noticed that the big guy at the bar was gone.

Wolfe crossed the promenade deck and turned starboard. He went out to the observation area, with its open louvered windows and its delicate decorated aluminum railings.

They were steering west-southwest, so there was still the last vestige of a late summer sunset out the windows. A slight breeze blew in, but much less than Wolfe had expected. He barely felt it in his thinning hair. There was also a hum, like the wind, barely noticeable.

The western sky, over the South China Sea, looked like a peeled pink Crayola left forgotten to melt against a dark blue windowpane. There were stars out up from the horizon. Wolfe looked down at the sea. It was like a flat sheet of dark leaded glass full of the dot and wink of stars, merging with pale red where it met the afterglow.

He heard people passing by toward the salon behind him and the subdued music. Part of him wanted to stay here, watching full night come on, the farthest from home he'd ever traveled. The other half wanted to drink in every note from the piano. There would always be beautiful evenings somewhere in the world; there might not always be a Fats Waller.

With a last puff, he took his cigarette from between his lips, gripped it between thumb and back-curled middle finger, and with a former paperboy's sure aim, flipped it far out away from the window railings.

He watched the orange dot blinking in a long arc; leaning closer to the window he saw it part of its way down the three thousand feet where it would land in the dark, star-pinned sea.

Looking up and out, he could see one of the ten Maybach twenty-cylinder engines that pushed the U.S.I.A.S. *Ticonderoga* through the cloudless sky. He imagined, as he looked at the propellers, that the hum in the air was louder, but it wasn't.

He turned and headed back down the promenade.

Ain't Misbehavin'

He finished "Honeysuckle Rose", the fingers of his left hand splayed far across the keys between each bass note. The right hand came down in another triplet, and the salon was still. Then the roar was deafening.

"My, my, yes," he said. He smiled at the crowd. "You better stay awake, because as soon as Fats is through, he's gonna be asleep for the entire rest of this trip. Them Japanese people done partied me for a week. I've eat more food and drank more *sake* than Carter has Little Liver Pills.

"What'll we do next, boys?" he asked the band. "Maybe we could do something I played with the Little Chocolate Dandies? Or McKenzie's Mound City Blue Blowers? How 'bout the 'West India Blues' I did with the Jamaica Jazzers?"

"We don't know that!" the band yelled back.

"Well, I could do something I learned from James P. Johnson. That's how I learned piano, you know, listening to his piano rolls. I used to turn the drum one note at the time, put my hand on the keys when they went down. Seemed like the only way to learn music to me." He grinned at the passengers. "Course I was only about nine years old then.

"I went in and auditioned for Willie 'The Lion' Smith—he needed a piano player for when he was taking a break. I was 'bout twelve years old, corner of Lexington and 114th, went down there and played for him. He pretended he wasn't even listening. I got through and says, 'what you think, Mr. Lion' and he says, 'no pissant gonna play intermission piano for me in *shorts*' and he marched me next door and bought me my first pair of long pants.

"Well, enough of this frothy badinage, let's get busy, boys! Hang on!"

He made a run, the bandleader started snapping along with his fingers, pulled his banjo up, and the band joined in on "(You're Just a) Square from Delaware".

Fats looked up as they played. "Uh. You know that, huh?" he said over the music. "Looka that man with the horn. Blow the end off it, Lips! Oh. Here comes that hard part again. There it comes. Think I got it. Yes, yes! Let's see if we can't get the last eight bars in six!" The music got faster, lost nothing. "O-Kay!" he said, as they slammed to a finish. During the clapping, Fats reached out and shook the bandleader's hand, nodded to the others.

Then they did "Abercrombie Had a Zombie", something Waller had recorded a few months before, which had become, for some obscure reason, a dance-band standard the world over.

"You boys can take a little break if you want to," said Fats. "I'll doodle around on this tin box here till you get back, and then we'll see if we can't blow all the rubber off this balloon."

The band rushed for the bar.

Fats straightened himself in his suit.

"You probably wonderin' what I was doing in Japan," he said to the audience. "I woke up yesterday wonderin' the same thing. No, no. Don't get me wrong. I been good lately."

Then he did an instrumental version of "Ain't Misbehavin'"

He stood up when he was through. "Y'all mind if Fats takes off his coat?" They yelled approval.

Two huge wet circles plastered his shirt under the arms. "Y'all tell me the second I begin to perspire, will you?" he asked.

He leaned forward, his hands only a fraction of an inch above the keys, and he played a Bach *partita*.

Until the Real Thing Comes Along

It had been the Olympics that brought him back, in many ways.

In those strange first days in Johns Hopkins, when he was meeting his mother and sisters and friends, for the second time, snatches of his former self would come to him unbidden, but isolated, with no indication which memory came first, or how far apart they were.

Then, like Faulkner's Benjy, things had quit spinning around and around and settled into a smoothness. The chronology sorted itself. First, he must have done this. This before that, this memory goes somewhere between *here* and *there*.

Still, there had been no linchpin holding it together, no relation to the 'me' he was.

It was in November, two months after the operation. He was still in Baltimore, in a hotel-apartment, looked after by his mother and sister.

"Well, Thomas," said his sister. "I'll be expecting you'll be wanting to see that film about the Olympic Games, especially since it's by that German woman."

"Whatever do you mean?" he'd asked from the couch.

"Well, you were *there*. It's all you talked about or wrote home about for six months."

"That's right," said his mother from the kitchen where she was shelling butterbeans she'd somehow found for supper in November.

He had a dim memory of crowds, moving colors, events of some kind. What he remembered mostly was a pretty woman's face. Who was she?

His mother wiped her hands on her apron, stood in the doorway.

"Don't tell me you forgot that, too? You were over there for two solid months, both sides of the Games. Then you hopped over to Austria and back to Holland, and who-knows-where-else you didn't tell us about."

"There are so many things, Mama. So many trips. They all run together. If you hadn't shown me the postcards, I wouldn't even have known I'd ever been in Seattle."

"Well, you went everywhere, and you was at the Olympics two year ago, and now there's a film about it," said his sister.

"I can't believe I did that and can't remember it," said Tom.

So they'd gone to the movie later that week. It was almost a mistake from the start. It was four hours long, and the first part of it was full of naked people throwing things around and running with torches with their willies out. Tom's sister covered her eyes when there were naked people up there. His mother kidded her about it.

Then the film switched to the '36 Olympics: the opening parade, the torch, events with shooting and horses, then the track and field. Lots of it was in slow motion, or from above or under the ground. Tom knew it was a great film, but he still had no sense of being there. Maybe he'd gone to Europe on a two-month bender and made up all the postcards?

Suddenly there was a Negro on the screen, getting down into starting blocks. Then a long shot of the race ready to begin. The camera lingered over the German entrant. You would think they would show more of the Negro man. Tom was irritated. The cameras panned over to the Chancellor's box. There was a shot of a fat man and a small man with a mustache. Get the camera off them, thought Tom, and back on the track. (It's a film, he reminded himself. These things are not happening right *now*.) Then the gun went off, and in slow-and-normal motion, the Negro man flew down the cinders, getting to the tape three steps ahead of the German and the rest.

There was a shot of the small man with the mustache turning his head sharply to the left, as did the others in the box, toward some commotion up and behind them.

Of course, thought Tom, that's when I yelled so loud for Jesse Owens from the American ambassador's box where I was sitting with Martha Dodd, that even Hitler was annoyed. Göring too.

"Why, Tom," asked his mother, "what's the matter?"

He was sitting still, tears running down his cheeks.

"I remember now, Mama," he said. "I *was* there."

And the pretty woman's name had been Thea Voelker.

"Mr. Wolfe?" asked a young male voice at his side.

"Yes?"

"I'm the social director on this trip," said the thin young man with black hair in a blue suit, holding out his hand. "Call me Jerry."

They shook hands.

"I'm not very sociable right now," said Wolfe. "What can I do for you?"

"Well, I have to ask you the usual questions and all. Like what do you like to do on trips like these?"

"Sleep and write. And drink."

"Hmmm. Mostly what I've got here is people who play checkers, chess, bridge, table tennis, the kinds of things young matrons—there are a few on this trip—like to do. There's skeet shooting tomorrow morning on the port side. Of course, you're welcome to come down to the activity room anytime—I see you're with us to Germany—to look over the stuff for the costume ball two nights from now. Lots of masks and things—I doubt we have any whole costumes themselves that will fit, but . . . we just might rig up something to make you very *mysterioso* . . ."

"Who's *not* going to know it's me?" asked Wolfe, quite seriously, then smiled.

The Jerry guy laughed. "I see what you mean. You're even bigger than your pictures make you look. And I saw the one of you with a German policeman under each arm."

"Really?" asked Wolfe. "Did that make the American papers?"

"I don't know. I was the games instructor on the *Bremerhaven* then. '37. When the chance came last year to sign on the *Ti*, I took it. Some way to travel, huh?"

Wolfe looked out over the dark ocean, heard the hum of the ten engines pushing them gently through the night sky at ninety miles per hour.

"It really is," he said. "My first time on an airship."

"We have tours tomorrow, eleven a.m. and three p.m. ship's time."

"I could maybe make the late one." Wolfe nodded toward the ballroom. "I'm going to watch him play till one of us drops."

"He's pretty good, isn't he? I'm not a boogie-woogie man myself," said Jerry, "but he sure beats . . ." he looked around conspiratorially, ". . . any of those guys in the ship's band."

Wolfe was looking once more at the darkened horizon aft.

"She's a great ship," he said.

"*He's* a great ship. Him," said Jerry. "That's left over from the

German zeps. They called them that, for obvious reasons. Half the crew on the *Ti* and his brother ships are old U.S. Navy men. Took them a long time to get used to it; Navy still calls all their airships *her*. Most of the new U.S.I. Airship Service people are trained in Germany, so it comes naturally to them. Still, there's just about a fight about it every week. President Scott, or the Congress Committee or somebody's going to have to make an official declaration, once and for all, is it *him* or *her*?"

"I didn't know that," said Wolfe.

Jerry looked around. "I didn't either, till I signed on the *Ti*. You know, Mr. Wolfe, there's one thing—"

Wolfe thought he knew what was coming. He'd heard it a thousand times since the operation, so it must have happened a million before then. There's one thing I always wanted to be—a writer, only I don't use words so good. But I've got this idea worth a million bucks. I'll tell it to you, and you write it up and we'll split the money fifty-fifty, right down the middle. Wolfe steeled himself, ready to make the usual polite denial, explain how with him, anyway, the ideas had to come from within, be driven by his experiences, his need to tell the story.

"—I bet you get tired of," said Jerry, "is people always coming up to you telling you they got an idea that'll make a million bucks, if only you'll write it up, they'll split the money with you."

Wolfe laughed nervously. Was this some new kind of preamble?

"Does that happen a lot, or am I just imagining it?" asked the social director.

"Way too much," said Wolfe, looking down at the official name tag on his blue suit coat. "Aren't you one of those people who wants to be a writer?"

"Me? Heck no!" said Jerry. "Give up a life of adventure and dames, flying all over the world, free drinks in the only official arm of the U.S. where it's legal to serve 'em? Give that up to sit in some crummy dump in the Bronx, collecting the Social, staring at a wall while the rats gnaw your feet, trying to think of something to write for *Swell Stories*? No thanks!"

Wolfe laughed again.

"Not that that's what *you* do, Mr. Wolfe," said Jerry. "I thought *0, Lost* was a really great first novel."

"Why, thank you."

"There's anything I can do for you on the trip, just let me know.

Office is always open—I'm not there just leave a message on the corkboard. It's really very nice to meet you." They shook hands again and he was gone back toward the salon.

After watching the darkness and the stars a little longer, Wolfe went back that way too.

It's a Sin to Tell a Lie

Fats took another swallow of gin.

He saw that the big guy who'd been watching from the bar was gone again. He'd seemed familiar somehow. But Fats had looked at a million faces in his time.

He ran his fingers over the keys, went *plink-plonk* at the end.

"I don't know about you," he said to the band, "but I ain't making this trip for my health, no, no." He made another rude noise with the keyboard. "I'm on my way to England, Ole Blighty, right now. Gonna make some records over there for Victorola. Only they don't call it that. Over there, it's His Master's Voice. From Nipper. I knew Nipper when he was just a pup. Why, I knew Nipper when he was so little he was listenin' to two tin cans with a string tied between 'em, instead of a phonograph. That's the truth!

"Gonna record with that Frenchman Grapply. Grape-Elly. I seen him bend a fiddle inside out once, had to play the music backwards so it would come out right. He can play better with his feet than Yehudi can with his teeth. I saw them do it myself. I'm also gonna record some music in a cathedral."

He began a slow melodious tinkling on the piano that wouldn't quite become a recognizable tune.

"Then I'll be coming back to good ol' New York City, U.S. of A. Incorporated. Me and my men will be closing out the New York World's Fair this year—well, we'll be closing it down completely, 'cause when we're done, it's through with."

The drummer hit his snare.

"Thank you, thank you. Any of you people out there come to N.Y.C., come on out and give us a listen. We'll be playing at the big Bandhouse there, for your dancing pleasure. To find us, just follow the firetrucks. I might even play the Mighty Wurlitzer organ for the Aquacade. While you're there, you might want to take in the fair, too."

Another drum roll.

"You can watch me on the new tele-vision there. Hey, you hear they got a robot-man there, the Electro-Man or something like that? He can talk. He can even play little tunes and stuff. I can hear his *repertoire* now: 'Junkyard Blues', 'Will You Love Me When I'm Oiled and Grey?', and 'Nobody Loves You When You're Rusty and Brown'. Maybe I can get him to sit in with the band.

"We could play duets. Can't be any worse than some of the stuff me and Andreamentano Razafinkierfo—or as he's better known to the American Society of Composers, Artists and Performers—Andy Razaf and me used to do. He used to say his playing was too mechanical, so working with Electro-Man'll be just like playing with Andy!"

Another snare drum shot, ending in a cow bell.

"Thank you. Okay, let's play something. Try to follow along, boys," he said to the Band in the Stars. "It gets too much for you, just lay down and take off your coats."

He counted off slow, then went into an easy melody with his right hand. After a couple of bars the band joined in, one and two at the time. "That's right, that's it," said Fats.

He sang "It's a Sin to Tell a Lie".

As he did so, he watched the big lunk come back in, knock back a drink, order another, pick it up and leave.

Either he don't like me, thought Fats, or the live experience of Victor's Cheerful Little Earful is too much for him.

Hold Tight (Want Some Seafood Mama)

The song, which had once had one powerful effect on Wolfe, now had another.

Intellectually, he remembered what it meant in the old days. Now, it no longer connected emotionally with anything in him, and that realization made him take his drink out of the ballroom, through the companionway, where the promenade, cabin and lower deck corridors met. His first impulse had been to go back to the reading and writing salon, but instead he went down the spiral aluminum staircase to the lower deck lounge area.

Most of the lower deck was the remainder of the cabins, two more observation areas, and farther back, crew's quarters and mess, and the freight and baggage compartments. He would see it all tomorrow; he knew this from the brochure they'd given him when he'd booked on the flight.

It was much quieter here. A few people sat about on the light but comfortably padded chairs and the settees. Most of the passengers were smoking, something impossible on the old dirigibles, before the Panhandle find of helium in Texas, and the other one in South Africa.

Two men sat at one of the only two cocktail tables—the other was occupied by a *pukka-sahib* type, and Wolfe could do without that right now.

One of the men at the table looked up—it was the R.A.F. sergeant he had seen writing earlier, the one with the sandy hair and blue eyes. Now he was in civilian clothing, khaki shirt, light wool pants—no vest, coat or tie. The other was a tall thin man with a large nose, receding hairline, dressed in a grey suit and vest, with a black tie.

The taller man said something to the other, then motioned Wolfe over. He carried his drink over to them.

"H—hello," said Wolfe, sticking out his hand.

"Join us, please?" asked the taller man. "My name's Norway. This is Sergeant Ross."

"Surely," said Wolfe. "Pleased to meet you Mr. Norway. Sergeant. I'm an American."

"Who doesn't know that, Mr. Wolfe?" asked the sergeant. "How's the music up there?"

"It's great!" said Wolfe, loosening his tie. "Too good. I had to get away for a few minutes, get some air. I—I've seen him before, long time ago. He was great then, too." He came to a stop, aware that he was sounding like a child who'd just seen his first puppet show.

"Perhaps we'll go listen soon, eh Ross?" asked Norway. The sergeant nodded.

"I suppose I'll just have to put on a coat," he said to Norway; then to Wolfe, "Do relax."

"We were just talking about your country, about the Technocrats. Do you have *any* idea what's next?" asked Norway.

Wolfe stammered, "I'm the last person to ask about anything political. For the first four years of the Depression, all I did was write. I came up for a breather around 1935, then got back to writing and traveling around for another three years. Then I got pretty sick. I'm just now getting on my feet again. So, sorry, I can't help you very much that way."

"Well," said Norway, "I don't think your case is much different than most other Americans."

Wolfe laughed. "It did seem like it happened overnight, I guess. Sort of like the Magna Carta with you people."

Sergeant Ross laughed. "I suppose so. But that wasn't in a democracy, with a constitution."

"People will do lots of screwy things when they're hungry," said Wolfe. "I try to steer clear of politics with other Americans. Saves a lot of wear and tear on my fists. Like I said, I haven't paid much attention since the '32 elections."

"That was—Long and Scott?—wasn't it? I was over there while that was going on," said Norway. "Seemed like a lot of consternation after—what's his name, governor with poliomyelitis . . . Roosevelt—choked on that ham sandwich—"

"It was a chicken bone, I think," said Wolfe.

"—chicken bone just before the convention."

"Whoever was nominated was going to beat Hoover," said Wolfe. "So it was Long, and he chose Scott for veep, not because he was a technocrat, but because he was a Yankee."

"Then Scott brought in all his technocratic colleagues. I met most of them back in '33," said Norway. "I never thought it had a chance of working."

"Well, I don't think it would have, if Long hadn't of been killed, and Scott took over. And the people hadn't voted in the Twentieth and Twenty-first Amendments."

"Well you certainly needed the first of those. You got back your 3.2 beer."

"All of America was drunk on 3.2 beer that day," said Wolfe. "That's one thing I *do* remember. You had to ask *not* to have it if you went to a restaurant. Scott himself said, 'a little beer is good for America'."

"He also said, 'a sober America is a working America'," said Norway.

"Spoken like a true engineer," said Ross.

The tall man looked at him.

Wolfe saw there was an intensity about Ross that he could almost feel, like this conversation was the most important thing in the world. He'd met people like that before, but usually going along with the intensity was a heaping helping of ego. Wolfe didn't feel that from this man.

"Uh, what do you do, Mr. Norway, *are* you some kind of engineer?"

Norway laughed. "Well, yes. Aeronautical engineering."

"Why, you must feel right at home!" said Wolfe, pointing all around them.

Ross laughed very hard.

Wolfe blinked. "Did I say something wrong?"

"No," said Ross. "You said something very funny. Norway built this airship. And all its sis—" Norway looked at Ross "—brother ships. Did the designs, top to bottom."

"Really?" asked Wolfe.

"I helped," said the engineer. "The U.S. Incorporated Airship Service called in a very *many* British and German consultants."

"Don't be quite so modest, Neville," said Sergeant Ross.

"You mustn't forget, I also helped with the *101*," said Norway, a little sourly.

There was a small pause. Wolfe remembered the disaster headlines from many years ago.

"Those were the old days. Things were different then. Hydrogen, for instance," said the sergeant.

"Hydrogen had nothing—"

"Well, Mr. Ross," asked Wolfe, "what brings you halfway around the world, and on an American airship? If I'm not prying."

"I assure you, I couldn't afford this trip on my non-commissioned officers' pay," he said, smiling. He looked away.

"Since he's too modest to tell you, I will," said Norway. "Sergeant Ross is being flown back to England to be a technical advisor on a motion picture."

"Really? What's it about? Flying? The Great War?"

Ross looked very embarrassed.

"It's about Lawrence," said Norway, looking at Wolfe, who creased his brow. "T. E.? Of Arabia?"

"Oh!" said Wolfe. "Did you serve with him?"

"I knew Lawrence in Palestine. Before the War. But the man I knew then was only slightly the one the film is being made about."

"But they still wanted you as technical advisor?"

"Yes. I told them that, but they insisted. I had studied all the man's writings, intimately. I think it was that they wanted." He struck a match against his thumbnail, watched it burn a few seconds, put it out. "It's going to be a very strange film. Not as strange as it would be if they could find out one-tenth of the truth about him. But still, very strange

— 34 —

indeed, if you view his life as a whole." The sergeant looked back down at his drink.

The ghost of a tune came down the stairwell. Wolfe thought at first it was one song, then it sounded like another.

Wolfe finished his bourbon and coke.

"Well," he said, rising, "I'd better get another drink. Can I bring you something? No? This is some spectacular airship, Mr. Norway," he said stamping his foot against the deck. "And I hope the film goes well for you, Sergeant. I'm sure we'll see each other again—I don't leave till we get to Germany. Come on up and hear the music or you'll be sorry you missed it."

Wolfe went up the circular stairs. As he rose, he looked through the aluminum trusses with the octagons cut out of them that formed the railing, saw that Ross and Norway were talking quietly again, as if he had never been there.

He was at the observation windows again. There was only a night full of stars out there. The interior lights had been dimmed to help the seeing, if there had been anything to watch. They were still running, according to the little ship they moved every hour on the world map beside the bulletin board, down the South China Sea before making the right turn that would take them to Karachi, India, the next stop on the *Ticonderoga*'s around-the-world flight. It had started in New Jersey and would end there. New Jersey — Akron — Ft. Worth (for helium) — San Francisco — Honolulu — Ichinomaya — Karachi — Cairo — Trevino — Friedrichshaffen — Paris — London — New Jersey. Wolfe would be leaving in Germany. He was going to see his German publisher. Now that Germany was back on Zone Time, money, which had been locked up during the years before the Army revolted against Chancellor Hitler after the Sudetenland Debacle, was again flowing in and out of the country. Wolfe was to pick up his royalties from the last two books, and was to meet a translator, Hesse, who had done the last book there, supposedly a very good job indeed. Then he would meet Thea again, and they would have six weeks together in Germany and France, ending up at the Oktoberfest in Munich.

Wolfe lit another cigarette, and as he did so he realized with a start that it was exactly two years to the day since he'd awakened in the bed at Johns Hopkins, after the tubercule had been taken out of his brain. He reached back and rubbed the scarred place on his head.

Two women's voices drifted over from the promenade, then one of them laughed at something.

He felt a small moment of dizziness. It was him, not the airship. He still occasionally had them. He reached his hand out to the aluminum railing past the window louvers, and the world came calm again.

At times like this, Wolfe truly felt something was wrong. Not wrong with him—the doctors reassured him on that—but with everything else. The times. The world. His present life. Like there was something fundamentally wrong with the whole business of living.

He'd felt it that evening two years ago in the hospital, when he'd first come to some of his senses. He'd remembered nothing of the weeks of delirium beforehand. They told him it had been six raving weeks since he had caught the cold that led to the flu that opened the old tubercular lesion. That he had been in Seattle. They might as well have told him that he was from Mars.

He had had the same dislocated feeling many times in the past two years. He talked to the psychiatrist friend of Dr. Dandy, the man who'd operated on him. The psychiatrist told him that it was a fairly common side effect of operations on the brain that entailed any memory loss of one kind or another, and that the feeling should go away with the return of memory. But it hadn't, not yet.

It had been his books and his older manuscripts that reinforced the feeling in him. He had read them all, sometimes again and again, in the past twenty-four months. Most of them were intensely personal writings, books about a writer writing books about a writer. When his memory had begun to return, he recalled some of the true incidents which had been transmogrified into the fiction.

But they no longer connected to the person he was. Phrases, words, sentences, sometimes whole pages spoke out to him; but they did so as to a reader, not as to the man who wrote them. It was like some other guy, with the same name, had written these works, and then taken off on a long vacation while Wolfe was sick, leaving only the words behind, like some jumbled private code. It had been up to Wolfe to discover who this person was, decipher the mystery. He had failed.

He'd gone through the long manuscript he and Perkins had broken off from *Time and the River* in '34, and that he had, evidently, later divided into *The Lost Helen* and *The October Fair*, both of which he had been adding and splicing to just before his illness.

There was an aborted, limited-third-person manuscript Perkins told him was the "Doakesology"—about a guy named Joe Doakes. In other places he was named Paul Spangler. Sometimes they were Eugene Gant, in other places it was "I", in others George Webber.

Wolfe had read the whole jumble over in two years. They were mostly full of great ringing apostrophes to night and America and food and trains. There was some good writing in them, lots of bad, too much of the mediocre. Mainly, they didn't interest him at all, because he no longer recalled the emotions that had made the Other Wolfe, as he referred to him sometimes, write them.

One chunk of manuscript from the two three-feet-by-four-feet pine packing crates full of them at the Scribner's office did interest him. It was a history, spare, told in the third person about (as Perkins and his mother told him) his North Carolina hill-country ancestors, called here the Pentlands and the Joyners. It was funny. It was exciting. It told a story. It wasn't like any of the other manuscripts that surrounded it.

It was this piece he had taken in the summer of '39, fleshed out and finished, and which Scribner's had published early this year as *The Hills Beyond Pentland*.

The reviewers, most of them, had gone crazy, taking it as a sign that a new, mature Thomas Wolfe was walking the field of letters, a writer more in control, one interested in narrative, who could write about people other than himself. (The entire narrative took place twenty years before he had been born.) That, they said, was worth the price of the book.

Others of course bemoaned the loss of the Wolfe who used to howl at the moon, the ones who wanted him to continue writing stories so that, as one of them said, "you couldn't tell if he was sitting down to a Thanksgiving dinner, or about to have sexual relations". (A line he would cherish forever.)

What neither set of critics knew was that some of the material had been written as far back as 1933. Most of it was in manuscript before the hospital stay. All he'd had to do was finish it just as he had started it; he had been capable of this book seven years before. As to the ones who wanted the Other Wolfe back, he was gone. He had disappeared into a hospital, and another writer, wearing his clothes and face, had come out. That man could no longer churn out dithyrambs at blinding speed, no longer overflowed with words like torrents of hot lava, was not a floodgate waiting to be opened by the business end of a stub pencil.

After the illness Wolfe found that sometimes the writing of a postcard could be an onerous chore. His work, his writing, now came slowly, slower than a mason with his bricks or a cabinetmaker with a piece of cedar. There were times when it did flow—a sentence, paragraphs, two, three: once a whole page. When it happened it left him feeling like he had been touched by the gods. But when it went away, there was nothing to do but go back to words, phrases, a sentence at a time. His manuscripts were now full of crossouts, big and little xxx's, six, seven, eight wrong word choices scratched through.

He asked Maxwell Perkins about it. He paused, in his Connecticut way, and then said:

"You used to write faster than any human being, Tom, but I had to have you take it out by the bucketfuls, whole chapters at a time. The stuff you're doing now is the best you've ever done. Don't worry. Just do it as it comes. You've got all the time in the world now, which you didn't used to think you had, which was what made you write too fast."

It was the longest speech he'd ever heard Perkins make.

There had been the time, just before he'd left on the western trip that made him sick, that he had almost broken with Scribner's. That terrible review by de Voto (rereading it lately, Wolfe could dispassionately see the places where it was right, the places where it was wrong) of the small book he did about the struggle to write *Time and the River*. Something about lawsuits they had settled out of court. Something that had gone on for months about a dentist's bill. (Wolfe had used Scribner's as a bank, drawing off his royalties ten and fifteen dollars at a time.) All those things meant zip now: Wolfe had found nothing so revealing as the ten, twenty, thirty page letters the Other Wolfe had written in the heat of rage, sealed in envelopes, but fortunately never mailed.

The Other Wolfe had been a bitter man in 1937 and '38.

But Maxwell Perkins had stuck with him. His had been the first face he'd seen at Johns Hopkins as he came out from under the sedative; it had been the last in New York when he set out on this journey that led to this dirigible over the South China Sea.

It was very late. Wolfe was tired (he was always tired these days—how had The Other Wolfe denied that body sleep and rest for so long without wearing it completely out?), but he wanted to hear more Fats Waller. If the man were as tired as Wolfe was, he would sleep for the rest of the flight once he quit.

The band kept up as best it could.

Fats slammed down on the last notes of "One O'Clock Jump". The sound was still holding in the air when he trilled his way up the scales in the opening to "Christopher Columbus". He sang, and the band joined in the vocals over the chorus. Waller went into the falsetto for the crewman's voice, and Columbus' basso, and then they went into an extended jam in the middle.

The ballroom was still two-thirds full, with other passengers coming in and going out continually. Crewmen, not allowed there except on duty, stood in the rear doorway that led to the kitchen; some danced in there, dimly seen through the cigarette smoke from the passenger tables.

The song kept growing and expanding; the bandleader took a kazoo from his breast pocket, blew it into the mike while continuing to slam-pick his banjo. He and Fats put their heads close together at the microphone, singing in good harmony.

The song rattled to its noisy close.

"Wowee!" said Fats. "Talk about a rumpus! My old heart can't take much of that. Let's see if we can't slow it down a little bit. Lessee, maybe I can think of something. Here's a thing we wrote for a Broadway revue, well, fewer years ago than it seems like. At least on the law books, this stuff don't cut it in the good old U.S. of A. anymore. Believe me, this song's still true."

The bandleader was looking at him expectantly, as if, for once, he knew what Waller was going to play. He whispered to the cornet player, who stood up. Fats had just finished speaking when the horn man blew the two-bar introduction, just like on Fats' recording, in front of Waller's slow piano notes. Fats smiled for a second at the horn man, before his face went back thoughtful, and he began to sing, in the smokiest, slowest voice of the night, his song "(What Did I Do To Be So) Black and Blue?"

The noise level in the salon dropped, then stopped completely. There was only Fats' voice, a few piano notes, the quiet accompaniment of the band, the muted cornet, slow violin, occasional *tum* from the banjo.

When he finished, there was no sound at all in the place. Then there was an explosion of applause and yells.

"Thankyou, thank you," he said, picking up the gin bottle. He leaned over and said something to the violin player, who put his instrument down on the edge of the aluminum piano.

Then he spun around on the piano bench, propped his immense feet up toward the audience. "You ever tried to buy a pair of Size Fifteen Torpedo Boats in Japan?" he asked. He saw, through the crowd, the big guy who'd been watching him all night from the bar suddenly break into a smile. "You saw these things coming at you on a dark night, you'd run screaming for the police." Then he looked down at himself. "Course, on me, they look positively dainty." He stood and struck a cupid pose. "But they're big, no doubt about it." He sat down and hit the opening *clump-clumps* of "Your Feet's Too Big", the song getting louder and more insistent as he played. Then, on the beginning of the chorus, he hit a note on the piano, stood up, missing two beats, picked up the violin and bow, and continued playing, pulling long vibrating sounds out of the strings, fingering rapidly. The violin looked like a toy in his huge hands, but the music from it filled the ballroom. The passengers yelled. Waller stopped, said; "It's easy, if you just knows how," in a mellifluous voice, finished the chorus on the violin, sat back down, again losing two beats, and ended the song on the piano.

He had been there a long time. Waller had taken off his vest and tie, rolled up his shirtsleeves. Someone brought him a garter, and someone else found a derby hat. He put both on, and posed while the ship's photographer snapped a picture.

"Boy, does this take me back!" he said. "Whoever thought when they was playing this music in the back parlors of sportin'—'scuse my Anglo-Saxonism—houses, we'd end up playin' it in the clouds over China? That's the charm of music, the Hegemony of Harmony, the Triumph of Terpsichore, and other melodious metaphors. Right now, you listen to the Band in the Stars, while ol' Fats has to visit the Necessary Room, or whatever they call the Head on this gasbag. I'll be right back."

"No, no!" yelled the passengers.

"You wanta see a big fat man explode all over a piano, or what?" he asked as he walked out the door, waving the derby.

The Band in the Stars played "Don't Get Around Much Anymore".

In three minutes, Waller was back.

Gonna Sit Right Down and Write Myself a Letter

Try as he would, Wolfe could hardly keep his eyes open, even standing against the bar. The drinks had worked on him, the smoke from the cigarettes and pipes scratched at his eyes. He could no longer drink like the Other Wolfe had. Coffee, which he'd been drinking since he was a child, now made him jumpy; it used to have a wakeful but calming effect on him. He had never really gotten his strength back after the operation.

The two men, Norway and Ross, had come into the ballroom at some point. They seemed to be enjoying Waller's antics as much as his musicianship, laughing quietly along with the rest of the crowd. At one time or another, every single person on the airship must have watched, crew included. The captain was at a corner table for a while—when he left, the second officer came back. Most of the crew Wolfe saw looked Old Navy, like the social director had said.

Fats and the band plunged ahead on "Darktown Strutters' Ball", which Wolfe knew had other lyrics than the ones usually sung in public. He was sure Waller knew them; maybe the violin player too: he had that seedy white musician look of a guy who spends his off-hours (back on the ground) at places where liquor (no matter how illegal) and other, stronger things always flow.

The passengers clapped along, faster on the climbing notes, slower on the descending ones, joining in on the chorus. Wolfe wished he felt as good as the audience sounded.

He waved away the barman coming toward him, nodded goodnight to Sergeant Ross, who happened to be looking his way, stepped through the perspex doorway with its stamped aluminum palm trees, and headed down the corridor.

He thought of looking at the stars one more time, maybe from the lower deck platform, but decided that if he were too tired for Waller, he was too tired for the most glorious night that ever was. There would be nothing to see; the little airship on the big map in the companionway was still over water.

He turned toward his cabin. Partway down the hall (outside half the doors people had set pairs of shoes to be shined by the steward) a woman in evening dress came out into the hall, Jerry behind her. She was newly-made-up and looked like a million dollars. The social director was readjusting his tie.

"Ah-mmmm," said Wolfe, pointing his right index finger at them, rubbing back and forth across it with his left index finger. The woman stepped back, looking up at him, and blushed. Jerry turned his head.

"Oh, Mr. Wolfe! Still want the tour tomorrow?"

"The late one, Jerry, please," he said, holding his head, feigning drunkenness.

"Sure thing! He still playing?"

"They'll have to beat him absolutely to death with a crowbar before he'll quit," said Wolfe.

The social director laughed. "We're on our way there now," he said.

"Have a good time. You won't be able to help yourselves. Good night."

He went to his cabin, opened the door, watched Jerry and the woman turn the corner, the guy slipping his arm around her waist in the instant just before they turned the corner, disappearing toward the far sound of music.

The steward had been in and folded the back of the couch up onto its chains for the upper, and pulled the cushions out on the lower. A two-foot-long ottoman formed an extension of the bottom bunk—one of the things Wolfe had requested when he'd booked the airship. (One thing Aline had done for him was to have him a long bed built for his apartment in those days in Brooklyn—the first he'd ever had in his life that his feet didn't hang off of.)

Wolfe undressed down to his undershirt and pants, took off his shoes (not quite Waller's size fifteens, but big enough) and socks. He hung up his other clothes on the open rack opposite the window. He went to it, and something out toward the horizon caught his eye.

It was a ship. He'd been on many ships before, but none like that one. It was huge, even at this distance, this far up from the ocean. It looked like a floating city, all lights and curves; unlike most steamships it was not open-decked, but streamlined, closed in, like it was a smooth, rounded battleship. There was deck upon deck, row upon row of lighted portholes, all the way down to the waterline. It must have been ten storeys tall above the first deck, with five more below that. The funnels looked like double shark fins, silhouetted in their own pools of light.

As he watched, the ship sent a hoot of greeting to the *Ticonderoga*, a long high blast that barely carried across the miles. There was a sudden pale light somewhere beneath Wolfe's vantage point. It revolved, red white blue, red white blue, then went off. One U.S.A. Incorporated vessel greeting another. Then the ship was gone, leaving a line of swirling phosphorescence to each side of the sea to mark where it had been. The *Ticonderoga* was going ninety miles an hour; the other ship must have been making fifty knots.

It had to be the *Columbiad*, bel Geddes-designed, commissioned last year. Like the *Ticonderoga*, it went anywhere it was needed, plied all the lanes, showed the flag in every port; anything from a Caribbean cruise to an around-the-world marathon.

A thin line glowing pale green was the only thing to look at out there on the dark. Wolfe closed his window, cranked it down; the air up here was a little chilly late at night.

His tiredness had lifted for a short while—either seeing Jerry and the woman, or the liner, or both, had taken some of his bone-weariness and drink fumes away.

He sat down at the writing desk, pulled up the folding backless stool, took out a sheet of paper. Of course he could wait to write anything until the night before he got off in Germany—nothing would get to New York faster than the *Ticonderoga* itself; it would drop off its mail sacks in New Jersey nine days from now. But he had many letters to write.

There was a light above the desk but Wolfe kept it off. He reached down inside one of the pockets in his huge traveling briefcase and came up with a box nine inches by four. As he lifted it, one of the flaps on the bottom came open and two C-cell batteries fell out and rolled across the decking.

"Damn!" he said, getting down and crawling after them, bringing them back. Then one of the spare bulbs fell out of the box. He caught it on the first bounce.

From inside its box he pulled out a child's nightlight. It was a figure of Mickey Mouse, made out of tin, leaning against a fake red candle at the top of which was a bulb shaped like a flame. Mickey was in his usual shorts with the two big buttons, he wore the shapeless bread-dough shoes, one white-gloved hand was waving, the other cupped around the candle, supporting his weight as he leaned against it like a lamppost. On his face was a confident grin.

Wolfe turned it on, then the light above the desk.

The nightlight had been the second thing he saw in the hospital—first Max's concerned face, then the beaming face of Mickey Mouse.

He'd found that his sister had bought it in those weeks of incoherence out west, before they brought him to Baltimore for the operation. She'd gone down the street from the apartment next to the Seattle hospital and had bought the first battery-powered nightlight she had found, since they knew they would be moving him cross-country on a train soon. She had bought it because Tom had seemed, while irrational, to be afraid of the dark.

He hadn't slept a night in the two years without Mickey being on. He smiled, took hold of Mickey's outstretched hand.

"Hello, Mickey," he said. Then he answered in a falsetto, as close to Walt Disney's as he could get, "Hello! Tom!"

He laughed in spite of himself. Then he took out his old Parker pen, unscrewed the cap, and got his reading glasses from his jacket pocket.

The stationery was official U.S.A. Incorporated Airship Service letterhead, with the embossed dirigible *Ticonderoga*.

Sept 15, 1940
16

Dear Max, (he wrote)

Somewhere way over the South China Sea or the Indian Ocean as I write this. We left six p.m. Tokyo time, it must be four a.m. (that damned Fats Waller has kept everybody up all night with his piano playing!) (just kidding!) The Olympics, as I told you last letter (but this might beat it there), were great. Watched Sunpei Uto set a new 100 meter freestyle record (better than Tarzan's). Since Owens wasn't there, we lost all the dash events in track, but won some distance (!) races—an American that can run more than a mile—unheard of in the 1930s! I'm sure you read all this in the papers—will tell you all about them when I get back in November.

Saw Scott F. in L.A. before I came over—has he written you?—he looks bad, Max (don't tell him I said that). He's writing some college movie for Columbia (he wrote a Republic Western under a pen name a few months ago)—when are they going to stop thinking of him as a freshman?—he's in his forties. He tried to get me to stay in Hollywood and write ("just till you get your health back, Tom—lot's of money to be made out here"). I told him I wouldn't have any health at all if I had to write for the little tin kings out there. Scott also says, "To hell with

Technocracy! I want to go in a bar in broad daylight and get drunk again".

It's not that way on this zep, Max. It flows like water. I'm glad you got me to take it, back in June when I was planning the Olympic trip. Smoother than a liner—we should already have come over 800 miles. Like riding in a fast hotel.

Did I tell you I watched the Olympics some on tele-vision? I know they have it at the World's Fair—but not like Japan. They wanted to keep the locals away from Olympic Stadium, so they broadcast it all over Japan—big department stores, town halls, etc. Saved most of the seats for the tourists. We're way behind them in the field of tele-vision. Tell Howard Scott that I said so next time you see him. Tell him to get his crackedest Technocrats on RCA's butt about it.

By the way, ask the accountant to make sure that if my U.S. Inc. shares get put in with my royalties, to turn them back in to my bank account (cashed!) please. I forgot to leave him a note before I left.

Harry and Caresse Crosby were supposed to be on the trip— but nobody's seen them. They either missed the zep, or maybe even never made it to Japan, or are in their cabin jazzing (Xcuse my French)—they saw Lindbergh land at Le Bourget, remember?— now everybody and his dog are zipping around the world in dirigibles (god, I'm beginning to sound like Fitzgerald!)

I think I saw the *Columbiad* below us a while ago. You can check the shipping tables and see if I'm hallucinating, or what, Max. Had to be. Looked like Philadelphia in a canoe. Or have they turned out another one since I left? (There I go again.)

This letter seemed important when I started it, now it just seems like a letter. Am looking forward to the rest of the trip— tomorrow (today) I get to take the tour. The Other Wolfe would have waxed poetic about it, the grandeur, the size, the mystery of all this, the zep, the people, their baggage, weighing less than this pen I'm writing with. (Somebody told me the pilots like to take off with the whole thing weighing around 200 pounds— something to do with the engines.) Once I would have waxed poetic, now I'm lucky if I can wax my shoes. (Sorry.)

Hear the German guy Hesse did a great job. Did you send Rohwolt the galleys of *Child By Tiger* (I'm sure you did) so they can start on that? *0, Lost* and *T.A.T. River* had great translations, everybody tells me *H.B. Pentland* (called—I forget what—*die Alpen Forever* or something) is even better than those. In German I mean. Am looking forward to the six weeks with Miss Voelker more than anyone knows. (She said she was writing you, but is ashamed of her English, which is better than mine, Max. Did she?)

Wolfe sat up and stretched his arms, rubbing his left shoulder. He looked toward the window. He couldn't tell if it was getting light, or what he saw was just the airglow off the ship's silver skin.

Now I'm tired Max, so will write more this afternoon. Will tell you all about the passenger list, starting with Herr Bock, Docteur Canard and Monsieur le Coq, and ascending upward to me. Also various other etceteras.

For now,
Tom

Wolfe lay naked on the bunk, orange in the glow from the nightlight. He smoked a last tired cigarette, stubbed it out in the weighted conical ashtray he'd taken off the desk and placed on the floor. There was a dull, not unpleasant throb on the deck. He put his hand up against the wall; it was there too. It must be there all the time, the tension of their passage through the air, the smooth vibrations of the engines against the structure of the ship. It was a calming thing.

He lay with his hands behind his head, staring up at the bottom of the unused bunk above him.

He was more than half a mile in the air, hurtling through the sky at nearly a hundred miles an hour, and he'd been listening to a band playing jazz as if he were in a Manhattan basement. He had never felt safer or more secure in his life.

He turned sideways, to face the dim light. All the familiar things were around him—his pen on the desk, his battered briefcase, his shoes and socks.

And the nightlight; grinning, confident, like President Scott in a pair of baggy shorts. Wolfe closed his eyes.

Into the future then, reeking of celluloid and Bakelite though it may be, with Mickey Mouse lighting the way.

The passengers in the salon felt as if they had been beaten with thousand-pound feathers most of the night. Fats took another drink from his bottle, looked at it, finished it.

He'd taken off the derby hat and the garter. His shirt was transparent, wet.

The band had quit two hours before, completely worn out. They'd packed up their instruments, left the stage, now sat at tables, watching, marveling, not believing the man. Not many people noticed they'd gone.

There was a sleeping child at one of the front tables. She began to wake up.

"Here's somethin' I should have played first," said Waller. "Way back when I started tonight."

He ran a bunch of high tinkling trills with his right hand, and in a high voice began singing "Cabin in the Sky".

He finished. The forty or fifty passengers left broke into applause.

He glanced out the door where he could get an angle on a window. The sky seemed paler, the stars beginning to fade.

He looked at the child who'd awakened. Her eyes were puffy as she rubbed them with her sleeve.

"Whose baby child is that?" he asked, pointing. The woman at the next table said "Mine." "Well, Ol' Fats is gonna sing one song, just for her, then he wants you to take her and put her in her little bitty bunk bed, and then come on back. But this one's gonna be for you, darlin'" he said, pointing to the girl. "You can help me sing it if you want to."

A man at another table looked at his Cartier wristwatch as Fats began the bass notes.

"Never mind the hour!" he said to the man, "I got the power!"

He started in, and they all—the little girl, her mother, the passengers, the band members, the crew—all joined in, shaking off their lethargy and sleepiness, as he began singing "Who's Afraid of the Big Bad Wolf?"

Afterword:

Going Home Again

> "Yeah, things are tough all over. Have you heard about Technocracy?"
>
> —Spanky McFarland to "Uncle George"
> in *The Kid From Borneo*, 1933

When people ask a writer, "What went into this story?", like as not the answer is "Disconnected reading, a lousy day job, and one bad-emotion night".

I've written plenty like that.

Sometimes though, the answer is "A whole life".

This was one of those.

There are certain writers that have to be read at a certain age. Too soon, or too late, and they never affect you in the same way.

Burroughs (E.R., not W.S.) you have to hit at twelve or thirteen so you can go sleep in trees and imagine a dry creekbed is the dead sea-bottoms of Barsoom. By mistake, the librarian in Arlington TX gave me my adult library card—which you weren't supposed to get till you turned twelve—on my eleventh birthday. The main benefit was you could check out six books a day, instead of the three *mere children* were allowed. But you could also check out *everything* in the library, even books with words like "damn" and "hell" in them, thought to burn the eyes out of anyone under twelve instantly, in those days. I walked into the room with real novels, and there, all thirty or forty of them, was everything Burroughs had ever written. I went through them six a day for ever-how-many days it took, then went to live in the trees all that fall.

H.P. Lovecraft is for the *summer* between junior and senior years in high school. Cosmic fear hits you about then anyway—you realize you'll soon have to Get a Real Job or Go To College or Both and, in those days, Be Drafted. A dose of Cthulhu helps put those feelings in perspective.

Bradbury's in there, along with what little Robert E. Howard was around before the Lancer paperbacks hit.

If you're going to eventually be a writer like I was there were other, more—literary?—figures. At the age of fourteen, I was going to be Dylan Thomas, the poet. I read all his poems and stories and books. I listened to the Caedmon recordings of him reading, endlessly reread John Malcolm Brinnin's *Dylan Thomas in America* and Rollie McKenna's photobook *The Days of Dylan Thomas*. I wrote horrible Welsh poetry, and worse American. By the time I was sixteen or so, I knew Dylan Thomas had been dead for nine years, and so had my poetry.

But Sidney Michael's play *Dylan* led me to drama, which led to Eugene O'Neill. Between say, seventeen and twenty, I was going to be Eugene O'Neill. Once again, I read everything by and about him: *Curse of the Misbegotten* by Croswell Bowen, *O'Neill* by Arthur and Barbara Gelb, even *Lost Plays*, a pirated edition of his first horrible attempts at being Strindberg back in 1914. Plays; I wrote plays. The Knights of the Round Table set in the Old West, with Barbed Wire in the place of Modred; the Holy Grail a pass the railroads didn't own—ideas worse than I can even *imagine* now. Plays that were, in the words of Sheldon Leonard in one of his last roles on *Dream On*, "fuckin' allegories". Me imitating O'Neill imitating Strindberg in Little Theater for four years.

Overlaid on that was James Agee, who first came to my dimbulb attention as a movie critic, then as author of *The Morning Watch* and *A Death in the Family*, but mostly for his unclassifiable *Let Us Now Praise Famous Men*. I remember writing rambling stream-of-consciousness letters to George R. R. Martin so long and heavy it took 8 cents to mail them (yes, he and I go back that far), under the influence of Agee's sharecropper book. Yow!

It all fits together, believe it or not, and I'm getting to it. Besides all these (as Ed Sanders says in *The Family*) "sleazo inputs", along with SF books, and plays and history, porn and movies, *Life Magazine* and *Uncle Scrooge Comics*, and television—and overriding most of them—was Thomas Wolfe.

Thomas Wolfe (1900-1938) died eight years to the day before I was born (as I pointed out in "Thirty Minutes Over Broadway" in George's *Wild Cards I* anthology). This shambling, stuttering, corn-fed North Carolina giant had four books published while he was alive: *Look Homeward, Angel* (1929), *Of Time and the River* (1935), the story collection *From Death To Morning* (1935) and his 'how-I-did-it' book, *The Story of a Novel* (1936). After his sudden death, three more books were edited from the literally chest-high pile of manuscript he left: *The Web and the*

Rock (1939), *You Can't Go Home Again* (1940), and another collection, *The Hills Beyond* (1941).

Go get a couple of biographies of him to find out about the Real Wolfe. The ones I knew growing up were Andrew Turnbull's *Thomas Wolfe*, Elizabeth Nowell's *Thomas Wolfe* and Richard S. Kennedy's *The Window of Memory: The Literary Career of Thomas Wolfe*. There are tons of newer, more definitive ones, like David Herbert Donald's *Look Homeward: A Biography of Thomas Wolfe*.

Well, such an impact he had you can't imagine. It started the day his first book was published, and it continued well into the '60s. (As Keith Ferrell says, now anyone talking about Tom Wolfe is talking about the mauve-glove guy.) Norman Mailer once wrote an article on the great American writers and said, "Wolfe wrote like the greatest 17-year-old who ever lived". (When he reprinted that article a few years later, he added a footnote to the line: "I should have said, 13-year-old".)

Look Homeward, Angel and its successors are the ultimate *romans-a-clef* (as the critics pointed out loudly), "novels about a novelist writing novels about a novelist". There were several libel suits during his short life, when someone thought he'd cut a little too close to the autobiographical, for-real-and-true, bone. Between 1929 and 1937 he really couldn't, he thought, go home to Asheville NC again.

Here were books about the long-striding, world-engulfing, book-swallowing, drinking, eating, fighting, fearless and foulmouthed days of a writer too large for any American-made chair. Some of it seems overblown and tortured now (a lot still holds up), but it didn't seem that way in 1929, and it sure as hell didn't to me in 1962.

And, as other people than me have said, Wolfe wasn't at his best in sprawling novels anyway, where the episodes were attenuated, but in the short novels—say 15-30,000 words—taken out, tightened up and published in the magazines; like "The Child By Tiger", "The Web of Earth" and "The Party at Jack's". Don't take our words for it; read them yourselves.

Along about five years ago I was looking to stretch my (so-called) literary muscles, and I was thinking and thinking. By and by I fell asleep. Then I woke up and lay on the couch, terrified because *two* ideas had come to me.

Usually ideas coming to me are a Good Thing, but not these. Because they came in the form of ideas for *novels*.

See, I'm a short story writer. (Before I go further: a) you can't make a living writing short stories, and b) you have to write novels if you want to make money.) So far, I have written two novels—one of them a collaboration published in 1974, one a real novel All By Myself published in 1984. Ten Years Apart. There's another one I've been thinking about for 26 years—I'll get to it Real Soon Now. Anyway, suddenly, two ideas for novels come to me in the space of, say, 45 seconds.

I applied the Shiner Method to them. Lewis Shiner says: if you think you have a novel, think about it real real hard, and it'll turn into a novella. If you think you have a novella, apply your brain; it's probably a novelette. If you have a novelette, turn it over and over, it'll become a short story. If you come up with the idea for a short story; hey presto! it's a short-short. If you have the idea for a short-short, forget it and go back to sleep.

Well, try as hard as I could, one of them stayed a novel—someday you'll read it as *The Moon World*. But, lo and behold, the other turned into a novella, the one you just read.

The image came to me just the way it seems to you it should have: Thomas Wolfe and Fats Waller returning from the 1940 Tokyo Olympics on a zeppelin.

Do yourself a favor: stop reading here and go listen to some Fats Waller. (There's a list of music I used while writing the story as an appendix to this.) Waller, the most exuberant performer, stride piano player and musician of his time, was the exact person I needed to counterbalance the Wolfe of my story—the one who didn't die at Johns Hopkins in 1938. (In the real 1940, Waller still had three years to go before catching pneumonia on the transcontinental train back east from L.A., and being taken, in a blizzard that had stopped all rail traffic in America, to die in the room always kept reserved, until the hotel called and asked, for the then-Senator Harry S. Truman at the Hotel Muehlbach in Kansas City. One piano-player to another, as it were.) If you want to see what the world lost, go rent the videotape of *Stormy Weather* (1943); you can't take your eyes off Waller anytime he shows up.

Well, I had Wolfe and Waller, and I knew about dirigibles. That left the Tokyo Olympics of 1940, which is where they *would* have been held. The tv coverage I mention would have happened, too. To leave most of the seats at the new stadium for the *gai-jen*, the Japanese were building viewing rooms in department stores, meeting halls and theaters for their *own* Imperial subjects. They would have, essentially, set up live remote coverage for the whole city of Tokyo.

So things had to be different. Like the small matter of there being no WW II.

Which brings us to the question asked by Mr. McFarland to the Wild Man From Borneo in the *Our Gang* short.

Most people remembered it looked like three choices in those depth-of-the-Depression, do-nothing late Hoover days of 1932: fascism, communism, anarchy. It takes a heap of depression to turn Democrats and Republicans into fascists or anarchists, but things seemed close to that point. Go read about the Bonus March.

But there weren't just three choices; there were too many, in fact. (Like in Santa Fe; *everybody* had a theory.) Huey Long had his Share-the-Wealth Plan ("Every Man A King"). There was the Townsend Plan; give all the old people in America a hundred dollars if they *promised* to spend every penny of it before the end of each month. There was a Single Tax movement: take away all taxes but one, and redistribute it—locally, statewide, nationally; everywhere that needs it. Upton Sinclair was running for Governor of California on what can only be described as the Home-Grown Hot-To-Trotsky Ticket; he even scared off support from FDR, the Democratic presidential candidate.

And if you were paying attention, even a three-year old like Spanky would know the word that kept coming up like a mantra: Technocracy.

It was the brainchild of a guy named Howard Scott. His idea was simple: build up a database of all the transportation, industrial, electrical, shipping and social engineers in America. Get them ready. When Things Went Blooey (sometime in early 1933, after Hoover was re-elected, it looked like from the summer of 1932), move them in. Get everything back on a supply-need basis; move goods and services from areas of surplus to scarcity; take over vital functions; put people to work on the what-we-would-now-call infrastructure—in some kind of credit arrangement—of all the things that the Depression had knocked the blocks out from under.

It took hold of the imaginations of all kinds of people, not just the poor. It seemed for the first time someone had pointed out that goods and food were still there, just like in 1929, but what was missing was the capital that moved them from one place to another. Replace the capital with brains; and somewhere in there get the exchange part on some other basis: either work credit, or some other funny-money. (One of their neat proposals was to divide the country into sectors by latitude and longitude, with major centers serving them. I used to write you from Austin, TX, Sector 9830.)

The Technocrats planned and waited. Scott was everywhere that fall and winter. Then something went terribly, terribly wrong for Technocracy. The wheels didn't come off America. The election came and went. FDR took office. His brain trust did a suck-job on some of the best Technocrat proposals. By early 1933 their time had come, and gone.

There are some still around; they're awfully old, but for a few minutes there they saw, like Wolfe, the shining, the golden opportunity.

There was a spate of real interest in Technocracy in 1932: books were published, magazines did feature stories on Scott (Dr. Seuss did a Technocracy cover for the old *Judge* magazine). There was an animated cartoon called *Techno-crazy* and a short called *Techno-cracked*.

I knew from the first time I read about it that I'd someday write a story set in Technocracy World (as surely as I'd known I'd write a story about the 1938 Westinghouse Time Capsule, when I first read about it as a kid: "Heirs of the Perisphere"). So, evidently, did Mack Reynolds, who wrote, as far as I know, the only other Technocracy story, called "Speakeasy". I haven't been able to find it to read it.

What I did was use some of Technocracy's ideas, cross them with some of the half-baked other schemes, and recast the U.S. in the form of a corporation, with dividends (of some kind) for all the shareholder-citizen Technocrats.

I was assuming a dirigible like the projected *Graf Zeppelin II*, a sort of next-step big brother to the *Hindenberg*, filled, of course with helium from the Texas Panhandle wells (Ft. Worth was a dirigible stop for the *Akron* and *Macon* in the thirties). I'd used the *Ticonderoga* before, in "Hoover's Men", set in yet another alternate past.

I worked hard to get the scene when you realize Wolfe's on a dirigible, not an ocean liner. I'd never done one before; they're hard to pull off without being hokey. There is never any reason to do this *unless* the surprise matters to the story. Nothing is changed to the characters, only the reader. Try it sometime.

I bring in T.E. Lawrence (as Sgt. Ross) for a good reason: after Alexander Korda had to stop filming *I, Claudius* due to Merle Oberon's car wreck, with only 40 minutes of Laughton in the can (there's an image), he immediately wanted to start a bio-pic on Lawrence, who had been a friend of Robert Graves. In my world, Lawrence never took that motorcycle ride that morning in 1935, and was posted to some Far Eastern part of the Empire with the R.A.F.

Same with Norway, who *really did* help design the R-101 and all the other British zeps (and a lot of Allied secret weapons of WW II). He was also Nevil Shute, who later wrote *On The Beach* (and an ignored book, now retro-sf, called *In The Wet*).

I also bring J. D. Salinger in for a scratch behind the ears. Hard as it is to believe, the most reclusive writer of the 20th Century *had* once been the social director of an ocean liner as one of his college summer jobs. (He could also have been Eugene O'Neill's son-in-law, instead of Charlie Chaplin. But that's another story . . .)

I wanted to do a couple of things, and there were a couple I *didn't* want to do.

When most people write about Wolfe, they try to write *like* Wolfe. I wasn't going to do that, except in the letter—and his letters weren't usually like his other writing.

Also, when people write about Wolfe somehow surviving the tuberculosis of the brain (brought on by influenza he probably got by sharing a bottle of whiskey with a seedy individual on the Seattle-Vancouver ferry), they have him continuing to be the free-swinging, logorrheic giant he'd always been.

Operations on the brain take it out of you, folks. I wanted to show a Thomas Wolfe who realistically wasn't the same man. He wouldn't remember some of the things he'd done before. I wanted to show a once-vital, exuberant man struggling to regain (he's not quite sure) what he's lost.

I tried to do that mostly through Waller and his music. Watching him, more than anything else, gives Wolfe some idea of what he, Wolfe, must have once been like, and the long struggle that lies ahead before he even gets close to it again.

Some of this is in the letter Wolfe writes Perkins at the end. He doesn't really know what he's trying to say (any more than he ever did), but he's trying to say *something*.

But with the aid of the Mickey Mouse nightlight, and the letter to Max, through Waller's music, and most of all through the *Ticonderoga*, Wolfe is going home again.

Thanks to George and Jan O'Nale, Charon Wood, Ms. Deborah Beale, Ellen Datlow and Keith Ferrell for help in various stages of this project.

Appendix: "A musical interlude"

This is a list of the music on the tapes I made and listened to while I was writing "You *Could* Go Home Again". You might want to make your own version. This fits on both sides of a 90-minute cassette and half a 60-minute one. You'll notice it's not all contemporary (either the music itself, like the Dylan, or the performer, like '30s music played by '60s neo-jug and jazz bands). What I was aiming at was a mood, something either to get me butt-jumping in my chair, or to calm me down. Besides, there's lots of good music here.

1. "The Joint is Jumpin'"—Fats Waller
2. "Gonna Sit Right Down (and Write Myself a Letter)"—Fats Waller
3. "Mood Indigo"—Jim Kweskin Jug Band
4. "The Sheik of Araby"—Jim Kweskin Jug Band
5. "It's a Sin to Tell a Lie"—Fats Waller
6. "Titanic"—Snaker Dave Ray & Spider John Koerner (*they have it going the wrong way . . .*)
7. "Ukelele Lady"—Jim Kweskin Jug Band
8. "Christopher Columbus"—Jim Kweskin Jug Band
9. "Your Feet's Too Big"—Fats Waller
10. "My Blue Heaven"—Fats *Domino*
11. "I Can't Give You Anything But Love"—Fats Waller
12. "Mississippi"—Turk Murphy Jazz Band
13. "Shipwreck Blues"—Bessie Smith
14. "Smokey Joe's Cafe"—Stampfel & Weber
15. "Corrina, Corrina"—Bob Dylan
16. "In The Mood"—Henhouse Five Plus Two (*chickens do Miller*)
17. "Aloha ka Manini"—Gabby Pahanui

18. "The Sheik of Araby"—Leon Redbone
19. "Emperor Norton's Hunch"—Queen City Jazz Band
20. "Bethena Waltzes"—Queen City Jazz Band
21. "Shine On Harvest Moon"—Leon Redbone
22. "Phonograph Blues"—Robert Johnson
23. "Willow Weep For Me"—Billie Holiday
24. "Mr. Jelly Roll Baker"—Leon Redbone
25. "Hang Out The Stars in Indiana"—New Mayfair Dance Orchestra
26. "After You've Gone"—Queen City Jazz Band
27. "If We Ever Meet Again This Side of Heaven"—Leon Redbone
28. "Ain't Misbehavin' "—Fats Waller
29. "Black Diamond Bay"—Bob Dylan
30. "Yellow Submarine"—The Beatles
31. "Wear Your Love Like Heaven"—Donovan
32. "Mississippi Rag"—Turk Murphy Jazz Band
33. "Gonna Sit Right Down (and Write Myself a Letter)"—Fats Waller (again)
34. "There Goes My Baby"—The Drifters
35. "Sea Cruise"—Frankie Ford
36. "Sincerely"—The Moonglows
37. "Goodnight Sweetheart Goodnight"—The Spaniels

Household Words; Or, The Powers-That-Be

"His theory of life was entirely wrong. He thought men ought to be buttered up, and the world made soft and accommodating for them, and all sorts of fellow have turkey for their Christmas dinner . . ."
— Thomas Carlyle

"He was the first to find out the immense spiritual power of the Christmas turkey."
— Mrs. Oliphant

Under a deep cerulean November sky, the train stopped on a turn near the road one half-mile outside the town of Barchester.

Two closed carriages waited on the road. Passengers leaned out the train windows and watched as a small man in a suit as brown as a Norfolk biffin stepped down from the doorway at the end of the third railcar.

Men waved their hats, women their scarves. "Hurray, Charlie!" they yelled. "Hoorah, Mr. Dickens! Hooray for Boz!"

The small man, accompanied by two others, limped across the cinders to a group of men who waited, hats in hand, near the carriages. He turned, doffed his stovepipe hat to the train and waved to the cheering people.

Footmen loaded his traveling case and the trunk of props from the train into the last carriage.

The train, with barely a lurch, moved smoothly on down the tracks toward the cathedral tower of the town, hidden from view by trees. There a large crowd, estimated at more than 3,000, would be waiting for the author, to cheer him and watch him alight.

The welcoming committee had met him here to obviate that indignity, and to take him by a side street to his hotel, avoiding the crowds.

When the men were all in, the drivers at the fronts of the carriages released their brakes, and the carriages made their way quickly down the road toward town.

Promptly at 8 p.m. the lights in the Workingman's Hall came up to full brilliance.

On stage were three deep magenta folding screens, the center one parallel to the audience, the two wings curved in slightly toward them. The stage curtains had been drawn in to touch the wings of the screen. Directly in front of the center panel stood a waist-high, four-legged small table. At the audience's right side of the desk was a raised wooden block; at its left, on a small lower projection, stood a glass and a sweating carafe of ice water; next to the water was an ivory letter opener and a white linen handkerchief. The top of the table was covered with a fringed magenta cloth that hung below the tabletop only an inch or so.

Without preamble, Charles Dickens walked with a slight limp in from the side of the stage and took his place behind the desk, carrying in his hand a small octavo volume. When he stood behind the thin-legged table his whole body, except for the few inches across his waist, was fully visible to the audience.

There came a thunderous roar of applause, wave after wave, then as one the audience rose to its feet, joyed for the very sight of the man who had brought so much warmth and wonder to their heater-sides and hearths.

He stood unmoving behind the desk, looking over them with his bright brown eyes above the now-familiar (due to the frontispiece by Mr. Frith in his latest published book, *Pip's Expectations*) visage with its high balding forehead, the shock of brownish hair combed to the left, the large pointed beard and connected thick mustache. He wore a brown formal evening suit, the jacket with black velvet lapels worn open showing his vest and watch-chain. His shirt was white, with an old-fashioned neck-stock in place of the new button-on collars, and he wore an even more old-fashioned bow tie, with two inches of end hanging down from the bows.

After two full minutes of applause, he nodded to the audience and they slowed, then stopped, sitting down with much clatter of canes and rustle of clothing and scraping of chairs, a scattering of coughs. From far back in the hall came a set of nervous hiccups, quickly shushed.

"My dear readers," said Dickens, "you do me more honor than I can stand. Since it is nearing the holiday season, I have chosen my reading especially, as suits that most Christian of seasons." Murmurs went around the hall. "As I look around me at this fine Barchester crowd, I see many of you in the proud blue and red uniforms of Her Majesty's Power Service, and I must remind you that I was writing in a time, more than two decades gone, when things in our country were neither as Christian as we should have liked, nor as fast and modern as we thought. To mention nothing of a type of weather only the most elderly—and I count myself among them—remember with absolutely no regrets whatsoever." Laughter. "As I read, should you my auditors be moved to express yourselves—in matters of appreciation and applause, tears, or indeed hostility"—more laughter— "please be assured you may do so without distracting or discomfiting me in any adverse way."

He poured a small amount of water from carafe to glass and drank. "Tonight, I shall read to you *The Christmas Garland.*"

There were oohs and more applause, the ones who guessed before nodding in satisfaction to themselves and their neighbors.

The house lights dimmed until only Dickens, the desk and the central magenta panel were illuminated.

He opened the book in his hand, and without looking at it said, "*The Christmas Garland.* Holly Sprig the First. 'No doubt about it, Marley was dead as a doorknob . . .'"

Dickens barely glanced at the prompt-book in his hand as he read. It was the regular edition of *The Christmas Garland,* the pages cut out and pasted in the center of larger bound octavo leaves. There were deletions and underlinings in red, blue and yellow inks—notes to himself, directions for changes of voice, alternate wordings for lines. The whole had been shortened by more than a third, to fit into an hour and half for these paid readings. When he had begun his charity readings more than ten years ago, the edition as printed had gone on more than two hours and a half. Through deletions and transpositions, he reduced it to its present length without losing effect or sense.

He moved continually as he read, now using the letter opener as Eben Mizer's quill, then the block of wood—three heavy blows with his left hand—as a doorknocker. He moved his fingers together, the book between them, to simulate Cratchitt's attempts to warm himself at a single glowing coal. His voice was slow, cold and drawn as Eben Mizer; solemnly cheerful as the gentleman from the charity; merry and bright as Mizer's nephew. The audience laughed or drew inward on itself as he read the opening scenes.

"For I am that Spirit of Christmases Past," said the visitant. "I am to show you things that Were. Take my hand."

Eben Mizer did so, and they were out the window casing and over the night city in a slow movement. They flew slowly into the darkness to the north.

And then they were outside a house and shop, looking through the window at a large man in old-fashioned waistcoat and knee-breeks, with his spectacles pushed back on his forehead.

"Why, old Mr. Fezziwigg, to whom I was 'prenticed!" said Eben Mizer.

"Ho!" said Fezziwigg. "Seven o'clock! Away with your quills! Roll back the carpets! Move those desks against the walls! It's Christmas Eve and no one works! . . ."

As Dickens acted out preparations for the party, his eyes going to the prompt-book only twice, he remembered the writing of this, his most famous story. It had been late October of the year 1843. He was halfway through the writing of *Martin Sweezlebugg*, had just, in fact, sent the young hero to America—the place he himself had returned from late in 1842, the place that had become the source of one long squeal of protest when he had published *Notes on the Americans* early in the year. He had gone from triumph to disdain in less than six months. For the first time in his life, the monthly numbers had been a chore for him—he was having troubles with *Sweezlebugg*, and the sales were disappointing. As they had been for *Gabriel Vardon: The Locksmith of London* of two years before. (The Americans who were outraged with his travel book were the same who had named a species of Far Western trout after Gabriel Vardon's daughter.) Between finishing the November number of

Sweezlebugg on October 18, and having to start the next on November 3, he had taken one of the steam-trains to the opening of the Manchester Institute of that city. Sitting on the platform, waiting his turn to speak, the idea for *The Christmas Garland* had come to him unbidden. He could hardly contain himself, waiting until after the speeches and the banquet to return to the quiet of his hotel to think it through.

And since he had a larger and larger family each year to support, more indigent brothers and sisters, in-laws and his importunate mother and father, he conceived the story as a separate book, to be sold at Christmas as were many of the holiday annuals, keepsakes and books of remembrance. Illustrated, of course, with cuts by John Leech. The whole plan was a fire in his mind that night and all the way back to London the next day. He went straight to Chapman and Hall and presented the notion to them. They agreed with alacrity, and began ordering up stock and writing advertisements.

He had had no wild success since the two books that had made his reputation, *Tales of the Nimrod Club* and *Oliver Twist*, parts of them written simultaneously, in overlapping monthly numbers, six years before. He had envisioned for *The Christmas Garland* sales that would earn him £3,000 or more.

"Show me no more, no more!" said Eben Mizer. "These are things long past; the alternate miseries and joys of my youth. Those times are all gone. We can no more change them than stop the tides!"

"These are things as they were," said the Spirit of Christmases Past. "These things *are* unchangeable. They *have* happened."

"I had forgotten both pleasure and heartache," said Mizer. "I had forgotten the firewood, the smoke, the horses."

"In another night, as Marley said, you shall be visited by another, who will show you things as they are now. Prepare," said the Spirit. As with the final guttering of a candle, it was gone. Eben Mizer was back in his bed, in his cold bedchamber, in the dark. He dropped his head to the horsehair pillow, and slept.

Twenty-two years had gone by since Dickens wrote the words he read. He remembered his disappointment with the sales of *The Christmas Garland*—"Disappointment?! Disappointment!" yelled his friend Macready, the actor, when he had complained. "Disappointment at selling 20,000 copies in six days! Disappointment, Charlie?" It was not that it had not sold phenomenally, but that it was such a well-made book—red cover, gilt-edged pages, four hand-tinted cuts, the best type and paper and, because of Dickens' insistence that everyone have one, priced far too low—that his half-copyright earnings through January 1844 only came to £347 6s 2p when he had counted on thousands. That had been the disappointment.

Dickens spoke on. This was the ninety-fourth public reading of *The Christmas Garland;* his most popular, next to the trial scene from *The Nimrod Club,* and the death of little Dombey. At home these days he worked on an abridgment of the scenes, including that of the great sea-storm, from *The Copperfield Record of the World As It Rolled,* which he thought would make a capital dramatic reading, perhaps to be followed by a short comic scene, such as his reading of Mrs. Gamp, the hit of the otherwise disappointing *Martin Sweezlebugg.*

What a winter that had been . . . the hostile American press, doing the monthly numbers of *Sweezlebugg,* writing and seeing to the publication of *The Christmas Garland* in less than six weeks, preparing his growing family—his wife, an ever-increasing number of children, his sister-in-law Georgina Hogarth, the servants and dogs—for the coming sojourn to Italy, severing his ties with *Bentley's Miscellany,* thinking of starting a daily newspaper of a liberal slant, walking each night through London streets five, ten, fifteen miles because his brain was hot with plans and he could not sleep or rest. He was never to know such energies again.

There was his foot now, for instance. He believed its present pain was a nervous condition brought on by walking twelve miles one night years ago through the snow. The two doctors who had diagnosed it as gout were dismissed; a third was brought in who diagnosed it as a nervous condition brought on by walking through the snow. Before each of his readings, his servant John had to put upon the bare foot a fomentation of the poppy, which allowed him to put on a sock and shoe, and make it the two hours standing up.

He still had a wife, though he had not seen her in six years; they had separated after twenty-three years of marriage and nine children. Some of the living children and Georgina had remained with Dickens, taking his side against the mother and sister. One boy was in the Navy, another in Australia, two others in school. Only one child, Mamie— "young Tinderbox", as Dickens called her—visited freely between the two households, taking neither side.

The separation had of course caused scandal, and Dickens' break with Anthony Trollope. They belonged to the same clubs. Trollope had walked into one; several scandalized members were saying that Dickens had taken his sister-in-law as mistress. "No such thing," said Trollope. "It's a young actress."

So it was; Trollope said he was averting a larger outrageous lie with the truth; Dickens had not seen it that way.

Her name was Ellen Ternan. She and Dickens had performed in charity theatricals together, *The Frozen Deep* and Jonson's *Every Man in His Humour*. She was of a stage family—her mother and two sisters were actresses. Her sister Fanny had married Anthony Trollope's brother Tom in Florence, Italy, where she had gone to be his children's tutor after the death of Tom's wife Theodosia.

The world had been a much more settled place when the young fire-eating Boz had published his first works, and had remained so for some time afterwards. But look at it now.

The Americans had just finished blowing the heads off first themselves, and then their President; had thrown the world in turmoil—which side should we take?—for four years, destroying a large part of their manpower and manufacturing capabilities. What irked Dickens was not their violent war—they had it coming—but that he would not be able to arrange a reading tour there for at least another year. An American had shown up two weeks ago at his publisher's office with an offer of £10,000, cash on the barrelhead, if Dickens would agree to a three-month tour of seventy-five readings. Both his friend Forster and the old actor Macready advised him against it for reasons of his health. Besides his foot, there had been some tightening in his chest for the last year or so, and his bowels had been in straitened circumstances long before that.

Ah, but what a trouper. He found even with his mind wandering he had not lost his place, or missed a change of voice or character; nor given the slightest hint that his whole being was not in the reading being communicated to his forward-leaning, intent auditors.

Eben Mizer opened his eyes. How long had he slept? Was the Spirit of Christmases Past that bit of undigested potato, that dollop of mustard? he thought.

There came to his bedchamber a slight crackling sound; the air was suffused with a faint blue glow. Mizer reached into the watch-catch above his bed and took down his timepiece. It was 12:00, he saw by the glow, which slowly brightened about his bed. Twelve! Surely not noon! And not the midnight before, when the Spirit of Christmases Past had come. Had he slept the clock round, all through the sham-bug Christmas Day? He grasped the bedclothes to haul himself out onto the cold bare floor. The overall bright glow coalesced in the corner nearest the chair.

The popping became louder, like faraway fireworks over the Thames on Coronation Day, or the ice slowly breaking on a March day. There was a smell of hot metal in the air; the sharp odor before a thunderstorm, but without heat or dampness. And then it was there, in the room behind the chair!

It was a looming figure, far above normal height, shrouded in a gown of copper and mica, and above its head, at its top, glowing green and jagged with purple, was one of Faraday's Needles . . .

The listeners jerked back, as always. There was a rustle of crinoline and starch as they hunkered back down. Most knew the story as they knew their own hearts, but the effect on them was always the same.

Dickens knew why; for when he had written those words more than two decades before, his own hair had stood on end as if he were in the very presence of the Motility Factor itself.

It was from that moment on in the writing of *The Christmas Garland* that he had never wavered, never slowed down; it was that moment when, overcome by tiredness at his desk, he had flung himself and his hat and cane out into the (in those days) dark London night, and had walked till dawn, out to Holborn, up Duckett Lane, across to Seven Sisters, and back up and down Vauxhall Bridge Road, to come in again just as the household was rising, and throw himself fully clothed across his bed, to sleep for an hour, and then, rising, go back to his ink bottle and quills.

The crackling sound grew louder as the Spirit shook his raiments, and a spark danced between the Needle and the ceiling, leaving a bright blue spot there to slowly fade as Eben Mizer watched, fascinated as a bird before a snake.

"Know that I am the Spirit of Christmases Current, Eben Mizer. Know that I am in the form that the men who hire your accountancy worship, as you worship the money that flows, like the Motive Force itself, from them to you."

"What do you wish of me?" asked Eben. The Spirit laughed, and a large gust of blue washed over the room, as if day had come and gone in an instant.

"Wish? Nothing. I am only to show you what takes place this Christmas."

"You mean this past day?"

"Past? Oh, very well, as you will!" The Spirit laughed again. "Take my hand."

"I will be vulcanized in an instant!" said Mizer.

"No, you shall not." It held out an empty sleeve. Mizer felt invisible fingers take his. "Come," said the Spirit. "Hold on to me."

There was a feeling of lightness in Mizer's head—he became a point of light, as the flash of a meteor across the heavens, or the dot of a lightning-bug against an American night, and they were outside his nephew's house in the daylight.

"As before, you are neither seen nor heard," said the Spirit of Christmases Current. "Walk through this wall with me." They did, but Mizer had the sensation that instead of walking directly through they had, in a twinkling, gone up the windowpane, across the roof tiles, down the heated air of the chimney, across the ceiling, and into the room just inside the window, too fast to apprehend. The effect was the same, from outside to inside, but Eben Mizer had the memory of doing it the long way . . .

Dickens' voice became high, thin and merry as he took on the younger tones of Mizer's nephew, his nephew's wife, their in-laws and guests at the party where they were settling in for a game of charades before the Christmas meal.

Actors on the stage of the time said that Dickens was the greatest actor of his age; others thought it beneath his dignity to do the readings—authors should be paid to publish books, not read them for money. Some of his readings he had dropped after they did not have the desired effect—comic or pathetic or terrific—on the audience. Others he had prepared but never given, because they had proved unsatisfying to him. By the time any reading had joined his repertoire, he had rehearsed it twenty-five times before its debut.

He knew that he was a good actor—if he had not gone into journalism, covering the courts and the Parliament when a youth, he would have gone on the stage—but he knew he was not great. He knew it was the words and the acting that had made his readings such a success. No matter how many times they had read and heard them, audiences still responded to them as if they had come newly dry from his pen that very morning.

Dickens paused for another drink from the glass, mopped his brow with the handkerchief that a moment before had been Mizer's nightcap. The audience waited patiently, the slight hum of the fans in the ceiling purring to let the accumulated warmth of 1,500 bodies escape into the cold night. The glow from the selenium lights against the magenta screen added nothing to the heat.

He put the glass down, eyes twinkling, and went back to his reading.

"If only my uncle were here," said his nephew.

"Oh, why bother?" asked his pretty young wife. "He's probably at his office counting out more profits from the Greater Cumberland and Smythe-Jones Motility Factory, or the United Batchford Motive-Force Delivery Service. And no doubt got poor Bob Cratchitt there with him, chained to his stool . . ."

"Hush, please," asked the nephew.

"Well, it's true. A man like Eben Mizer. He does sums for seventeen different power-brokers, yet his office is still lit with candles! He lets poor Cratchitt freeze in the outer office. And poor Bob with the troubles he has at home. Your uncle should be ashamed of what he pays him, of how he himself lives . . ."

"But, after all," said her father the greengrocer, "it is a free market, and he pays what the trade will bear."

"That's wrong too," said the young wife, hands on hips. "How the workingmen are to better themselves if their wages are so low they have to put their children working at such early ages is beyond me. How are they to make ends meet? How are they to advance themselves if there are no better wages in the future, perhaps even lower ones, and they can't live decently now?"

"The Tories won't be happy if women such as yourself get the suffrage," said her father with a laugh. "Neither would anyone on the board of directors of a motive-power company!"

"If I did not love you as a father," said the young wife, "I should be very cross with you."

"Come, come," said her husband the nephew. "It's Christmas Day. Where's your charity?"

"Where's your uncle's?"

"He does as the world wills," said the nephew.

"Only more so," said another guest, and they all laughed, the young wife included.

"Well, I invited him," said Mizer's nephew. "It's up to him to come or no. I should welcome him with all the gladness of the season."

"As would I," said his wife. "Only you might as well wish for Christian charity to be carried on every day, in every way, throughout the year, in every nation on Earth!"

"Why show me this?" asked Eben Mizer of the Spirit. "No love is lost betwixt my nephew's wife and myself. My nephew means very well, but he does not grasp the full principles of business to his bosom. He has done well enough; he *could* do much better."

"Come," said the Spirit of Christmases Current, grabbing Mizer's hand in its unseen own. There was another crackle of blue lightning, and they were away, up a nail, across the roof, down the gutter pipe and off into the day.

After this reading, Dickens had two more in the provinces, then back to St. James Hall in London for the holiday series. He would read not only *The Christmas Garland* there, but also both *The Chimes* and *The Haunted Man*, his last Christmas book from back in 1848.

In London he would also oversee the Christmas supplement of *Household Words*, his weekly magazine. This year, on a theme superintended by Dickens, and including one short story by him, was the conceit of Christmas at Mugby Junction, a station where five railway lines converged. Leaning over the junction would be the bright blue towers of the H.M.P.S., from which the trains drew their force. Indeed, Wilkie Collins's contribution was the story of a boy, back in London, who proudly wore the crisp blue and red uniform, imagining, as he sat on duty with his headset strapped on, Mugby Junction and the great rail lines that he powered, on one of which was coming to London, and to whom he would be introduced on his fortnight off duty, his brother-in-law's cousin, a girl. Dickens had, of course, made Collins rewrite all the precious parts, and bring Father Christmas in for a scratch behind the ears—"else it might as well take place during August Bank Holiday!" said Dickens in a terse note to Collins when the manuscript had caught up with him at his hotel in Aberdeen yesterday.

Just now, the letter opener in his hand had become the cane of old Mr. Jayhew as he walked toward the Cratchitts' door.

Such a smell, like a bakery and a laundry and a pub all rolled together! The very air was thick with Christmas, so much so that Eben Mizer wondered how he detected the smells, unseen and unheard as he was, as the sputtering blue and purple Spirit stood beside him.

"Where's your father?" asked Mrs. Cratchitt.

"He's just gone to fetch Giant Timmy," said the youngest daughter.

"Your brother's name is Tim," said Mrs. Cratchitt. "It's just the neighbors call him that," she added with a smile.

The door came open without a knock, and there stood Katy, their eldest, laden with baskets and a case, come all the way from Cambridge, where she worked as a nanny.

"Mother!" she said. "Oh, the changes on the trains! I thought I should never reach here!"

"Well," said Mrs. Cratchitt, hugging her, "you're here, that's what matters. Now it will be a very merry Christmas!"

"I must have waited in ten stations," said Katy, taking off her shawl, then hugging her sisters and giving them small presents. "Every line its own train, every one with its own motive-car. Absolutely nothing works right on Christmas Eve!" She looked around. "Where's father? Where's Tim?"

"Your father's off fetching him . . . and his pay," said Mrs. Cratchitt.

"When can I go to work, mumsy?" asked Bobby, pulling at his pinafore.

"Not for a long time yet," said Mrs. Cratchitt. "Perhaps you'll be the first one in the family goes to University."

"Don't tease him so," said Katy.

"Well, it's possible," said his mother.

"Not with what Mr. Mizer pays father, and what I can send when I can, nor even with Tim's pay," said Katy. "And unless I am mistaken, his rates have gone down."

"All of them are down," said Mrs. Cratchitt, "what with the Irish and the potato blight. The streets here are full of red hair and beards, all looking for work."

There was a sound outside in the street, and the door came open, Mr. Cratchitt's back appearing as he turned. "This way. No, no, this way." He tugged twice, and then was followed.

Behind Mr. Cratchitt came Tim. He weighed fifteen stone though he was but twelve years old. He wore a white shapeless smock, with the name *Wilborn Mot. Ser.* written in smudged ink across the left chest, and white pants. His skin was translucent, as if made of waxed parchment, and his head had taken on a slight pearlike appearance, not helped by the short bowl-shape into which his hair had been cut. There were two round notches in the bowl-cut, just above the temples, and small bruised and slightly burnt circles covered the exposed skin there.

But it was the eyes Mizer noticed most—the eyes, once blue-green like his father's, had faded to whitish grey; they seemed both starting from their sockets in amazement, and to be taking in absolutely nothing, as if they were white china doorknobs stuck below his brows.

"Tim!" yelled Katy. She ran to him and hugged him as best she could. He slowly lifted one of his arms to wrap around her shoulders.

"Oh! You're hurting!" she said, and pulled away.

"Here, sit here, Tim," said Bob Cratchitt, making motions towards the largest chair. It groaned as the boy sat down.

"There is a small bonus for Christmas," said Mr. Cratchitt. "Not much." He patted the corner of the pay envelope in his pocket. "Not enough to equal even the old pay rates, but something. They've been working especially hard. The paymaster at Wilborn's was telling me they've been hired as motive power for six new factories in the last month alone."

"Oh, Tim," said Katy. "It's so good to see you and have you home for Christmas, even for just the day."

He looked at her for a long time, then went back to watching the fireplace.

Then there was the steaming sound of a goose coming out of the oven, hissing in its own gravy, and of a pudding going in, and Mr. Cratchitt leapt up and started the gin-and-apple punch, with its pieces of pineapple, and oranges, and a full stick of cinnamon bark.

Halfway through the meal, when healths were going round, and Mr. Mizer's name mentioned, and the Queen's, Giant Timmy sat forward suddenly in the big chair that had been pulled up to the table, and said, "God Bless . . . us all each . . . every . . ." Then he went quiet again, staring at his glass.

"That's right, that's exactly right, Tim," said Bob Cratchitt. "God Bless Us All, Each and Every One!"

Then the Spirit and Eben Mizer were outside in the snow, looking in at the window.

"I have nothing to do with this," said Eben. "I pay Cratchitt as good as he could get, and I have *nothing* to do, whatsoever, with the policies of the companies for whom I do the accounts." He looked at the Spirit of Christmases Current, who said nothing, and in a trice, he was back in his bedchamber, and the blue-purple glow was fading from the air. Exhausted as if he had swum ten miles off Blackpool, he dropped to unconsciousness against his stiff pillow.

Dickens grew rapidly tired as he read, but he dared not now let down either himself or his audience.

In many ways that younger self who had written the story had been a dreamer, but he had been also a very practical man in business and social matters. That night in Manchester as he waited for Mr. Disraeli to wind down, and as the idea for *The Christmas Garland* ran through his head, he thought he had seen a glimpse of a simple social need, and with all the assurance and arrogance of youth, what needed to be done. If he could strike the hammer blow with a Christmas tale, so much the better.

So he had.

The Spirit of Christmases Yet to Come was a small imp-like person, jumping here and there. It wore no mica or copper, only a tight garment and a small cloth skullcap from which stood up only a single wire, slightly glowing at the tip. First the Spirit was behind the chair, then in front, then above the bureau, then at one corner of the bed.

Despite its somewhat comic manner, the Spirit frightened Eben Mizer as the others had not. He drew back, afraid, for the face below the cap was an upturned grin, whether from mirth or in a rictus of pain he did not know. The imp said nothing but held out a gutta-percha covered wand for Mizer to grasp, as if it knew the very touch of its nervous hand would cause instant death, of the kind Mizer had feared from the Spirit before. Mizer took the end of the wand; instantly they were on the ceiling, then out in the hall, back near the chair, then inside something dark, then out into the night.

"I know you are to show me the Christmas Yet to Come, as Marley said. But is it Christmas as it *Will Be*, or only Christmas Yet to Come if I *keep on* this way?"

The imp was silent. They were in the air near the Serpentine, then somewhere off Margate, then back at the confluence of the Thames and Isis, then somewhere over the river near the docks. As Eben Mizer looked down, a slow barge transformed into a sleek boat going an unimaginable speed across the water. As he watched, it went in a long fast circle and crashed into a wharf, spewing bodies like toy soldiers from a bumped table.

He looked out towards the city. London towered up and up and up, till the highest buildings were level with his place in the middle of the air. And above the highest buildings stood giant towers of every kind and shape, humming and glowing blue in the air. Between the tall stone and iron buildings ran aerial railways, level after crossing level of them, and on every one some kind of train; some sleek, some boxlike, moving along their spans. The city was a blaze of light; every corner on every street glowed, all the buildings were lit. Far to the horizon the lights stretched, past all comprehension; lights in a million houses, more lights than all the candles and lamps and new motility-lights in Eben Mizer's world could make if all lit at once. There was no end to the glow—the whole river valley was one blue sheen that hurt his eyes.

Here and there, though, the blue flickered. As he watched, some trains gathered speed on their rails three hundred feet above the ground, and on others higher or lower they stopped completely. Then he and the imp were closer to one of the trains that had come to a halt. The passengers were pressed to the windows of one of the carriages, which had no engines or motive-cars attached, and then in a flash around a building came a spotted snake of light that was another train, and there was a great grinding roar as the two became one. The trains were a wilted salad of metal and wheels, and people flew by like hornet larvae from a nest hit by a shotgun blast. They tumbled without sound down the crevasses between the buildings, and cracked windows and masonry followed them as rails snapped like stretched string.

Something was wrong with the sky, for the blue light flickered on and off, as did the lights of the city, and the top of one of the towers began to glow faint red, as if it were a mulling poker.

Then he and the imp were on the ground, near a churchyard, and as they watched, with a grinding clang that died instantly, a train car from above went through the belfry of the church. Bodies, whose screams grew higher and louder, thudded into the sacred ground, snapping off tombstones, giving statues a clothing of true human skin.

The imp of Christmases Yet to Come drew nearer a wooden cross in the pauper's section, pointing. Eben Mizer stood transfixed, watching the towers of buildings, stone attached to iron, and the twisting cords of the railways above come loose and dangle before breaking off and falling.

With a deafening roar a ground-level railway train came ploughing through the churchyard wall, tearing a great gouge in the earth and, shedding passengers like an otter shakes water, burst through the opposite wall, ending its career further out of sight. It left a huge furrow through the cemetery, and at the cemetery's exact center a quiet, intact railway car in which nothing moved. Here and there in the torn earth a coffin stood on end, or lay cut in two, exactly half an anatomy lesson.

Eben Mizer saw that one of the great towers nearby had its side punched open, as neat a cut as with a knife through a hoop of cheese. From this opening shambled an army, if ever army such as this could be . . .

They were huge, and their heads too were huge, and the sides of their heads smoked; the hair of some was smouldering, which they did not notice, until some quite burst afire, and then those slowly sank back to the ground. Others walked in place, only thinking their thin legs were moving them forward. A higher part of the tower fell on twenty or thirty of them with no effect on the others who were walking before or behind them.

Great fires were bursting out in the buildings overhead. A jagged bolt lanced into the Thames, turning it to steam; a return bolt blew the top from a tower, which fell away from the river, taking two giant buildings with it.

A train shot out of the city a thousand feet up. As it left, the entire valley winked out into a darkness lit only by dim blazes from fires. Mizer heard the train hit in Southwark in the pitch blackness before his night vision came back.

All around there was moaning; the small moanings of people, larger ones of twisted cooling metal, great ones of buildings before they snapped and fell.

He began to make out shapes in the churchyard slowly, here and there. There were fires on bodies of people, on the wooden seats of train benches. A burning chesterfield fell onto the railway car, showering sparks.

The staggering figures came closer; they were dressed in loose clothing. By the light of fires he saw their bulbous shapes. One drew near, and turned towards him.

Its eyes, all their eyes, were like pale doorknobs. They moved towards him. The closest, its lips trying to say words, lifted its arms. Others joined it, and they came on slowly, their shoulders moving ineffectually back and forth; they shuffled from one foot to the other, getting closer and closer. They lifted their white soft grub-worm fingers towards him—

WHAP!!! Dickens brought his palm down hard on the wooden block. The whole audience jumped. Men and women both yelped. Then nervous laughter ran through the hall.

Eben Mizer opened the shutter. The boy in the street had another snowball ready to throw when he noticed the man at the window. He turned to run.

"Wait, boy!" Eben Mizer called. "Wait! What day is this?"

"What? Why, sir, it's Christmas Day."

"Bless me," said Eben Mizer. "Of course. The Spirits have done it all in one night. Of course they have. There's still time. Boy! You know that turkey in the shop down the street? . . ."

His foot was paining him mightily. He shifted his weight to the other leg, his arms drawing the giant shape of the man-sized turkey in the air. He was Eben Mizer, and he was the boy, and he was also the poulterer, running back with the turkey.

And from that day on, he was a man with a mission, a most Christian one, and he took to his bosom his nephew's family, and that of all mankind, but most especially that of Bob Cratchitt, and that most special case of Giant Timmy—who did not die—and took to his heart those great words, "God Bless . . . us all each . . . every . . ."

Charles Dickens closed his book and stood bathed in the selenium glow, and waited for the battering love that was applause.

Afterword to:

Household Words; Or, The Powers-That-Be

Here's how I killed *Amazing Stories*, world's oldest SF magazine.

Me (and the British Postal Service) seemed to be about the only two entities in the world who noticed that 1993 was the 150th Anniversary of *A Christmas Carol*.

Unfortunately, it took me till late July to realize it. That's normally way too late, since magazines are normally made up anywhere from five months to almost a year ahead of time, the ephemera like book reviews and editorials going in at the very last. Which normally meant I was out of luck, even if I was the only person who noticed.

But . . . a few months before, at Wiscon (In Madison, Wisconsin. In February. What's wrong with this picture?), Kim Mohan, editor of *Amazing* and me sat down to a beer or something and he told me he'd been astounded that I'd only had half a story in *Amazing* in its and my long career. ("Men of Greywater Station" with George R. R. Martin, March 1976.) And that I should probably do something about it. I told him what I always tell editors: "Sure thing. Soon."

But he'd also told me he was editing only about three months ahead, which meant if I fired off something real quick, and he liked it, there was a chance he could get it into print before Christmas.

So I did two things at once: I fired off a letter to Kim asking if the lead time was still the same *and* I hit Peter Ackroyd's *Dickens* again.

I'd been researching Dickens on and off for five or six years (he's very important to *The Moon World*, if I ever finish *that*) and had read the up-to-then standard biographies: Edgar Johnson's *Charles Dickens: His Tragedy and Triumph* (2 vols.), Hesketh Pearson's *Dickens: His Character, Comedy and Career*, and the volume *Dickens at Work*. But a couple of years before, Ackroyd's book had come out. When I'd read it then, I knew what biographies *should* be.

I went back there to get the details of writing *A Christmas Carol* right. I already knew I was going to set the story in the 1860s, during one of Dickens' reading tours, and that it was going to be a work of memory and reconciliation.

The image of the pylons and Giant Timmy came to me about a week later. I had the "thing" that makes a story fall into place. For what did the Victorians do but give their children to the Empire for service?

On August 15-17 I wrote the first and second drafts, and on the 18th Express-mailed it to Kim.

Who called me on the 24th accepting it. It was then he said, all the time he was reading it, the middle spirit should be called Christmas Current. "Do it," I said, and changed it to that in my manuscript.

Charles Dickens was pretty much a phenomenon, and a cautionary one. Family fallen on hard times; the blacking factory; then, shorthand clerk, court reporter, journalist, novelist, newspaper and magazine editor, philanthropist, reformer, speaker, long distance walker, insomniac, actor; the most famous reader of his own works who ever lived; Patriarch of a large family (to paraphrase Carla Tortelli on *Cheers*: they popped out of Mrs. Dickens like a Pez dispenser) and supporter of failed parents, siblings, strangers; involved in scandal the last ten years of his life. Some of his children (and his sister-in-law) stayed with him after the separation from his wife, as against the wife's family.

And those books and stories. Yow! They'll probably last as long as there's readin' and writin'.

Ackroyd's book (and the others) can tell you all that. I wanted to do some of the same things in "Household Words . . ." only in an alternate Dickensian England, with another Scrooge, another Cratchitt, another nephew, but the same fat turkey. And, as I remember (like Mel Torme says of writing "The Christmas Song (Chestnuts Roasting on an Open Fire)") it was written on the hottest day of the year, in Texas, without air-conditioning; a story of a cool England and a remembered older Christmas.

When this was published (more later) I got a nice note (via Michael Moorcock, who'd heard me read it in November and asked for a copy) from Peter Ackroyd. Yow! At that same reading, David Hartwell came up and said he wanted it for his *Christmas Magic* paperback, which appeared in December 1994.

Back to *Amazing*. The story was supposed to be out in the December 1993 issue. I went haring off, on an existential adventure, to be Writer in the Classroom in Telluride, Colorado (the two days after I'd read the story were spent driving 1,000 miles to arrive at the hell-hole of Telluride just at dusk the second day) for six weeks (I'm *not* a skier, I'm a fisherman, and the San Miguel froze slowly over, day by day) from Nov 10 to Dec 17 of 1993.

In the middle of teaching hellbound 7th graders (and a good class of high school seniors) some ways of expressing themselves not involving knives, a package arrived from home: *Amazing,* with a great illo for the story. Only instead of December 1993 it said Winter 1994.

Uh oh.

You guessed it. That was the last one. 68 years, and it took me to kill it.

Sorry, Kim. If it's any consolation, I have killed, by having a story in the very last of each, the following things: *Vertex, Galaxy, Crawdaddy* (twice!), *Eternity SF, New Dimensions, Shayol.* But I admit it, it took some *doing* to kill the very first, oldest SF magazine.

Waldrop: The Legend Continues.

The Effects of Alienation

It always seemed to be snowing in Zurich that winter, but as Peter walked toward the café, he found himself looking up at an astonishingly blue sky.

Cold, still colder than a well-digger's ass, but clear nonetheless. He was so taken aback he stopped. There was a dull sun, looking as frozen as an outdoor Christmas tree ornament, over to the west. The houses and buildings all seemed new-washed; even the slush on the sides of the street was white, not the usual sooty gray. Perhaps the crowd for the opening night might be larger than even he had hoped. If Brecht were still alive, he would have said, "Weather good for a crowd, good for a crowd."

There was a stuttering hum in the air, a summer sound from another country and time, the sound of a fan in a faraway room. It got louder. Then above the lake the airship *Hermann Göring II* pulled into view like an art deco sausage on its daily run from Freidrichschaffen across the border to Berne. Some mighty Germans aboard; an admiral's and two generals' pennants flew from the tail landing ropes just below the swastikas on the stubby fins. Peter's eyes were getting worse (he was in his fifties) but he noticed the flags while the thing was still two kilometers away. The airship passed out of sight beyond the nearest buildings. Its usual course was far north-west of Zurich—one of the Aryans must have wanted a look.

Higher up in the sky he saw the thin slash of white made by the Helsinki-Madrid jet, usually invisible far above the snowy clouds over Switzerland. Peter hadn't seen it for months (not that he'd even been looking). To people here, the passenger planes were something you only occasionally saw, like summer. Well, maybe that will change tonight, he thought. They'll never look at a jet plane or a rocket the same way again.

Then he asked himself: Who are we fooling?

He went on down the street to the Cabaret Kropotkin.

The actor doubling in the role of the blind organ grinder was having trouble with his Zucco, so in the last run-through he had to sing *a cappella*. Another headache, thought Peter. Brecht's widow sent the offending instrument out: the *one* thing you could get done in Switzerland was have things fixed. More trouble: the ropes holding some of the props had loosened; they had to be restrung.

Peter tugged on a carabinier. "Zero," he said to the actor, "you really *should* lose some weight." Peter had the voice of a small, adenoidal Austrian garter snake.

The other actor (in the Cabaret Kropotkin *everyone* was an actor, everyone a stagehand, an usher, waiter, a dish-washer) pulled himself to his full height. He towered over Peter and blocked his view of the stage. He let go of his end of the rope.

"What? And lose my personality?" said Zero. "It's glands!"

"Glands, my ass," said Peter. "On what we make, I don't know how you gain weight." He pulled on the guy rope.

"Do what? Gain? Back in America, I used to weigh—"

"Back in America," said Shemp, the other actor with a leading role in the play, "back in America, we all had jobs. We also knew how to keep a rope tight." He jerked it away, burning their hands.

"Quit trying to be your late brother!" said Zero, sucking on his fingers. "You just don't have Moe's unique personality."

"And he didn't have my looks. Eeep Eeep Eeep Eeep!"

Peter shook his head, twisted a turnbuckle past the stripped place on the threads.

"Vaudeville!" said Zero. "God, how I don't miss it!"

"Eight shows a day!" said Shemp. "Your name up in lights!"

"The only thing your name is going to be up in is the pay register," said Brecht's widow from the cabaret floor where she had returned without a sound, "if you don't get those ropes straightened out."

"Yes, comrade Ma'am," said Shemp for all of them.

A little after 5 p.m. they finished the last rehearsal and it was time for supper. They'd had to cook that, too. A healthy cabbage soup with potatoes and a thick black bread Zero had kneaded up that morning.

Madame Brecht, who wore her hair in a severe bun, joined them. The conversation was light. The Poles, Swedes, English, Americans, Germans, French and Lithuanians who made up the ensemble had been together for such a time they no longer needed to talk. One look, and everybody knew just how everybody else's life was going. When they did speak, it was in a sort of pig-Esperanto comprised of parts of all their languages, and when the Madame was around, great heaping doses of Hegelian gibberish.

Not that a single one of them didn't believe that being *right there right then* wasn't the only place to be.

Bruno, the old German gaffer, was staring into his soup bowl like it was the floor of Pontius Pilate's house.

Shemp whispered to Peter, "Here comes the fucking Paris story again."

"I was there," said Bruno. "I was in the German Army then. What did I know? I was fifty-three years old and had been drafted."

Madame Brecht started to say something. Peter caught her eye and raised his finger, warning her off.

"Paris!" said the old man, looking up from the table. "Paris, the second time we took it. There we were in our millions, drums beating, bugles blaring, rank on rank of us! There was the Führer in his chariot, Mussolini following behind in his. There they were pulling the Führer down the Champs Élysées, Montgomery and Eisenhower in the lead traces, de Gaulle and Bomber Harris behind. Poor Bomber! He'd been put in at the last moment after they shot Patton down like a dog when he refused. Then came all the Allied generals with their insignia ripped off. It was a beautiful spring day. It was fifteen years ago."

There were tears streaming down his face, and he looked at the Madame and smiled in a goofy way.

"I remember it well," continued Bruno, "for that night, while looting a store, under the floor-boards, I found the writings of Mr. Brecht."

"Thank you for your kind reminiscence, Bruno," said the Madame.

"Suck up!" said Zero, under his breath.

"Just another hard-luck story," said Shemp.

"I like it very much," said Peter to Zero quietly. "It has a certain decadent bourgeois charm."

"Does anyone else have an anecdote about the Master?" asked the Madame, looking around expectantly.

Peter sighed as someone else started in on yet another instructive little dialectic parable.

Arguing with Brecht had been like talking to a Communist post. When the man's mind was made up, that was that. When it wasn't was the only time you could show him he was being a Stalinist *putz*; only then had he been known to rewrite something.

The first time Peter had met Brecht, Peter had been nineteen and fresh off the last turnip truck from Ludow. All he wanted was a Berlin theater job; what Brecht wanted was a talented marionette. He'd ended up doing Brecht's comedy by night and Fritz Lang's movies by day, and in his copious free time learning to spend the increasingly inflated Weimar money, which eventually became too cheap to wipe your butt with. Then Peter found himself in America, via Hitchcock, and Brecht found himself in Switzerland, via Hitler.

Peter sighed, looking around the table. Everybody here had a story. Not like mine, but *just like* mine. I was making movies and money in America. I was nominated for the Academy Award *twice*, after playing Orientals and psychopaths and crazy weenies for ten years. There was a war on. I was safe. It was that fat old fart Greenstreet, God rest his soul, who talked me into the U.S.O. tour with him. There we were, waiting for Glenn Miller's plane to come in, near the Swiss border, six shows a day, Hitler almost done in, the biggest audiences we'd ever played to when BLAM!—the old world was gone.

And when I quit running, it's "Hello, Herr Brecht, it is I, your long-lost admirer, Peter, the doormat."

"And you?" asked Madame. "What can *you* tell us of our late departed genius?"

Peter ran through thirty years of memories, those of the first, and the ones of the last fifteen years. Yes, age had mellowed the parts of Brecht's mind that needed it. Yes, he had begun to bathe and change clothes more often after his second or third heart attack, which had made things much more pleasant. He had exploited people a little less; possibly he'd forgotten how, or was so used to it that he no longer noticed when he wasn't. No, the mental fires had never gone out. Yes, it was hard to carry on their work without the sharp nail of his mind at the center of their theater. He could also have said that Brecht spent the last three years of his life trying to put *The Communist Manifesto* into rhymed couplets. He *could* have said all that. Instead, he looked at the Madame. "Brecht wanted to live his life so that every day at 6 p.m. he could go into his room, lock the door, read cheap American detective stories, and eat cheese to his heart's content. The man must have had bowel muscles like steel strands."

Then Peter got up and left the room.

Walter Brettschneider was the Cultural Attaché to the Reichsconsul in Zurich and was only twenty-five years old. Which meant, of course, that he was a major in the Geheime Staats Polizei. His job at the Consulate included arranging and attending social and cultural affairs, arrangements for touring groups from the Fatherland to various Swiss cities (Zurich, he thought, rather than Berne, being the only city in the country with *any* culture at all). His other job was easier—he could have been assigned to one of the Occupied Lands, or South America, or as liaison with the Japanese, which every day was becoming more and more of a chore for the Reich; his friend back in Berlin in the Ministry of Manufacture told him the members of the Greater East Asia Co-Prosperity Sphere had come up with many technical innovations in the last few years; they were now making an automobile as good as the Volkswagen and had radio and televiewing equipment that required only three tubes.

That second job of his consisted of forwarding to Berlin, each year or so, a list of thirty to forty names. Of these, a dozen or fifteen would be picked. These people would suddenly find that their permanent resident alien status in Switzerland was in question, there were certain charges, etc. And then they would be asked by the Swiss to leave the country.

Everyone was satisfied with the arrangement, the Swiss, the Reich, in some strange way the resident aliens, as long as they weren't one of the dozen or so. Switzerland itself was mined and booby-trapped and well-defended. If the Reich tried to invade, the Alps would drop on them. Germany controlled everything going in and out—it surrounded the country for two thousand kilometers in every direction: the New Lands, New Russland, New Afrika, New Iceland, the lands along the shiny new Berlin-Baghdad *eisenbahn*—except the contents of the diplomatic pouches, and some of those, too.

If the Fatherland tried to use the Weapons on the Swiss, they lost all those glittery numbered assets, and endangered their surrounding territory.

So the system was understood. After all, as the First Führer had said, we have a thousand years; at a dozen a year we will eventually get them all.

Edward, his assistant, knocked and came in.

"Heil Bormann," he said, nonchalantly raising his hand a few inches.

"OK," said Brettschneider, doing likewise.

"You remember that the two younger cousins of the Swabian Minister for Culture are arriving Thursday?" asked Edward.

"I had tried to forget," said Brettschneider. He opened the big 1960 calendar on his desk to February 13th, made a note. "Will you *please* make sure the schedule in the hall is marked? Why, why do people come to Switzerland in the *winter*?"

"I certainly have no idea," said Edward. "What's doing?"

"There's a new show at the Kropotkin tonight. They're not saying what it is, so of course I have to go see."

"Not the kind of place you can take the cou—"

"Most assuredly not. But then again, last month they did the decadent American classic *Arsenic and Old Lace*. Quite amusing in its original version. Of course, in theirs, the Roosevelt character wasn't Theodore. And Jonathan was made up to look like the Second Führer—" Brettschneider looked up at the three photos on his wall—Hitler, Himmler, Bormann—Himmler's was one of the old official ones, from eleven years ago, before the chin operation, not the posthumous *new* official ones—"No, not really the kind of place, the type of plays two young women should see."

"Have a good time," said Edward. "*I* have to accompany the Reichsminister's wife to the Turkish thing."

"Oh? Yes? How's your Turkish?"

"It's being given in English, I am led to believe. I'll drop back in later today, in any case."

Edward left. Brettschneider stared at the doorway. For all he knew, Edward might be a *colonel* in the G.S.P.

"It's too bad they don't make Zambesi cigarettes anymore," said Caspar, the scene designer, as he smoked one of Peter's cheap German cigars. "We'd have them free. It was before your time, before you met Brecht, back in the early Twenties. He was always trying to write pirate movies and detective novels. Before Marx. He designed an ad campaign for the tobacco company. He took an unlimited supply of Zambesis in payment. He grew to detest them before the company went out of business. I thought them quite good."

"I'd give anything to smoke a Camel again," said Shemp. They were putting down tablecloths and ashtrays, and lighting the candles out front. Zero was pumping up the beer spigots over behind the bar. Madame was, as usual, nowhere to be seen, but, say something wrong, you could be sure she would hear it. The woman was fueled by the thought that someone, somewhere, wasn't thinking about Bertolt Brecht.

"I heard they don't make them over there anymore," said Caspar. "The Turks, you know? They claim, in Germany, Airship Brand is the same thing as Camels used to be."

"They're as full of shit as Christmas geese," said Shemp. "God, what I wouldn't give for a slice of goose!"

And so it went until time to open, when the Madame suddenly appeared in front of Peter and said, "You work the door until 1930 hours. *Then* you may get into costume."

"Yes, comrade Madame," he said.

There was no use arguing with her. It would have been like asking Rondo Hatton, "Why the long face?".

He went to the door. Under the covered walkway quite a nice crowd had gathered early. Peter looked at the sign out front with its double silhouette of Kropotkin and Brecht and the hand-painted legend: *Tonight!—Cabaret Kropotkin—The Zürcher Ensemble—new BRECHT play!*

It wasn't really Brecht. It wasn't exactly a play. It wasn't exactly new. They'd been working on it steadily in the three years since Brecht's death.

He undid the latches as the people surged expectantly toward him. He opened the doors, stood back, nodded his head toward the tables.

"Trough's open," he said.

Brettschneider arrived a few minutes to eight, went in, nodded to Caspar, who was bartending, and found a spot at a table near the stage with three Swiss students. He listened to their talk a while—it must be nice to live in their world. They were treating the night as a lark; a dangerous place, reputed to be filled with drugs and lady Bolsheviks with mattresses tied to their backs.

Hesse was over in the corner. Brettschneider nodded to him. He doubted the old man saw him, as his eyes were becoming quite bad (he was, after all, 83 years old now); he would go over and say hello during the interval.

There were a few of what passed as Swiss celebrities present, some Germans, a few Swiss arms dealers.

Across the length of the stage was the patented Zürcher Ensemble half-curtain let down on a length of pipe. Behind it was the bare back wall. Across this were strung a few twinkling lights, like a Christmas tree with too few bulbs. People moved back and forth across the stage, quite visible to the audience from the neck up.

The band took its place in front of the curtain—banjo, piano, clarinet—and began a jazz arrangement of "The Internationale"; one or two people stood, and the rest began clapping along. When that was done, they played the old favorite "Moon of Alabama" from *Mahoganny*, and "Don't Sit Under the Apple Tree with Anyone Else but Me". Brettschneider drank a chocolate schnapps and began to feel quite warm. The cabaret was already thick with the blue smoke of a hundred different tobaccos.

Then the lights went down. From the ceiling a sign dropped: *Cabaret Kropotkin*—a hand came down from above and beat on the top of the sign, which unfolded into three parts: *Cabaret Kropotkin—The Zürcher Ensemble Presents Bertolt Brecht's—Die Dreiraketenmensch Spaceoper!* The half-curtain came up. Another sign dropped in: *Scene: The Rocket Men's Club. Time: The Future. Moritaten.*

An actor dressed as a blind man came on with a barrel organ and began singing "The Night We Dropped the Big One on Biggin Hill".

Zero, Peter, and Shemp, in their Rocket Men Cadet uniforms, walk by the beggar who is then escorted offstage by a policeman.

"Here we are at last!" says Zero. "Just out of Basic Training! Our first taste of the Outer Reaches!"

"I'm ready for some inner reaches!" says Shemp.

"Beer again!" says Peter.

The flies pulled up revealing a bar's interior, tables. Dropping in were huge posters of von Braun and Dornberger, and a portrait in the frame reserved for Führers. The audience found it hilarious.

Brettschneider wrote in his notebook: *Unnecessary fun made of Himmler Jr.*

When things quit falling, unfurling and drooping in from the overheads, there were swastikas whirling like propellers and a giant, very pink rocket with a purple nose cone to be seen.

The three students then sang, as appropriate title cards were revealed, "It's Me for the Stars, and the Stars for Me", followed by Zero's "Once You Get Up There". Then one of their instructor officers, Major Strasser, came in and had a drink with them.

"But don't you find it cold here?" asks Peter.

"We Germans must get used to all climates, from the Sahara to the poles of Saturn," says the major.

Then the chorines danced on and sang "Dock Your Rocket *Here*" and a chorus line, not of cadets but true Rocket Men, danced on, including one small grotesque figure in sunglasses.

Brettschneider wrote: *more " " " " H. Jr.*, beneath his first entry.

The cadets and Rocket Men ran off with the chorines, and a new card dropped in: *The Field for Rockets. Training.* On one side of the fence the three cadets stood at attention; on the other a girl skipped rope to the chant:

"My girlfriend's name is Guernica

Her Daddy bombed 'Merika . . ."

The Drill Instructor, called Manley Mann, comes on and yells at the cadets.

"Where you going, you stupid lot?"

"Up Up Up."

"How you goin'?"

"Fast Fast Fast."

"At night, whatcha see inna sky?"

"Nazi Socialist Moon!"

"Gimme a thousand pushups."

The cadets dropped down, began to count, "One Vengeance Weapon, Two Vengeance Weapon, Three Vengeance Weapon . . ." There was stage business with the pushups, most of it dealing with Zero's attempts to do nothing while yelling at the top of his voice.

When they finished, Manley Mann said, "Right. Today we're gonna learn about the MD2D3 Course Plottin' Calculator. Walk smart follow me follow me—" and off.

Another card: *Six Weeks Later. Cadet Barracks. Night.*

Then came Shemp's solo, as he looked out the window at a bored-looking stagehand holding up a cardboard moon. He did some comic patter, then went on to sing "I Wish I Had a Little Rocket of My Own".

Then the lights went up, the Intermission sign dropped down, and the half-curtain was lowered to the stage.

Backstage the Madame was furious. "I *told* you we must take that song out!" she yelled at Shemp. "You realize you made the audience identify with your character? You know that's against all the Master's teachings! You were supposed to sing the 'Song of the Iron Will'." Shemp weaved like a punch-drunk boxer, running his hands through his dank, lanky hair. "I got mixed up," he said. "They played the wrong music, so I sang it. Yell at the band."

"You must always *always* remember the *Verfremsdungeffekt*. You must always remind people they are watching a performance. Why do you think the stagehand holds the prop moon so everyone can see him? Are you an idiot? What were you thinking?"

Shemp paused, ticking off on his fingers. "I do. I always do. I don't know. Yes. Nothing."

"*Why* must I be saddled with morons?" Shemp said something under his breath.

"What?! What did you say?!"

"I said I gotta get a drink of water, or I'm gonna lose my voice next act."

"That's not what you said!"

"Yes it is, comrade Ma'am."

"Get out of my sight!"

"At once," said Shemp, and disappeared offstage.

Zero sat on a crate in the alleyway. It was bitterly cold, but this was the only place he was sure Madame wouldn't follow him. Peter came out, lit up a butt one of the waiters had brought him from a customer's ashtray.

"We gotta find another way to make a living," said Zero, his breath a fog.

"We've said that every night for sixteen years now," said Peter. "Christ, it's cold!"

"Wasn't it Fitzgerald that said nothing much starts in Switzerland, but lots of things end there?"

"How the fuck should I know?" said Peter.

"Well, I don't want to be one of the things that ends here," said Zero.

Peter thought of lines from a movie he'd been in long ago, lines dealing with exile, expatriation, and death, and started to say one of them, but didn't. Besides, they'd already used the best lines from that movie in the play.

"It's like I told that fat great Limey actor once," said Peter. "'Chuck,' I said, 'if you *have* to pork young men, just go for god's sake and *do* it, and come back and learn your goddamn lines; just quit torturing yourself about it!'"

"Are you saying I should pick up a little boy?" asked Zero.

Peter shrugged his shoulders. "Where else is there to go but here, Zero?" he asked.

Zero was quiet. Then: "Sometimes I get so tired, Pete. Soon we'll be old men. Like Bruno. Then dead old men . . ."

"But theater!—" began Peter.

"—and Brecht!—" said Zero.

"—will live forever!" they finished in unison. They laughed and Zero fell off his crate into the snow. Then they brushed themselves off and went back inside.

Brettschneider had made his rounds of the tables during the break. He looked over his notes, made an emendation on one of them. He ate a kaiser roll, then drank a gin-and-tonic, feeling the pine-needle taste far back in his throat.

Then the band came back, played the last-act overture, and cards dropped back in.

There was a classroom lecture on the futurist films of Fritz Lang, *Metropolis* and *Frau im Mond*, which then went backwards and forwards to cover other spaceward-looking films: *Himmelskibet*, *F.P.1 Antwortet Nicht*, *Der Tunnel* and *Welttraumschiff I Startet*, at which Zero insisted on confusing Leni Reifenstahl with the Dusseldorf Murderer.

Brettschneider wrote: *Unacceptable reference to Reichsminister for Culture.*

Then the play moved on to Graduation Day, where the massed cadets (represented by the three actors, some mops and brooms with mustaches painted on them, and a boxful of toy soldiers) sang "Up Up for the Fatherland" and were handed their rocket insignia.

The actors changed onstage into their powder-blue uniforms (overalls) with the jackboots (rubber galoshes) as a sign came down: *First Assignment. Rocket Man City Peënemünde.*

Another sign: *Suddenly—A Propaganda Crisis!*

Major Strasser comes up to the three Rocket Men. "Suddenly," he says, "a propaganda crisis!"

"Eeep Eeep Eeep Eeep!" says Shemp, staggering.

"Attention!" says the major. "Our enemies in the U.S.R. far beyond the Urals have launched one of their primitive reaction-motor ships. It is bound for the far reaches of the Solar System. Our information is that it is filled with the Collected Works of Marx and Lenin, and the brilliant but non-Aryan playwright Bertolt Brecht."

(There was a boo from the audience, followed by laughter. The actors on-stage held still until it was over.)

"Your first assignment is to intercept this missile before it can spread unapproved thinking to Nazi Socialist space and beyond, and to destroy it."

There was a blackout; four signs were illuminated, one after the other:

Three Go Out.
One Gets Killed.
One Goes Mad.
One Doesn't Come Back.

The first two signs were lit. In the darkness, Zero is in a balsawood frame-work shaped like a small rocket. To his uniform has been added a bent coat hanger representing a space helmet.

His voice is roaring, he is determined. The band is raucous behind him but his singing overpowers it.

"Target in sight!
It's easy, all right!
Just line up the guns and watch all the fu—
Ooops!"

A papier-mâché meteor, painted red and trailing smoke vertically, comes out of the darkness. It smashes into Zero's ship, which flies to flinders. Zero, his coat-hanger helmet now gone, floats up into the air on wires in the dark, a hideous grin on his face.

The spot-lit placard: *One Goes Mad.*

Shemp's balsawood spaceship. Zero floats directly in front of it. "Whoa!" yells Shemp. He punches things on his instrument panel, running his hands over his coat hanger. "Eeep Eeep Eeep Eeep!" Then he sits bolt upright, unmoving except for the lips, making perfect sense in a monotonous voice, reciting the successive graph plots on a Fibonacci curve, as he and his ship, trailing vertical smoke, are pulled by ropes out of the light into the darkness at the back of the stage.

The spotlight searches around, finds the sign: *One Doesn't Come Back.* Peter in his ship. He is mumbling the Soldier's Creed. At the other side of the stage, light comes up on a toy rocket. Peter takes out a dart gun, fires twice at the toy, his arm outside the ship's framework as he reloads the rubber-tipped darts. One finally hits the toy rocket— it explodes like a piñata.

Then an *oogah* klaxon horn is blown backstage, causing the audience to jump, and Peter's ship is bathed in flickering red light. "Uh-oh," he says. "Trouble." Then the band begins to play softly, and he sings "I Wonder What Deborah's Doing in Festung Amerika Tonight?"

The ship tilts downwards. Blackout. A sign: *Mars.*

When the lights come back up the stage is clear. A red silk drop cloth covers the ground. For a full minute, nothing happens. Then Peter's balsawood ship, him inside, flies out of the wings and he lands flat on his ass, legs straight out while pieces of wood bounce all over.

He stands up, brushes himself off. As he does so, stage-hands begin to ripple the red silk, making it look like drifting, gently blowing sand. Peter takes off his coat hanger, takes a deep breath. A book falls from above, bounces at the rear of the moving red stage. Then another follows. Peter looks up. A book slowly lowers toward him on a wire. He reaches up and plucks it from the air. Others fall around him occasionally throughout the scene. Peter begins to read. His eyes widen even more. He looks up at the audience. He reads more. Then he stands up. "Holy dialectical shit!" he says.

Then the lights came up, and the chorines, stagehands, actors, ushers and dishwashers came in, taking their bows. Zero floated down from the ceiling on his wires, blowing kisses. Then the Madame came out, glaring at Zero, turned and took a bow to the audience for having survived Brecht.

Then they all passed among the tables, holding out baskets for donations.

Brettschneider stayed at his table drinking, while the audience mingled with the members of the Ensemble. He noticed that he'd written nothing in his notebook since the couple of entries just after intermission. When he saw Peter take something from Madame, put on his coat and go out the door, Brettschneider wrote: *Suspects then all followed their usual routines.* Then he gathered up his own things, nodded to Caspar who was still tending bar, and went back to his home and to bed.

Christ, it's even colder than this morning, thought Peter. He turned off the main avenue, went down a side street. The snow, which this morning had seemed so white and pure, was now gray, crusted ice. Even so, as he turned into a small courtyard, he saw that only a few sets of footprints had come and gone that way the whole day.

Near the middle was a rusty iron gate. He went in with a loud groaning squeal from the metal. On the wall was a brass plate that said *Union of Soviet Republics Consular Offices.* Peter went to the mail drop, took the envelope out of his thin overcoat pocket. On the outside, written in Madame's florid script was *From Your Comrades at the Cabaret Kropotkin.* Peter tore open the envelope, took out a few hundred francs, slapped some medical adhesive tape over the torn flap, tied it around twice with some twine, and dropped it in the slot.

As Brecht had said: First the beans, then the morals.

He went back up the avenue, crunching through the frosty ice on the way. The night was still clear, bitterly frigid. He looked up at the winking stars, and saw the slow moving dot of Space Platform #6 on its two-hour orbit.

He heard a streetcar bell. He knew of a place he could go and get a cup of real coffee and watch a fireplace burning for an hour or two, where the thought of Herr Brecht would never cross his mind. He began whistling "In the Hall of the Mountain King".

Afterword to:

The Effects of Alienation

Schickelgrubers on Parade:

Most writers, when they write alternate-Nazi stories (*The Man in the High Castle, SS-GB, Fatherland*) do it to find out what would happen, to say, the U.S., the world, great historical figures.

I wrote this to find out what effect Hitler winning World War II would have had on Peter Lorre.

I also knew it would be about Bertolt Brecht, Kurt Weill, Weimar Germany, the alienation effect etc., only transposed, and later. And have some of my favorite character actors in it.

So I read and read. And made tapes of Brecht-Weill songs, "Mack the Knife", "Alabama Song", which I played while reading.

Then I was flown to England for the first and only time in my life and was one of the guests of honor at Mexicon IV held in Harrowgate. It was like being in a foreign country where they speak much the same language. They're all dying of alcoholism, nicotine poisoning and despair. I walked around with a pint and a half of Guinness Stout in me for a week (nobody would let the level drop) until I told them, "You know, I'm not much of a drinking man."

"You could have fooled us," they said.

In an existential programming moment, I (just having finished it) read the story to the assembled convention, and Roz Kaveny did an on-the-spot critical talk/interview.

"Gee whiz, Roz!" I said.

I came back from England, slept for a week or so, then rewrote it and sent it to Ellen Datlow at *Omni* so I could get "Why Did?" back to re-write it (see *that* afterword for *that* story), but since I'd already been paid, I didn't make any money on the deal.

A lot of the feel of the story, I think, was from writing it in a foreign country—well, slightly foreign—where they *do* do things differently.

And Peter Lorre goes back a long way with me. I once wrote a play called "The Long Goodnight" about Lorre and the dying Bogart—only Bogart as Sam Spade/Philip Marlowe—while I was in college, during the Bogart boom of the 1960s. Then Woody Allen wrote *Play It Again, Sam*. Also in college, I played the kid in *A Thousand Clowns* because I was the only one who could do Peter Lorre.

If you watch his films, you can look at one of the most phenomenally-talented actors of this century. Beneath the twitches and quirks ("I *told* you to keep that *monkey* away from me!" "This is my wife. You can look at her, but you can't *touch* her."—*Island of Doomed Men*, 1940) was a versatile performer. While he was being the child-killer in M (1930) in the afternoons for Fritz Lang he was doing musical comedy at night.

He arrived in England knowing three words of English: *Milk, Hamburger, Yes*. He got his first job with Hitchcock because someone told him Hitch liked to tell long boring shaggy-dog stories. Lorre went in, shook his hand, watched Hitchcock's lips move for five minutes. When they stopped moving Lorre fell down laughing. Hitch shook his hand again, and Lorre was in *The Man Who Knew Too Much* (1934). He learned English in a week or two. And so on, through the next 30 years, through the illness that took him from being a slim twitchy actor to being an overweight twitchy one, the best ever. He was a survivor, and in my story he survives Nazis, WW II and the Dragon-Lady Comrade Madam. He's the only one who learned the message at the heart of Brecht's didacticism.

And, I got to write a play I never got to write in college.

Life is a *song*.

The Sawing Boys

There was a place in the woods where three paths came together and turned into one big path heading south.

A bearded man in a large straw hat and patched bib overalls came down one. Over his shoulder was a tow sack, and out of it stuck the handle of a saw. The man had a long wide face and large thin ears.

Down the path to his left came a short man in butternut pants and a red checkerboard shirt that said *Ralston-Purina Net Wt. 20 lbs.* on it. He had on a bright red cloth cap that stood up on the top of his head. Slung over his back was a leather strap; hanging from it was a big ripsaw.

On the third path were two people, one of whom wore a yellow-and-black striped shirt, and had a mustache that stood straight out from the sides of his nose. The other man was dressed in a dark brown barn coat. He had a wrinkled face, and wore a brown Mackenzie cap down from which the earflaps hung, even though it was a warm morning. The man with the mustache carried a narrow folding ladder; the other carried a two-man bucksaw.

The first man stopped.

"Hi yew!" he said in the general direction of the other two paths.

"Howdee!" said the short man in the red cap.

"Well, well, well!" said the man with the floppy-eared hat, putting down his big saw.

"Weow!" said the man with the wiry mustache.

They looked each other over, keeping their distance, eyeing each others' clothing and saws.

"Well, I guess we know where we're all headed," said the man with the brown Mackenzie cap.

"I reckon," said the man in the straw hat. "I'm Luke Apuleus, from over Cornfield County way. I play the crosscut."

"I'm Rooster Joe Banty," said the second. "I'm a ripsaw bender myself."

"I'm Felix Horbliss," said the man in stripes with the ladder. "That thar's Cave Canem. We play this here big bucksaw."

They looked at each other some more.

"I'm to wonderin'," said Luke, bringing his tow sack around in front of him. "I'm wonderin' if 'n we know the same tunes. Seems to me it'd be a shame to have to play agin' each other if 'n we could help it."

"You-all know 'Trottin' Gertie Home'?" asked Felix.

Luke and Rooster Joe nodded.

"How about 'When the Shine comes Out'n the Dripper'?" asked Rooster Joe.

The others nodded.

"How are you on 'Snake Handler's Two-Step'?" asked Luke Apuleus.

More nods.

"Well, that's a start on it," said Cave Canem. "We can talk about it on the way there. I bet we'd sound right purty together."

So side by side by bucksaw and ladder, they set out down the big path south.

What we are doing is, we are walking down this unpaved road. How we have come to be walking down this unpaved road is a very long and tiresome story that I should not bore you with.

We are being Chris the Shoemaker, who is the brains of this operation, and a very known guy back where we come from, which is south of Long Island, and Large Jake and Little Willie, who are being the brawn, and Miss Millie Dee Chantpie, who is Chris the Shoemaker's doll, and who is always dressed to the nines, and myself, Charlie Perro, whose job it is to remind everyone what their job is being.

"I am astounded as all get-out," says Little Willie, "that there are so many places with no persons in them nowise," looking around at the trees and bushes and such. "We have seen two toolsheds which looked as if they once housed families of fourteen, but of real-for-true homes, I am not seeing any."

"Use your glims for something besides keeping your nose from sliding into your eyebrows," says Chris the Shoemaker. "You will have seen the sign that said one of the toolcribs is the town of Podunk, and the other shed is the burg of Shtetl. I am believing the next one we will encounter is called Pratt Falls. I am assuming it contains some sort of trickle of fluid, a stunning and precipitous descent in elevation, established by someone with the aforementioned surname."

He is called Chris the Shoemaker because that is now his moniker, and he once hung around shoestores. At that time the cobbler shops was the place where the policy action was hot, and before you can be saying Hey Presto! there is Chris the Shoemaker in a new loud suit looking like a comet, and he is the middle guy between the shoemakers and the elves that rig the policy.

"Who would have thought it?" asked Little Willie. "Both balonies on the rear blowing at the same time, and bending up the frammus, and all the push and pull running out? I mean, what are the chances?"

Little Willie is called that because he is the smaller of the two brothers. Large Jake is called that because, oh my goodness, is he large. He is so large that people have confused him for nightfall—they are standing on the corner shooting the breeze with some guys, and suddenly all the light goes away, and so do the other guys. There are all these cigarettes dropping to the pavement where guys used to be, and the person looks around and Whoa! it is not night at all, it is only Large Jake.

For two brothers they do not look a thing alike. Little Willie looks, you should excuse the expression, like something from the family Rodentia, whereas Large Jake is a very pleasant-looking individual, only the pleasant is spread across about three feet of mook.

Miss Millie Dee Chantpie is hubba-hubba stuff (only Chris the Shoemaker best not see you give her more than one Long Island peek) and the talk is she used to be a roving debutante. Chris has the goo-goo eyes for her, and she is just about a whiz at the new crossword puzzles, which always give Little Willie a headache when he tries to do one.

Where we are is somewhere in the state of Kentucky, which I had not been able to imagine had I not seen it yesterday from the train. Why we were here was for a meet with this known guy who runs a used furniture business on South Wabash Street in Chi City. The meet was to involve lots of known guys, and to be at some hunting lodge in these hills outside Frankfort, where we should not be bothered by prying eyes. Only first the train is late, and the jalopy we bought stalled on us in the dark, and there must have been this wrong turn somewhere, and the next thing you are knowing the balonies blow and we are playing in the ditch and gunk and goo are all over the place.

So here we are walking down this (pardon the expression) road, and we are looking for a phone and a mechanically inclined individual, and we are not having such a hot time of it.

"You will notice the absence of wires," said Chris the Shoemaker, "which leads me to believe we will not find no blower at this watery paradise of Pratt Falls."

"Christ Almighty, I'm gettin' hungry!" says Miss Millie Dee Chantpie of a sudden. She is in this real flapper outfit, with a bandeau top and fringes, and is wearing pearls that must have come out of oysters the size of freight trucks.

"If we do not soon find the object of our quest," says Chris the Shoemaker, "I shall have Large Jake blow you the head off a moose, or whatever they have in place of cows out here."

It being a meet, we are pretty well rodded up, all except for Chris, who had to put on his Fall Togs last year on Bargain Day at the courthouse and do a minute standing on his head, so of course he can no longer have an oscar anywhere within a block of his person, so Miss Millie Dee Chantpie carries his cannon in one of her enchanting little reticules.

Large Jake is under an even more stringent set of behavioral codes, but he just plain does not care, and I do not personally know any cops or even the Sammys who are so gauche as to try to frisk him without first calling out the militia. Large Jake usually carries a powder wagon—it is the kind of thing they use on mad elephants or to stop runaway locomotives only it is sawed off on both ends to be only about a foot long.

Little Willie usually carries a sissy rod, only it is a dumb gat so there is not much commotion when he uses it—just the sound of air coming out of it, and then the sound of air coming out of whomsoever he uses it on. Little Willie has had a date to Ride Old Sparky before, only he was let out on a technical. The technical was that the judge had not noticed the big shoe box full of geetas on the corner of his desk before he brought the gavel down.

I am packing my usual complement of calibers which (I am prouder than anything to say) I have never used. They are only there for the bulges for people to ogle at while Chris the Shoemaker is speaking.

Pratt Falls is another couple of broken boards and a sign saying Feed and Seed. There was this dry ditch with a hole with a couple of rocks in it.

"It was sure no Niagara," says Little Willie, "that's for certain."

At the end of the place was a sign, all weathered out except for the part that said 2 MILES.

We are making this two miles in something less than three-quarters of an hour because it is mostly uphill and our dogs are barking, and Miss Millie Dee Chantpie, who has left her high heels in the flivver, is falling off the sides of her flats very often.

We are looking down into what passes for a real live town in these parts.

"This is the kind of place," says Little Willie, "where when you are in the paper business, and you mess up your double sawbuck plates, and print a twentyone-dollar bill, you bring it here and ask for change. And the guy at the store will look in the drawer and ask you if two nines and a three will do."

"Ah, but look, gentlemen and lady," says Chris the Shoemaker, "there are at least two wires coming down over the mountain into this metropolis, and my guess is that they are attached to civilization at the other end."

"I do not spy no filling station," I says. "But there does seem to be great activity for so early of a morning." I am counting houses. "More people are already in town than live here."

"Perhaps the large gaudy sign up ahead will explain it," says Little Willie. The sign is being at an angle where another larger dirt path comes into town. From all around on the mountains I can see people coming in in wagons and on horses and on foot.

We get to the sign. This is what it says, I kid you not:

BIG HARMONY CONTEST!
BRIMMYTOWN SQUARE SAT MAY 16
$50 FIRST PRIZE
Brought to you by Watkins Products
and CARDUI, Makers of BLACK DRAUGHT
Extra! Sacred Harp Singing
Rev. Shapenote and the Mt. Sinai Choir.

"Well, well," says Chris. "Looks like there'll be plenty of *étrangers* in this burg. We get in there, make the call on the meet, get someone to fix the jalopy, and be on our way. We should fit right in."

While Chris the Shoemaker is saying this, he is adjusting his orange-and-pink tie and shooting the cuffs on his purple-and-white pinstripe suit. Little Willie is straightening his pumpkin-colored, double-breasted suit and brushing the dust off his yellow spats. Large Jake is dressed in a pure white suit with a black shirt and white tie, and has on a white fedora with a thin black band. Miss Millie Dee Chantpie swirls her fringes and rearranges the ostrich feather in her cloche. I feel pretty much like a sparrow among peacocks.

"Yeah," I says, looking over the town, "they'll probably never notice we been here."

They made their way into town and went into a store. They bought themselves some items, and went out onto the long, columned verandah of the place, and sat down on some nail kegs, resting their saws and ladders against the porch railings.

Cave Canem had a big five-cent RC Cola and a bag of Tom's Nickel Peanuts. He took a long drink of the cola, tore the top off the celluloid bag, and poured the salted peanuts into the neck of the bottle. The liquid instantly turned to foam and overflowed the top, which Canem put into his mouth. When it settled down, he drank from the bottle and chewed on the peanuts that came up the neck.

Rooster Joe took off his red cap. He had a five-cent Moon Pie the size of a dinner plate and took bites off that.

Horbliss had a ten-cent can of King Oscar Sardines. The key attached to the bottom broke off at the wrong place. Rather than tearing his thumb up, he took out his pocketknife and cut the top of the can off and peeled the ragged edge back. He drank off the oil, smacking his lips, then took out the sardines between his thumb and the knife blade and ate them.

Luke had bought a two-foot length of sugarcane and was sucking on it, spitting out the fine slivers which came away in his mouth.

They ate in silence and watched the crowds go by, clumps of people breaking away and eddying into the stores and shops. At one end of town, farmers stopped their wagons and began selling the produce. From the other end, at the big open place where the courthouse would be if Brimmytown were the county seat, music started up.

They had rarely seen so many men in white shirts, even on Sunday, and women and kids in their finest clothes; even if they were only patched and faded coveralls, they were starched and clean.

Then a bunch of city flatlanders came by—the men all had on hats and bright suits and ties, and the woman, a goddess, was the first flapper they had ever seen. The eyes of the flatlanders were moving everywhere. Heads turned to watch them all along their route. They were moving toward the general mercantile, and they looked tired and dusty for all their fancy duds.

"Well, boys," said Luke. "That were a right smart breakfast. I reckon usall better be gettin' on down towards the musical place and see what the otherns look like."

They gathered up their saws and ladders and walked toward the sweetest sounds this side of Big Bone Lick.

"So," says Little Willie to a citizen, "tell us where we can score a couple of motorman's gloves?"

The man is looking at him like he has just stepped off one of the outermost colder planets. This is fitting, for the citizen looks to us vice versa.

"What my friend of limited vocabulary means," says Chris the Shoemaker to the astounding and astounded individual, "is where might we purchase a mess of fried pork chops?"

The man keeps looking at us with his wide eyes the size of doorknobs.

"Eats?" I volunteers.

Nothing is happening.

Large Jake makes eating motions with his mitt and goozle.

Still nothing.

"Say, fellers," says this other resident, "you won't be gettin' nothing useful outin him. He's one of the simpler folks hereabouts, what them Victorian painter fellers used to call 'naturals'. What you want's Ma Gooser's place, straight down this yere street."

"Much obliged," says Chris.

"It's about time, too," says Miss Millie Dee Chantpie. "I'm so hungry I could eat the ass off a pigeon through a park bench!"

I am still staring at the individual who has given us directions, who is knocking the ashes out of his corncob pipe against a rain barrel.

"Such a collection of spungs and feebs I personally have never seen," says Chris the Shoemaker, who is all the time looking at the wire that comes down the hill into town.

"I must admit you are right," says Little Willie. And indeed it seems every living thing for three counties is here—there are nags and wagons, preggo dolls with stair-step children born nine months and fifteen minutes apart, guys wearing only a hat and one blue garment, a couple of men with what's left of Great War uniforms with the dago dazzlers still pinned to the chests—yes indeedy, a motley and hilarity-making group.

The streets are being full of wagons with melons and the lesser legumes and things which for a fact I know grow in the ground. The indigenous peoples are selling everything what moves. And from far away you can hear the beginnings of music.

"I spy," says Chris the Shoemaker.

"Whazzat?" asks Little Willie.

"I spy the blacksmith shop, and I spy the general mercantile establishment to which the blower wire runs. Here is what we are doing. William and I will saunter over to the smithy and forge, where we will inquire of aid for the vehicle. Charlie Perro, you will go make the call which will tender our apologies as being late for the meet, and get some further instructions. Jacob, you will take the love of my life, Miss Millie, to this venerable Ma Gooser's eatatorium where we will soon join you in a prodigious repast."

The general mercantile is in the way of selling everything on god's green earth, and the aroma is very mouth-watering—it is a mixture of apple candy and nag tack, coal oil and licorice and flour, roasted coffee and big burlap sacks of nothing in particular. There is ladies' dresses and guy hats and weapons of all kinds.

There is one phone; it is on the back wall; it is the kind Alexander Graham Bell made himself.

"Good person," I says to the man behind the counter, who is wearing specs and a vest and has a tape measure draped over his shoulder, "might I use your telephonic equipment to make a collect long-distance call?"

"Everthin's long-distance from here," he opines. "Collect, you say?"

"That is being correct."

He goes to the wall and twists a crank and makes bell sounds. "Hello, Gertie. This is Spoon. How's things in Grinder Switch? . . . You don't say? Well, there's a city feller here needs to make a co-llect call. Right. You fix him up." He hands me the long earpiece, and puts me in the fishwife care of this Gertie, and parks himself nearby and begins to count some bright glittery objects.

I tells Gertie the number I want. There are these sounds like the towers are falling. "And what's your name," asks this Gertie.

I gives her the name of this known newspaper guy who hangs out at Chases' and who writes about life in the Roaring Forties back in the Big City. The party on the other end will be wise that that is not who it is, but will know I know he knows.

I hear this voice and Gertie gives them my name and they say okay. "Go ahead," says Gertie.

"We are missing the meet," I says.

"Bleaso!" says the voice. "Eetmay alledoffcay. Ammysays Iseway! Izzyoway and Oemay erehay."

Itshay I am thinking to myself. To him I says: "Elltay usoway atwhay otay ooday?"

"Ogay Omehay!"

He gets off the blower.

"I used to have a cousin that could talk Mex," says Spoon at the counter. I thank him for the use of the phone. "Proud as a peach of it," he says, wiping at it with a cloth.

"Well, you should be," I tell him. Then I buy two cents worth of candy and put it in a couple of pockets, and then I ease on down this town's Great White Way.

This Ma Gooser's is some hopping joint. I don't think the griddle here's been allowed to cool off since the McKinley Administration. Large Jake and Miss Millie Dee Chantpie are already tucking in. The place is as busy as a chophouse on Chinese New Year.

There are these indistinguishable shapes on the platters.

A woman the size of Large Jake comes by with six full plates along each arm, headed towards a table of what looks like two oxdrivers in flannel shirts. These two oxdrivers are as alike as all get-out. The woman puts three plates in front of each guy and they fall into them mouth first.

The woman comes back. She has wild hair, and it does not look like she has breasts; it looks like she has a solid shelf across her chest under her work shirt. "Yeah?" she says, wiping sweat from her brow.

"I'd like a steak and some eggs," I says, "over easy on the eggs, steak well-done, some juice on the side."

"You'll get the breakfast, if 'n you get anything," she says. "Same's everybody else." She follows my eyes back to the two giants at the next table. Large Jake can put away the groceries, but he is a piker next to these two. A couple of the plates in front of them are already shining clean and they are reaching for a pile of biscuits on the next table as they work on their third plates.

"Them's the Famous Singin' Eesup Twins, Bert and Mert," says Ma Gooser. "If 'n everybody could pile it in like them, I'd be a rich woman." She turns to the kitchen.

"Hey, Jughead," she yells, "where's them six dozen biscuits?"

"Comin', Ma Gooser!" yells a voice from back in the hell there.

"More blackstrap 'lasses over here, Ma!" yells a corncob from another table.

"Hold your water!" yells Ma. "I only got six hands!" She runs back towards the kitchen.

Chris the Shoemaker and Little Willie comes in and settles down.

"Well, we are set in some departments. The blacksmith is gathering up the tools of his trade and Little William will accompany him in his wagon to the site of the vehicular happenstance. I will swear to you, he picks up his anvil and puts it into his wagon, just like that. The thing must have dropped the wagon bed two foot. What is it they are feeding the locals around here?" He looks down at the plates in front of Large Jake and Miss Millie. "What is *dat?*"

"I got no idea, sweetie," says Miss Millie, putting another forkful in, "but it sure is good!"

"And what's the news from our friends across the ways?"

"Zex," I says.

He looks at me. "*You* are telling *me* zex in this oomray full of oobrays?"

"No, Chris," I says, "the *word* is zex."

"Oh," he says, "and for why?"

"Izzy and Moe," I says.

"*Izzy and Moe?!* How did Izzy and Moe get wise to this deal?"

"How do Izzy and Moe get wise to anything," I says, keeping my voice low and not moving my goozle. "Hell, if someone could get *them* to come over, this umray unningray biz would be a snap. If they can dress like women shipwrecks and get picked up by runners' ships, they can get wind of a meet somewhere."

"So what are our options being?" asks Chris the Shoemaker.

"That is why we have all these round-trip tickets," I says.

He is quiet. Ma Gooser slaps down these plates in front of us, and coffee all round, and takes two more piles of biscuits over to the Famous Singing Eesup Twins.

"Well, that puts the damper on my portion of the Era of Coolidge Prosperity," says Chris the Shoemaker. "I am beginning to think this decade is going to be a more problematical thing than first imagined. In fact, I am getting in one rotten mood." He takes a drink of coffee. His beezer lights up. "Say, the flit in the *Knowledge Box* got *nothing* on this." He drains the cup dry. He digs at his plate, then wolfs it all down. "Suddenly my mood is changing. Suddenlike, I am in a working mood."

I drops my fork.

"Nix?" I asks nice, looking at him like I am a tired halibut.

"No, not no nix at all. It is of a sudden very clear why we have come to be in this place through these unlikely circumstances. I had just not realized it till now."

Large Jake has finished his second plate. He pushes it away and looks at Chris the Shoemaker.

"Later," says Chris. "Outside."

Jake nods.

Of a sudden-like, I am not enjoying Ma Gooser's groaning board as much as I should wish.

For when Chris is in a working mood, things happen.

They had drawn spot #24 down at the judging stand. Each contestant could sing three songs, and the Black Draught people had a big gong they could ring if anyone was too bad.

"I don't know 'bout the ones from 'round here," said Cave Canem, "but they won't need that there gong for the people we know about. We came in third to some of 'em last year in Sweet Tater City."

"Me neither," said Rooster Joe. "The folks I seen can sure play and sing. Why even the Famous Eesup Twins, Bert and Mert, is here. You ever hear them do 'Land Where No Cabins Fall'?"

"Nope," said Luke, "but I have heard of 'em. It seems we'll just have to outplay them all."

They were under a tree pretty far away from the rest of the crowd, who were waiting for the contest to begin.

"Let's rosin up, boys," said Luke, taking his crosscut saw out of his tow sack.

Felix unfolded the ladder and climbed up. Cave pulled out a big willow bow strung with braided muletail hair.

Rooster Joe took out an eight-ounce ball peen hammer and sat back against a tree root.

Luke rosined up his fiddle bow.

"Okay, let's give 'er about two pounds o' press and bend."

He nodded his head. They bowed, Felix pressing down on the big bucksaw handle from above, Rooster Joe striking his ripsaw, Luke pulling at the back of his crosscut.

The same note, three octaves apart, floated on the air.

"Well, that's enough rehearsin'," said Luke. "Now all we got to do is stay in this shady spot and wait till our turn."

They put their instruments and ladder against the tree, and took naps.

When Chris the Shoemaker starts to working, usually someone ends up with cackle fruit on their mug.

When Little Willie and Chris first teamed up when they were oh so very young, they did all the usual grifts. They worked the cherry-colored cat and the old hydrophoby lay, and once or twice even pulled off the glim drop, which is a wonder since neither of them has a glass peeper. They quit the grift when it turns out that Little Willie is always off nugging when Chris needs him, or is piping some doll's stems when he should be laying zex. So they went into various other forms of getting the mazuma.

The ramadoola Chris has come up with is a simple one. We are to get the lizzie going; or barring that are to Hooverize another one; then we cut the lines of communication; immobilize the town clown, glom the loot, and give them the old razoo.

"But Chris," says I, "it is so simple and easy there must be something wrong with your brainstorm. And besides, it is what? Maybe a hundred simoleons in all? I have seen you lose that betting on which raindrop will run down a windowpane first."

"We have been placed here to do this thing," says Chris the Shoemaker. We are all standing on the porch of Ma Gooser's. "We cut the phone," says Chris, "no one can call out. Any other jalopies, Large Jake makes inoperable. That leaves horses, which even we can go faster than. We make the local yokel do a Brodie so there is no Cicero lightning or Illinois thunder. We are gone, and the news takes till next week to get over the ridge yonder."

Miss Millie Dee Chantpie has one of her shoes off and is rubbing her well-turned foot. "My corns is killing me," she says, "and Chris, I think this is the dumbest thing you have ever thought about!"

"I will note and file that," says Chris. "Meantimes, that is the plan. Little William here will start a rumor that will make our presence acceptable before he goes off with the man with the thews of iron. We will only bleaso this caper should the flivver not be fixable or we cannot kipe another one. So it is written. So it shall be done."

Ten minutes later, just before Little Willie leaves in the wagon, I hear two people talking close by, pointing to Miss Millie Dee Chantpie and swearing she is a famous chanteuse, and that Chris the Shoemaker is a talent scout from Okeh Records.

"The town clown," says Chris to me in a while, "will be no problem. He is that gent you see over there sucking on the yamsicle, with the tin star pinned to his long johns with the Civil War cannon tucked in his belt."

I nod.

"Charlie Perro," he says to me, "now let us make like we are mesmerized by this screeching and hollering that is beginning."

The contest is under way. It was like this carnival freak show had of a sudden gone into a production of *No, No Nanette* while you were trying to get a good peek at the India Rubber Woman.

I am not sure whether to be laughing or crying, so I just puts on the look a steer gets just after the hammer comes down, and pretends to watch. What I am really thinking, even I don't know.

There had been sister harmony groups, and guitar and mandolin ensembles, three guys on one big harmonica, a couple of twelve-year-olds playing ocarinas and washboards, a woman on gutbucket broom bass, a handbell choir from a church, three one-man bands, and a guy who could tear newspapers to the tune of "Hold That Tiger!"

Every eight acts or so, Reverend Shapenote and the Mt. Sinai Choir got up and sang sacred harp music, singing the notes only, with no words because their church believed you went straight to Hell if you sang words to a hymn; you could only lift your voice in song.

Luke lay with his hat over his eyes through two more acts. It was well into the afternoon. People were getting hot and cranky all over the town.

As the next act started, Luke sat up. He looked toward the stage. Two giants in coveralls and flannel shirts got up. Even from this far away, their voices carried clear and loud, not strained: deep bass and baritone.

The words of "Eight More Miles To Home" and then "You Are My Sunshine" came back, and for their last song, they went into the old hymn, "Absalom, Absalom":

> Day-Vid The King—He-Wept—and Wept
> Saying—Oh My Son—Oh my son . . .

and a chill went up Luke's back.

"That's them," said Rooster Joe, seeing Luke awake.

"Well," said Luke Apuleus, pulling his hat back down over his eyes as the crowd went crazy, "them is the ones we really have to beat. Call me when they gets to the Cowbell Quintet so we can be moseying up there."

I am being very relieved when Little Willie comes driving into town in the flivver; it is looking much the worse for wear but seems to be running fine. He parks it on Main Street at the far edge of the crowd and comes walking over to me and Chris the Shoemaker.

"How are you standing this?" he asks.

"Why do you not get up there, William?" asks Chris. "I know for a fact you warbled for the cheese up at the River Academy, before they let you out on the technical."

"It was just to keep from driving an Irish buggy," says Little Willie. "The Lizzie will go wherever you want it to. Tires patched. Gassed and lubered up. Say the syllable."

Chris nods to Large Jake over at the edge of the crowd. Jake saunters back towards the only two trucks in town, besides the Cardui vehicle, which, being too gaudy even for us, Jake has already fixed while it is parked right in front of the stage, for Jake is a very clever fellow for someone with such big mitts.

"Charlie Perro," says Chris, reaching in Miss Millie Dee Chantpie's purse, "how's about taking these nippers here," handing me a pair of wire cutters, "and go see if that blower wire back of the general mercantile isn't too long by about six feet when I give you the nod. Then you should come back and help us." He also takes his howitzer out of Miss Millie's bag.

"Little William," he says, turning. "Take Miss Millie Dee Chantpie to the car and start it up. I shall go see what the Cardui Black Draught people are doing."

So it was we sets out to pull the biggest caper in the history of Brimmytown.

"That's them," said Rooster Joe. "The cowbells afore us."

"Well, boys," said Luke, "it's do-or-die time."

They gathered up their saws and sacks and ladder, and started for the stage.

Miss Millie Dee Chantpie is in the car, looking cool as a cucumber. Little Willie is at one side of the crowd, standing out like a sore thumb; he has his hand under his jacket on The Old Crowd Pleaser.

Large Jake is back, shading three or four people from the hot afternoon sun. I am at the corner of the general mercantile, one eye on Chris the Shoemaker and one on the wire coming down the back of the store.

The prize moolah is in this big glass cracker jar on the table with the judges so everybody can see it. It is in greenbacks.

I am seeing Large Jake move up behind the John Law figure, who is sucking at a jug of corn liquor—you would not think the Prohib was the rule of the land here.

I am seeing these guys climb onto the stage, and I cannot believe my peepers, because they are pulling saws and ladders out of their backs. Are these carpenters or what? There is a guy in a straw hat, and one with a bristle mustache, and one with a redchecked shirt and red hat, and one with a cap with big floppy earflaps. One is climbing on a ladder. They are having tools everywhere. What the dingdong is going on?

And they begin to play, a corny song, but it is high and sweet, and then I am thinking of birds and rivers and running water and so forth. So I shakes myself, and keeps my glims on Chris the Shoemaker.

The guys with the saws are finishing their song, and people are going ga-ga over them.

And then I see that Chris is in position.

"Thank yew, thank yew," said Luke. "We-all is the Sawing Boys and we are pleased as butter to be here. I got a cousin over to Cornfield County what has one uh them new cat-whisker crystal *raddio* devices, and you should hear the things that comes right over the air from it. Well, I learned a few of them, and me and the boys talked about them, and now we'll do a couple for yew. Here we're gonna do one by the Molokoi Hotel Royal Hawaiian Serenaders called 'Ule Uhi Umekoi Hwa Hwa'. Take it away, Sawing Boys!" He tapped his foot.

He bent his saw and bowed the first high, swelling notes, then Rooster Joe came down on the harmony rhythm on the ripsaw. Felix bent down on the ladder on the handle of the bucksaw, and Cave pulled the big willow bow and they were off into a fast, swinging song that was about lagoons and fish and food. People were jumping and yelling all over town, and Luke, whose voice was nothing special, started singing:

> "*Ume hoi uli koi hwa hwa*
> *Wa haweaee omi oi lui lui . . .*"

And the applause began before Rooster Joe finished alone with a dying struck high note that held for ten or fifteen seconds. People were yelling and screaming and the Cardui people didn't know what to do with themselves.

"Thank yew, thank yew!" said Luke Apuleus, wiping his brow with his arm while holding his big straw hat in his hand. "Now, here's another one I heerd. We hope you-all like it. It's from the Abe Schwartz Orchestra and it's called 'Beym Rebn in Palestine'. Take it away, Sawing Boys."

They hit halting, fluttering notes, punctuated by Rooster Joe's hammered ripsaw, and then the bucksaw went rolling behind it, Felix pumping up and down on the handle, Cave Canem bowing away. It sounded like flutes and violins and clarinets and mandolins. It sounded a thousand years old, but not like moonshine mountain music; it was from another time and another land.

Something is wrong, for Chris is standing very still, like he is already in the old oak kimono, and I can see he is not going to be giving me the High Sign.

I see that Little Willie, who never does anything on his own, is motioning to me and Large Jake to come over. So over I trot, and the music really washes over me. I know it in my bones, for it is the music of the old neighborhood where all of us but Miss Millie grew up.

I am coming up on Chris the Shoemaker and I see he has turned on the waterworks. He is transfixed, for here, one thousand miles from home, he is being caught up in the mighty coils of memory and transfiguration.

I am hearing with his ears, and what the saws are making is not the Abe Schwartz Orchestra but Itzikel Kramtweiss of Philadelphia, or perhaps Naftalie Brandwein, who used to play bar mitzvahs and weddings with his back to the audience so rival clarinet players couldn't see his hands and how he made those notes.

There is maybe ten thousand years behind that noise, and it is calling all the way across the Kentucky hills from the Land of Gaza.

And while they are still playing, we walk with Chris the Shoemaker back to the jalopy, and pile in around Miss Millie Dee Chantpie, who, when she sees Chris crying, begins herself, and I confess I, too, am a little blurry-eyed at the poignance of the moment.

And we pull out of Brimmytown, the saws still whining and screeching their jazzy ancient tune, and as it is fading and we are going up the hill, Chris the Shoemaker speaks for us all, and what he says is:

"God Damn. You cannot be going *anywhere* these days without you run into a bunch of half-assed *klezmorim*."

For Arthur Hunnicutt and the late Sheldon Leonard.

Glossary

Balonies — tires
Bargain Day — court time set aside for sentencing plea-bargain cases
Beezer — the face, sometimes especially the nose
Bleaso! — 1. an interjection — Careful! You are being overheard! Some chump is wise to the deal! 2. verb — to forgo something, change plans, etc.
The Cherry-colored Cat — an old con game
Cicero Lightning and Illinois Thunder — the muzzle flashes from machine guns and the sound of hand grenades going off
Do a minute — thirty days
Dogs are barking — feet are hurting
Fall Togs — the suit you wear going into, and coming out of, jail

Flit — prison coffee, from its resemblance to the popular fly spray of the time

Flivver — a jalopy

Frammus — a thingamajig or doohickey

Geetas — money, of any kind or amount

Glim Drop — con game involving leaving a glass eye as security for an amount of money; *at least* one of the con men should have a glass eye . . .

Glims — eyes

Goozle — mouth

Hooverize (pre-Depression) — Hoover had been Allied Food Commissioner during the Great War, and was responsible for people getting the most use out of whatever foods they had; the standard command from parents was "Hooverize that plate!"; possibly a secondary reference to vacuum cleaners of the time

Irish buggy (also Irish surrey) — a wheelbarrow

Jalopy — a flivver

Lizzie — a flivver

Mazuma — money, of any kind or amount

Mook — face

Motorman's gloves — any especially large cut of meat

Nugging — porking

The Old Hydrophoby Lay — con game involving pretending to be bitten by someone's (possibly mad) dog

Piping Some Doll's Stems — looking at some woman's legs

Push and Pull — gas and oil

Sammys — the Feds

Zex — Quiet (as in bleaso), cut it out, jiggies! Beat it! Laying zex—keeping lookout

Rules of pig Latin: initial consonants are moved to the end of the word and -ay is added to the consonant; initial vowels are moved to the end of the word and -way is added to the vowel.

Afterword to:

The Sawing Boys

Ellen Datlow called me up in 1992 and wanted a story for her and Terri Windling's *Snow White, Blood Red*, retellings and recastings of fairy tales. "Sure thing," I said. "Real Soon Now."

I wasn't in *that* one.

Six months later she called back. "We're doing a second one. I want you in *that*. What do you want to do?"

"The Brementown Musicians," I said.

"Great," said Ellen.

Later that day. I looked in Grimm. I read The Brementown Musicians.

The musicians meet, decide to go to Brementown, go to a house and make some noise and run off some robbers. The end.

Nothing happens in the story. What had I done?

Well, okay, I'll show Ellen. I'll write that *same exact story* and see how she likes it. I did.

The musicians meet. They decide to go to Brementown. They make a lot of noise and run off some robbers.

Yes or no?

I've always liked the musical saw. There's a great book, which of course I found too late to use for this story, called *Scratch My Back*, a history of the instrument. I knew the musicians were going to play saws. Cave Canem is about your average Arthur Hunnicutt/Denver Pyle figure from the old *Andy Griffith Show*. There's lots of corncob humor here, references to figures of myth from my youth.

Then for the robbers. I did something like this before, in *A Dozen Tough Jobs*, where I got tired after 80 pages or so of writing Southern Black '20s dialect and brought in T. Harris Stottle from Chicago to talk Runyonese for a few pages. Anyone who thinks Runyonese is easy is wrong. Not only do you have to use the ongoing present tense, you have to write out of the side of your mouth. Hence Sheldon Leonard, and there are lots of Leonard in-jokes here. (Among other things, Leonard was the producer of the *Andy Griffith Show*.)

I wanted two distinct styles for the sections so there'd be no mistake about where and with whom you were, and two more different ones I couldn't think of.

And, of course, the gang is Hans (Chris)tian Anderson, the Brothers Grimm, Charles Perrault and Mlle. Sophie Leroyer de Chantepie, a friend of Flaubert's who also wrote fairy tales. You have to watch me every minute . . .

I did the first draft of this, as usual, read it alternating a fedora and a mule's straw hat in St. Louis (actually Collinsville, Ill., home of Cahokia Mound) in June of 1993, and shot the revised draft off to Ellen a few days later. She and Terri took it instanter, only she made me add the Glossary. The book wasn't called *Snow White, Blood Red II*, it was called *Black Thorn, White Rose*. After it appeared, Gardner Dozois picked up "The Sawing Boys" for his *Year's Best SF: 12th Annual Collection*. I was pleased as butter.

I tell people this is actually a story about the spread of mass communications in the early 20th Century, and its effects on the populace. They look at me funny.

Well, it *is*.

Why Did?

Now me thinks on a sudden I am wakened as if it were out of a dream, I have had a raving fit, a phantastical fit, ranged up and down, in and out, I have insulted over most kinde of men, abused some, offended others, wronged myself: and now being recovered and perceiving my error, cry *Solvite me!* pardon that which is past.

— Robert Burton, *Anatomy of Melancholy*, 1621

Leonard:

For a long time he did not remember anything. The moon was just rising. He must have come from the river because his footprints led from it to where he stood. His head hurt.

He walked for a very long way and he was hot. He wished he hadn't left the water; now he needed a drink. He felt something heavy on the top of his head. He didn't think it was his cap. He reached up and his hand came away with something dark and something gray and blue in the moonlight.

"*Ahhh!*" he yelled. "*Ahhh!*" He began to run, falling down twice, flopping around in the dirt until he could get up. His left arm did not work. He ran and ran, then he passed out.

When he came to again he was walking and it was either just after sunset or just before dawn, he did not know which. He walked and walked. His head was pounding now but he was afraid to reach up and touch it again. He was so tired and so hungry but he could not stop. He knew that if he stopped he would die.

It was morning.

He hobbled onto the edge of a field. It stretched away forever with the stubble of some crop. There was a man far away on the other side doing something with a tractor. There was a truck parked there, too. He walked toward the man at the tractor and the man heard him coming and looked up. The man's eyes got wide and bright behind his glasses and he put one hand up over his face a second.

"Holy Mother of Christ!" the man said.

"*Unhh! Unhh!*" he said, holding his right arm out.

"Jesus! You're really hurt? How did that happen?"

"*Unhh!*"

"Hold still. Don't move." The man went to the truck and came back with a flour sack covered with grit. "It's all I got. Let me put that on your head."

He held still.

The man made a strange noise behind him.

"I don't know how you're walking, buddy," the man said. "It . . . it looks like you been shot in the back of the head and the bullet came out the top. That's brains hangin' there."

"*Unhh! Unhh!*"

"Easy now. If you come this far you ain't gonna die yet. Ease over into the truck here—I'll take you over to the hospital in Salinas. Watch your head gettin' in. There's more of it on top than you think . . ."

He got into the truck. Soon they were bouncing along the road and the gravel was flying in a big V out behind. His head hurt more and soon he was asleep.

All he remembered was pieces of the next few days. There were rooms and lights and doctors and nurses and they put something in his head. Then he was in a big bed and they brought him food and asked all about him.

Then some other doctors came and a state trooper in a smart uniform with a shiny badge, and a few days later they took him to another place.

It was there that something began to happen to his head, not on the outside where all the bandages and the tin were, but inside. Small flashes of who he was would come back then go away, like a bird hopping closer and closer behind a tree you were leaning against but which would hop away before you could turn around and see it. There had been a ranch or a farm. He'd done something that made people mad at him. He couldn't remember. There had been a running through the woods to the river.

And then G—

It was a name. He did not know who the name was.

He couldn't remember and it made him cry.

This place wasn't so nice. There were people who were always making him do things and move from his bed or chair and they talked to him but he could not understand.

A long long time went by, maybe a month or two. He wished he could leave and go find some work or something. He did not like it here.

Sometimes he wished he had a rabbit to hold.

And then one day when they had him outside bouncing the ball he looked up and there standing in front of him was a funny little clown in a black clown suit with a pointed hat and big buttons down the front.

He looked at the clown and he smiled because he knew from then on everything was going to be okay.

Benjamin:

It was day and rain and my sister held me while I held the slipper and the grandmother was in the house then my brother came home mad and I was taken somewhere with lots of doors and white and I didn't like it and was going to say and going and they put the thing on my arm that hurt and I went away and then it was day again and my pushing-man took me outside in the buggy-chair and put me under the tree the tree like the one in the pasture where the boy and I were walking and he was looking for the money "Money Money" said my brother. "You're all bleeding me white" and then I was in this place under the tree watching and watching for my sister to come to the gate so I could see her and she climbed the pear tree to look in at my grandmother like the horse in the ditch and the people wouldn't let me go to the gate and the men were hitting and calling my sister's name and there was the girl who wasn't my sister who yelled and yelled at the gate and the fire went around and around and it was rain and I couldn't sleep and it was day again and they were saying "Benjamin, Benjamin, don't yell so, just show us where it hurts" and I tried to tell them and the black woman cook said "Grab his hand" and I put it in my mouth it hurt so and I pointed where it hurt and they made it stop it was day again and they let me stand at the gate only it was tall and I was little that time and my pushing-man put me under the tree then the man came and the man had a clown with him like the one that came to town only he had on a black suit and he hugged me like my sister used to do in the buggy-chair and the clown and the man were in the little box with me that bumped and bumped and pastures and houses went by the windows real fast and there was a bridge and a river and hills going by too and then it was day and night again and I was in the big house which was my grandmother's house only it was big and I was little in it and sometimes the clown was big and stuck out of the house and sometimes he was little and walked around and sat in his swing.

The gateman let the car, a new '51 Kaiser, into the grounds.

In the front seat beside the driver from the motor pool, Dr. Ernest Seeker stared up the drive toward the mansion. It was a three-storey stone building. At the front, over the portico was the head of a giant clown, mechanical eyes slowly rolling, tongue lolling out of the mouth.

The grounds, ten or eleven rolling acres, were surrounded by a twelve-foot high narrow iron spiked fence. Here and there as he watched, solitary men and women moved on missions of their own.

Far off, near a little copse of trees, someone who was dressed like Koko the Clown from the old Betty Boop cartoons sat in a board-and-rope swing, winding himself up with little movements of the feet and letting the twisted ropes spin him around again.

In another direction, a patch of what looked like wheat bordered the fence. There was no one waiting for him out front when the car pulled to a stop.

Seeker got out. He pulled his briefcase from the back seat. He looked back beyond the gate to the far hill where the construction on the new housing subdivisions had begun.

After waiting a few more moments, he stepped to the wide double doors and went inside.

The place was light and airy and had peculiar, not unpleasant, smells. The hallway led to a large sitting room with overstuffed Victorian furniture, worn looking but clean. From somewhere far off to the left he heard the rattle of a pot or pan, low talk. To the right was another hallway. A man was coming out of the room pushing his hair back with both hands.

"Mr. Seeker," he said. "Willard Beemer. Sorry I didn't hear your car—we don't have a telephone at the gate. I wouldn't have known you were here except one of our guests went by the window—he goes to meet every car. Usually that's just the help arriving for work, but it's too late for that so I knew it had to be you."

Seeker shook his hand.

"I'm sure the department explained why I'm here."

"They told me we'd need a license for the facility. I tried to explain why I didn't think it came under your purview, but they insisted. So I told them, send their best investigator out and look the place over, and we'd talk about it."

"You realize, of course, that if you were an M.D. or this were under the direct supervision of a neurosurgeon or psychiatrist, I wouldn't be here?"

"I know, I know. But we didn't *ask* to be licensed; you called us. My guess is it's because of the guy building the houses all across the hills that you got called. Some people are afraid of things they don't understand. See, we don't consider ourselves a place for treatment. We're, like, a big family who live in a big house with a fence and mind our own business."

"You can understand the concerns of the county and state when there are complaints that there's an unlicensed mental facility in the middle of what will become a high-density residential area."

"Well, the county can't do anything because they got a grandfather clause in all their zoning stuff. And you're the state, so I just have to convince you, right?"

"That is essentially correct."

"Okay. Let's get to it."

"How long have you been here?"

"Twelve years. Since 1939."

"How many patients do you have?"

"Twenty-seven. Only they're not patients, they're guests. Five have been here since the beginning; the others came one or two at a time. Either we went out to find them, or some just showed up, over the years."

"You went out to find them? Where?"

"Some from state hospitals. Some from private. One we found kept in a cage out behind an alligator farm in Florida."

"You go get them from state hospitals?"

"Most states are only too happy to find someone to take them off their hands. Look," said Beemer, "I'm not explaining myself very well. Leave your briefcase here. Come outside with me. Take a look around."

He followed Beemer back through the parlor, out the double doors to the driveway where the car sat. A man stood near the steps, his head moving back and forth, eyes wide, staring at the car and driver.

"I better start at the beginning. I didn't found this place: my father did—though he died on the trip West with the first five guests. I'm the executor of his estate, which makes me also the guardian of the Democritus Trust. That's where we get the money."

Seeker looked out toward the field near the back of the grounds. A young person, a lone boy, stood in the middle of the half-acre patch.

"That's the newest one, Holden. I'm not sure he should be here, but the Little Moron wanted him to stay."

"We don't like to refer to anyone as a moron, Mr. Beemer . . ."

"That's what he calls himself. He's the one all the stories are about."

Seeker looked at Beemer. "You mean, the Little Moron jokes?"

"That's him. Elwood Democritus, Jr. His father was richer than Croesus. He appointed my father executor on his deathbed. Elwood Jr.'s mother had died years before; he was an only child on a dead-end branch of the family tree. Then the Little Moron and my father came West, setting up the place, getting the original five guests, setting it all up; then my father died and I came out here and here we are."

The clown face overhead suddenly straightened to the vertical. Its eyes rolled and the mouth opened. "Yum Yum Yum!" said a voice over the P.A. system. "Yum Yum Yum!"

"Lunchtime," said Beemer. "Want to join them?"

"I've already eaten," said Seeker.

From the far corners of the grounds, people walked toward the house. Some had hobbling steps. One walked but his arms didn't swing with his steps; they remained at his sides. There were six or eight women. A microcephalic in a spotted blue dress with her hair in a bow came up and hugged Beemer, then went inside. An old man dressed like the Little King in a tiny child's pedal car raced up to the steps, hopped out and ran through the double doors.

The lone boy stayed out in the field. "Those that don't want to eat don't have to," said Beemer. "The cooks leave them sandwiches and stuff. Not your pickle loaf or baloney, either."

"How do you choose who stays here and who doesn't?"

"I don't. The Little Moron does."

"He chooses them?"

"He'll let me know he wants to go somewhere. We'll go. One in a thousand sometimes. We'll go ten places, nothing. Eleventh place he gets out of the car, walks right up to someone, or they come up to him. He breaks out in a big smile. That's the one."

"And you take procedures to get them here?"

"Yep."

"Don't you find that a little . . . arbitrary?"

"Beats me. It's worked every time."

"All right. You've been here twelve years. How many pa— guests have died?"

"None."

"How many escaped?"

"None."

"Can you explain this?"

"They're happy here. Why would they want to leave?"

"What kind of therapy do you use?"

"None whatsoever."

"None?"

"Okay," Beemer paused, "happy therapy. They get to do pretty much whatever they want to do. If they're happy, they're okay."

The man in the Koko suit came by.

His face was covered with clown white. His baggy black suit had big white buttons on it, and his pointed hat had three white puffs down the front. He walked over, picked up Beemer, carried him to the stairs and set him down. Then he went inside.

"He wants a step-father," said Beemer.

"Who?"

"Elwood Jr. The Little Moron."

"He doesn't talk," said Beemer. "Most of them can't, or won't. Elwood can write though; mostly they're little rebuses or riddles that I can make out. Or he'll take me and show me. Sometimes it's hard. But he doesn't ask for much, and not often. I can show you his room, if you want me to, while he's eating. It'll give you some idea."

They went upstairs. There was a long hall with bedrooms off each side. They came to one. Outside was a pile of hay. Beemer opened the door. In the center of the floor was a carpet with a hole cut in it. There was a bed with springs sticking out one end, on the wall was a calendar with some of the numbers missing. On the other side above the wash basin was a medicine cabinet with a pair of padded slippers on the floor in front of them. At an open window was a box of clocks, and there was another pile of timepieces under the desk in the corner. In another corner was a refrigerator. Beemer opened it. There were no shelves inside. There was a second handle so it could be opened from the inside.

"He thinks of me as his father, sometimes," said Beemer. Seeker didn't understand the reference but said nothing.

At the bottom of the refrigerator was a sack of fish with their noses cut off. On the wall above a chair was a huge clock. On the wash basin was a hairbrush and a box of candy bullets.

There were several sheets of paper on the desk. One was a picture of an elephant with a howdah on it and an arrow pointing toward the bottom and a question mark.

"Oh, that's for me," said Beemer. He studied it a moment, then drew a picture: the word NO, a comma, an arrow pointing toward the bottom of the page, and a waterfowl of some kind.

"What's that?" asked Seeker.

"That was an easy one," Willard Beemer said. "He wanted to know how you got down off an elephant. I said, you don't get down off an elephant, you get down off a goose."

Seeker stared at him a moment.

"You're telling me he thinks on a tertiary *conceptual level?*"

"No. No. He thinks on a literal level. *His* father, Elwood Sr., never could figure out a damn thing he was trying to do, because *he* thought on a tertiary level all the time. Me and my father could figure out pretty much everything, 'cause we didn't. There are two or three of these things I still can't answer, though."

"Have you ever had him tested? Or any of them?"

"Tested for *what?* Like I said, if Elwood Jr. wants them here, that's good enough for me. Come on. Let's go outside again. You see how he lives here."

Outside, they walked up the drive. The kid who had been in the wheat (or whatever-it-was) field was gone now. The clown head on the house was immobile.

"See, what we got here is like people coming to visit who never leave. That's the best way I can describe it. The help comes here and takes care of them and leaves at night. Nobody comes to visit, because most of them don't have *anybody*. We're not trying to put anything over on anyone."

Then Beemer stopped. "Just remembered one for Elwood Jr.," he said. He took a piece of paper and drew on it: ?, then a baby, ? NO, then another baby. He put the paper in a crack in one of the wood columns of the portico. The clown head above the porch began to move. "Ha Ha Ha!" it said, its tinny voice echoing over the grounds, "Ha Ha Ha!"

"Playtime," said Beemer. "They'll all be coming out again."

"Mr. Beemer," said Seeker. "I'm not going to advise you on how to run your business, or to circumvent the laws. But you'll have to get at least a private facility license. You'll have to get a physician or psychiatrist to apply for you. I understand your care and concern. But suppose something happens to you or Elwood Jr? It could be chaotic for everyone involved, especially with the three housing developments going up nearby. They're even thinking of putting in a new golf course over there. If something should happen—I'm thinking of your pa—guests here. There needs to be some supervision, some treatment program." He paused.

"I'm not saying this officially. Plenty of medics will put their names on an application blank for a fee and not bother you at all. I'd like you to find one who does care, who can see what you've done here—maybe there's something medicine can learn from it."

"I didn't do it. The Little Moron did."

"Well, what's been done here, then. It's hard to believe you've managed for a dozen years."

"We don't manage, Mr. Seeker. We're here. This is what we are, always will be."

"I'd like to believe that, too. But get a psychiatrist to apply for you. Have him take an active part so nothing goes wrong."

As they were talking, Seeker watched the guests coming out from lunch. The Little King came out and jumped in his pedal car and tore off up the driveway, knees like blurs. Elwood Jr. stopped at the porch post, took out the piece of paper. He wrote something on it, put it back in the crack and walked toward the thicket with a book in his hand. Seeker watched him sit down, place the book in front of him, open and stare at it.

Beemer followed his gaze. "It's fall," he said, as if by way of explanation. The Little Moron continued to stare at the book all the time they walked back to the department's car.

The man still stood on the porch watching the car, his head moving back and forth. The driver, reading a magazine, paid no attention.

"We can handle almost anything," said Beemer. "One of our guests, when we found him, had been shot in the back of the head. Went right through the corpus callosum and out the top. We got no idea who he is, but that's him out yonder with the chickens at the rabbit hutch. He's been here since almost the beginning."

"I'll turn in my report on the place," said Seeker. "We'll send a team out next week to see if there are any modifications needed to bring it up to state standards. Meanwhile, you should shop around for a resident psychiatrist."

"Money's no object," said Beemer, shrugging. "Just the idea's not to my liking."

Willard went to the post while Seeker put the briefcase in the back seat. Beemer unfolded the paper and smiled, showing it to Seeker.

? then baby NO then baby?

under it was drawn:

= then a very tiny cross mark.

Seeker said nothing about the paper, then: "I'll be back after the team. It's been a pleasure talking to you, Mr. Beemer. Please remember what I said."

"I will. Goodbye."

The car started up the driveway. Seeker watched the boy in the field, the giant man near the chicken yard, Elwood Jr. on his swing, still staring at the open book before him.

Back at the house, the big clown head laughed its scratchy laugh again.

Beemer hired Dr. Winfred Rance.

She called Seeker a few months into her residency.

"I've never seen a smoother-running place in my life," she said. "And Beemer doesn't do anything, like he told you. It's all Elwood Jr. I've seen just about everything in my time, but nothing like him, or his effect on the others around him."

"I'm glad you're taking such an interest in their—somewhat unusual— procedures," said Seeker.

"I'm beginning to think Elwood Jr. likes me," she said, sounding unprofessional for the first time since Seeker had known her. "He's started leaving those little puzzle things for me. The ones for me have the stick figure of a girl at the top; Beemer's don't. Mine at first were easy, then they got harder. I don't think he's testing me or anything, I just think that's the way they come to him. He usually leaves them in the door handle of my car."

Seeker remembered Elwood Jr. in his swing, staring at the open book's pages in front of him, as if waiting for something to happen. "It's fall," Beemer had said as if by way of explanation.

"I also want to talk to Holden a little. No prying. It's just that he doesn't seem like the others at all."

"I'm glad it's working out well," said Seeker. "I'll be up for a visit in—" he glanced at his calendar "—the customary six-month inspection time."

"I'll keep you informed," said Winfred.

He opened a letter from Beemer that arrived about three weeks later.

Dear Doc—

Thanks for putting me on to Winfred. She's a corker, and most of the time you wouldn't even know she was here. I think she's gonna get a big fat article out of the Democritus System, as she calls it. Okay by me.

Like I said, I was pretty peeved at those realtor assholes when they sold all that land around me; I woulda been glad to buy it up myself, but somebody in the Chamber of Commerce had dropped dead or something, which led to all this.

But it did turn out okay 'cause we got Winfred.

Thanks again Doc.

Your Pal,
Willard Beemer

PS: I think Elwood Jr. likes her, too. But I can tell he's getting antsy again, more than usual, that probably means we'll go get some more guests soon.

"They've been gone two weeks," said Winfred, on the phone. "I'm not quite sure what was going on with Elwood Jr.—neither Willard nor I got any puzzles from him for the last week they were here, before he took Willard out to the car that morning two weeks ago. He seemed, well, troubled."

Seeker wondered, for an instant, how you could tell if someone whose mind was a rebus was having a mood swing.

"I've often wondered," said Seeker, "what would happen if Elwood Jr. couldn't tell the difference between, let's say, alternative thought patterns, and perhaps, those of a sociopath . . ."

"His sense hasn't failed him yet," Winfred laughed. "And you know what? I think if someone like that did end up here, they might just cure themselves."

"Are you losing your objectivity, Winfred?"

"Well, just kidding, sort of. Or maybe I'm gaining a *new* kind of objectivity. Hold it!—speak of the devil. Beemer and Elwood Jr. just pulled up in the driveway. Looks like they've got . . . a very old geezer and, and a young girl with them. I'll see what's up and call you back later."

The Little Girl:
I had such a pretty grandmother! That was after all the trouble with my mother and father and the spelling-bee medal. My grandmother was *so* nice so long to me. Then she told me that we had to move far away, and that I was going to have to go to one of those schools where you sit in church and wear a plaid dress, and I asked her *please* not to do that, but she said it was *best* for me. I was so unhappy for a while. Then I begged and pleaded, and was just so nice for my grandmother, but she still said we couldn't stay where we were. So then I played with my jacks on the stairs, and played with the tacks on the runner carpet, ever so little at a time, and a little more each day, and then one morning when we were ready to go out shopping for new suitcases for the trip, I went up to help my grandmother down the stairs.

And then I was *so unhappy* for the longest time, because I used to have a pretty grandmother.

Dr. Rance sat at her desk.

A shadow fell over it.

She looked up. It was Holden. He never left his small patch of grain field from sunup to sundown, except when it was raining. He rarely ate with the others and stayed in his room at night. "Yes Holden?" she asked.

He stared at her a moment, then looked left and right. He started to form words, then quit.

"Is there something wrong?" she asked.

"That new little Rhoda girl," he said. "She's a goddamn phony and all."

Then he left.

Dr. Rance sat at her desk a while, then went to look out the window. Holden was already back in his patch, looking far out over the hills like he always did.

She wondered if she imagined it. When she saw the new little girl later that day, she was standing near the trees, watching Elwood Jr. in his swing.

When Beemer came in from the kitchen, she said, "Holden spoke to me today."

"No shit?" said Beemer. "I didn't figure him for the talking type. Need anything in town, Doc?"

"No, I'm leaving soon myself," she said.

"Be in tomorrow?"

"No, Tuesday."

"See you then."

The Little Girl:

He thinks he can fool me, but *I* know what he's up to. Sitting there in his swing, running things, making people do things without even *thinking* about it. He pretends to be *so* nice to me, but I know there's only room for one person in charge here, and it's not that dumb Willard or that pretend-nice Dr. Rance, she's like *all* the others, trying to get inside my head to see if the loud clock there is still working, or that Holden; I don't like the way he looks at me; I'll take care of *him* after I settle the Little Moron's hash. I know where they keep the matches here, and I know when they're all going to be eating, and I know what's in the basement. And later, it'll be just me, and that nice Leonard, and the rabbits and mice, and we'll have *ever so much fun* . . .

Leonard:

Uh-oh. Now someone's really gonna get it!

It wasn't me, no sir. I was out by the rabbit hutch and then there was a roar like when a train used to come by real close when me and my friend was sleeping in the 'bo jungles and the whole house blew up and caught on fire and then I saw the little houses across the golfing place blow up and catch on fire and then I was running as fast as I could only I stopped and went back to get the rabbits out of their cages and then it started raining fire.

I ain't never seen it rain fire before. It came down just like water only things was turning brown and gray and going away.

And then it was real hard to breathe and real hot and I dropped the rabbits cause my hands hurt real bad and then the rabbits caught on fire too. I started crying only nothing came out. When I screamed I couldn't get my breath back in and I ran with my head down and my hair caught fire and the tin place on my head was hot as a stove. I was yelling and running and got one eye open and my clothes was on fire and I remembered you could roll, only the ground was on fire too but I yelled and rolled.

Then I was up and running again toward the wheat field and Holden was jumping up and down and biting his hand and looking at the house and screaming.

I looked back and the big clown head blew up and one of its eyes popped out and went past the fence. I looked again and saw the fence was down over to the other side of the house and Benjamin who always stood there looking was nowhere in sight.

I went running that way to get away from the fire. I wanted to get as far away as I could and jump into one of those water puddles they have by the sandpiles. I ran and ran.

Somebody was sure gonna get it but it wasn't me, no sir. I was out by the hutch . . .

Then I remembered the rabbits and started crying.

Then I saw Benjamin lying way out in the middle of the golf place and I forgot about jumping in the water because I couldn't feel the burning any more.

He was laying there and he looked like a newspaper that's been in the fireplace. There was smoke coming out of his mouth.

I ain't ever seen smoke come out of anybody's mouth unless they had a cigarette.

I tried to let him know it was okay but I must have been yelling.

I didn't know what to do. I stood there crying and crying and I heard noises and whistles and sirens yelling from all around.

Benjamin looked at me with his blue eyes but I couldn't tell if he saw me or not.

If I'd of had a mouse I would have given it to him to hold; I sure would have.

Benjamin:

For the first time in his life he was neither confused nor caught in an eternal present. Since the explosion, things had slowed down, pulled, come apart into separate distinct moments. He had seen parts of the big house come by him and realized that they had not been there before, that this was a new thing to him.

He had been near the fence, watching the men play golf and calling his sister's name. He still had his sister's slipper in his back pocket. Before the blast he expected her to come anytime to the fence, especially with the men calling her name so often.

Then pieces of the house and something else came by and hit the men out there and the houses beyond the pasture. As he was lifted through the air he thought again the world was turning around like it did when the black boy fed him the whiskey at his grandmother's house.

He saw the ground hit him three or four times and every time he bumped things got more still and calm inside him.

Then he was looking up at the quiet blue sky with some smoke going through it. Every time he breathed, more smoke came up. He watched it. Then he began to see that this, too, was a new thing. Before this, he had been at the fence; now he was somewhere else.

He saw that all the things he knew were different things, that his sister must have been gone many many many days. He saw that the big house which had come to pieces in fire was not his grandmother's house and that that was not the place he had been in before he came here. This was a wonderful thing.

That meant that all the people were different people. The black cook was not the one in the house here who was a man. The man here was not his brother though he had the same job. The car out front had not been the one of his other brother—it was shinier and lower and did not have a top on it where the people sat. The blue sky now had more smoke in it. It had not always had smoke. Sometimes it was blue or gray; sometimes it rained and you could watch it from inside the houses.

Then he saw there were insides and outsides to houses, and that they were the same. That meant the outside had to be bigger than the inside to hold the people though they sometimes looked little when you had walked away from them and you had gotten bigger. That must mean it was you who made them little by being farther away from them.

He lay there, calm. What else could all this mean? He found himself trying to think of one thing, and it came to him, what he was trying to think about. He tried something else, and it came to him, too. Not like in a flow, where one thing led to another like it used to do . . .

He could not contain this new knowledge. He wanted to yell it, tell everyone. Not like in other days before the house came apart when he tried to say things and everyone said he was bellowing. He wanted the words to let everyone know that he had found these new things.

He smiled with exultation. Now if only Leonard would quit pushing and prodding him and yelling. It was beginning to bother him.

He closed his eyes.

Seeker heard about the explosion on the radio. It took almost a day to get through, but he finally found a phone Winfred was at late the next morning.

"Only five of the guests are still alive," she said. "One of them's critical. They found what they're sure are Elwood Jr.'s and Beemer's bodies and the new little girl's. They suspect arson—the propane tanks."

"I was just going to call you yesterday morning, before it happened. For the first time, one of the guests was missing, but evidently had been since the night before, and we don't think he had anything to do with it.

"We've got people with the survivors," she went on. "Beemer's will's going to be read in two days. I'm sure he provided for everything for them through the trust. We'll do whatever the will says, no matter what, or how strange it sounds."

Then she began to cry. "Holden's the only one who *saw* it happen. The ones who lived through it, the ones inside eating lunch, probably didn't understand what happened at all."

"I wish I could tell you how sorry I am," said Seeker. He made arrangements to come down for the reading of the will. He offered her the department's help in anything she might need.

"I'll see you day after tomorrow," he said.

"Thanks." She hung up.

He was doodling on his desk pad when he first noticed the honking of car horns outside the office. He went to his second floor window and looked out. Then he ran downstairs and out onto the street.

There was a slow-moving line of cars coming toward him. At the front of it, the Little King, looking neither left nor right, was coming up the street in his pedal car. People were yelling "stupid asshole!" out the windows of their cars and trucks. The Little King paid no attention and pulled to a stop in front of Dr. Seeker as the traffic roared around him.

He climbed out of the pedal car. He wore an orange-red robe trimmed in ermine, and on top of his head was a crown that looked like the top half of a gold-yellow ball-jack. His beard and mustache were clipped and curled.

He took off his crown. His head was bald and red, with only a fringe of hair where the crown sat. He handed Dr. Seeker a folded piece of paper that had been inside.

Seeker opened it.

At the top was a stick figure of a man with a briefcase in his left hand.

On the paper, in Elwood Jr.'s drawing, was the following: ?, then the Little Moron figure with XX's over the eyes, then a duck and a big X and a cow, and a test tube over a Bunsen burner. Seeker remembered what Beemer had said about literal levels.

How was the Little Moron killed in a eugenics experiment? it was asking.

Seeker took out his Parker T-Ball Jotter. He wrote an equals sign, then drew a giant firecracker with a sputtering fuse and a X and a road full of cars with speed lines coming from them, and an exclamation point.

How was the Little Moron killed in a eugenics experiment? it asked.

He was trying to cross a busy highway with a lit stick of dynamite! Seeker had answered.

He refolded the paper and handed it back to the Little King. The tiny old man replaced it in his crown, jumped back in his pedal car, made a U-turn and started back the way he had come, causing another giant screeching of brakes and cursing sounds. Seeker watched for a moment: a man who thought he was a king taking a joke back from a man who thought he was a doctor to a man who was dead. Then he went back inside, to call Winfred to tell her one of the guests had been found, but that he would probably be late for dinner.

Afterword to:

Why Did?

More than any other, this story's the reason this book's got afterwords instead of intros with the stories.

It has a long and complex history, and you're going to get it, like it or not.

For some reason, when I was a kid in the Fifties, and heard Little Moron jokes ("Why did the Little Moron throw the clock out the window?" "He wanted to see Time Fly."), I always envisioned him as looking like Koko the Clown from the old *Out of the Inkwell* Fleischer cartoons, many of which, silents included, were just showing up on television for the first time. Don't ask me why; it's just kid association. I am not responsible.

(Don't you wish sometimes you lived in a Fleischer cartoon world, with Betty Boop, Bimbo, Koko and Pudge? That when things were going great, and you were dancing, all the buildings and people and the moon and stars were dancing along with you? And when things were bad, even the trees would chase you?)

Anyway, sometime in the Eighties I started referring to the "Little Moron Story" I was going to write soon.

Along comes a convention in New Orleans in June of 1989. Sick as a dog for the first time in years (no eating alligator and sucking crawdad heads for me!), I had fever and chills. I'd go to bed, get the shakes, get up and do a panel or whatever, come back to the room, work on the story, get fever, etc. Anyway, I finished it and read it there.

People stared at me when I was through. *Then* they applauded. (On the way back to Austin, Hurricane David hit, to cap off my fun week.) A month later I rewrote the story, sent it off to Ellen Datlow, and she bought it.

Then, a rare thing with me, I had some second thoughts. The version Ellen bought was different from the one you just read; there was lots more chaff: the *deus ex machina* of the explosion was a real one, the Bell X-1E rocket plane if I remember correctly. I was vaguely dissatisfied, since my reasoning had been Other-directed by some kind of fever fugue while writing it.

The money, of course, having been frittered away on food and rent, I did the only honorable thing I could do, since I didn't want to re-write it then and there.

I wrote another story ("The Effects of Alienation") and sent it to Ellen with the proviso that, if she wanted it, she had to send "Why Did?" back.

I got a call from her (I had a *phone* in those days): "I want them both," she said. "Unh-uh. Can't have the new one unless you send the old one back," I said.

Ellen: "But you've already been paid."

Me: "Take out the contract. Where it says 'Why Did?', cross it out and write in 'The Effects of Alienation'. See how easy this publishing stuff is?"

Ellen: "I don't like this."

Me: "Trust me."

An interval of time descends over the proceedings while I'm busy with other stuff.

It says here I did one rewrite on it October 8, 1992 and another on Pearl Harbor Day, 1992—a really long space for me—and that I sent it back to Ellen a couple of days later.

And she bought it *again*.

When it was published in the April 1994 *Omni*, it got the same reaction as "Springtime For Hitler" in *The Producers*.

Okay, as George R. R. Martin says (he was there when I read it in New Orleans): a tour of the Twentieth Century with the great idiots of literature (and a couple of schizoids and sociopaths).

All the stuff in Elwood Jr.'s room is from Little Moron jokes: the fishes don't have noses so they won't smell, etc.

And the whole thing's a reverse *Parsifal:* the wise man's asking questions of the fool. Sometimes my life's a lot like "Why Did?".

Yours too, I bet.

Occam's Ducks

Producers Releasing Corporation Executive: Bill, you're 45 minutes behind your shooting schedule.

Beaudine: You mean, someone's *waiting* to see this crap??

— William "One-Shot" Beaudine

For a week, late in the year 1919, some of the most famous people in the world seemed to have dropped off its surface.

The Griffith company, filming the motion picture *The Idol Dancer*, with the palm trees and beaches of Florida standing in for the South Seas, took a shooting break.

The mayor of Fort Lauderdale invited them for a 12-hour cruise aboard his yacht, the *Grey Duck*. They sailed out of harbor on a beautiful November morning. Just after noon a late-season hurricane slammed out of the Caribbean.

There was no word of the movie people, the mayor, his yacht, or the crew for five days. The Coast Guard and the Navy sent out every available ship. Two seaplanes flew over shipping lanes as the storm abated.

Richard Barthelmess came down to Florida at first news of the disappearance, while the hurricane still raged. He went out with the crew of the Great War U-boat chaser, the *Berry Islands*. The seas were so rough the captain ordered them back in after six hours.

The days stretched on; three, four. The Hearst newspapers put out extras, speculating on the fate of Griffith, Gish, the other actors, the mayor. The weather cleared and calm returned. There were no sightings of debris or oil slicks. Reporters did stories on the *Marie Celeste* mystery. Hearst himself called in spiritualists in an attempt to contact the presumed dead director and stars.

On the morning of the sixth day, the happy yachting party sailed back in to harbor.

First there were sighs of relief.

Then the reception soured. Someone in Hollywood pointed out that Griffith's next picture, to be released nationwide in three weeks, was called *The Greatest Question*, and was about life after death, and the attempts of mediums to contact the dead.

W. R. Hearst was not amused, and he told the editors of his papers not to be amused, either.

Griffith shrugged his shoulders for the newsmen. "A storm came up. The captain put in at the nearest island. We rode out the cyclone. We had plenty to eat and drink, and when it was over, we came back."

The island was called Whale Cay. They had been buffeted by the heavy seas and torrential rains the first day and night, but made do by lantern light and electric torches, and the dancing fire of the lightning in the bay around them. They slept stacked like cordwood in the crowded belowdecks.

They had breakfasted in the sunny eye of the hurricane late next morning up on deck. Many of the movie people had had strange dreams, which they related as the far-wall clouds of the back half of the hurricane moved lazily toward them.

Neil Hamilton, the matinee idol who had posed for paintings on the cover of *The Saturday Evening Post* during the Great War, told his dream. He was in a long valley with high cliffs surrounding him. On every side, as far as he could see, the ground, the arroyos were covered with the bones and tusks of elephants. Their cyclopean skulls were tumbled at all angles. There were millions and millions of them, as if every pachyderm that had ever lived had died there. It was near dark, the sky overhead paling, the jumbled bones around him becoming purple and indistinct.

Over the narrow valley, against the early stars a strange light appeared. It came from a searchlight somewhere beyond the cliffs, and projected onto a high bank of noctilucent cirrus was a winged black shape. From somewhere behind him a telephone rang with a sense of urgency. Then he'd awakened with a start.

Lillian Gish, who'd only arrived at the dock the morning they left, going directly from the Florida Special to the yacht, had spent the whole week before at the new studio at Mamaroneck, New York, overseeing its completion and directing her sister in a comedy feature. On the tossing, pitching yacht, she'd had a terrible time getting to sleep. She had dreamed, she said, of being an old woman, or being dressed like one, and carrying a Browning semi-automatic shotgun. She was being stalked through a swamp by a crazed man with words tattooed on his fists, who sang hymns as he followed her. She was very frightened in her nightmare, she said, not by being pursued, but by the idea of being old. Everyone laughed at that.

They asked David Wark Griffith what he'd dreamed of. "Nothing in particular," he said. But he *had* dreamed: there was a land of fire and eruptions, where men and women clad in animal skins fought against giant crocodiles and lizards, much like in his film of ten years before, *Man's Genesis*. Hal Roach, the upstart competing producer, was there, too, looking older, but he seemed to be telling Griffith what to do. D.W. couldn't imagine such a thing. Griffith attributed the dream to the rolling of the ship, and to an especially fine bowl of turtle soup he'd eaten that morning aboard the *Grey Duck*, before the storm hit.

Another person didn't tell of his dreams. He saw no reason to. He was the stubby steward who kept them all rocking with laughter through the storm with his antics and jokes. He said nothing to the film people, because he had a dream so very puzzling to him, a dream unlike any other he'd ever had.

He had been somewhere; a stage, a room. He wore some kind of livery; a doorman's or a chauffeur's outfit. There was a big Swede standing right in front of him, and the Swedish guy was made up like a Japanese or a Chinaman. He had a big mustache like Dr. Fu Manchu on the book jackets, and he wore a tropical planter's suit and hat. Then this young Filipino guy had run into the room yelling a mile a minute, and the Swede asked, "Why number-three son making noise like motorboat?" and the Filipino yelled something else and ran to a closet door and opened it, and a white feller fell out of it with a knife in his back.

Then a voice behind the steward said, "Cut!" and then said, "Let's do it again," and the guy with the knife in his back got up and went back into the closet, and the Filipino guy went back out the door, and the big Swede took two puffs on a Camel and handed it to someone and then just stood there, and the voice behind the steward said to him, "Okay," and then, "This time, Mantan, bug your eyes out a little more."

The dream made no sense at all.

After their return on the yacht, the steward had performed at the wrap party for the productions. An Elk saw him, and they hired him to do their next initiation follies. Then he won a couple of amateur nights, and played theaters in a couple of nearby towns. He fetched and carried around the mayor's house in the daytime, and rolled audiences in the aisles at night.

One day early in 1920, he looked in his monthly pay envelope and found it was about a quarter of what he'd earned in the theater the last week.

He gave notice, hit the boards running, and never looked back.

So it was that two years later, on April 12, 1922, Mantan Brown found himself, at eight in the morning, in front of a large building in Fort Lee, New Jersey. He had seen the place the year before, when he had been playing a theater down the street. Before the Great War it had been part of Nestor or Centaur, or maybe the Thantouser Film Company. The Navy had taken it over for a year to make toothbrushing and trench-foot movies to show new recruits, and films for the public on how to spot the Kaiser in case he was working in disguise on your block.

It was a commercial studio again, but now for rent by the day or week. Most film production had moved out to the western coast, but there were still a few—in Jersey, out on Astoria, in Manhattan itself—doing some kind of business in the East.

Mantan had ferried over before sunup, taken a streetcar, and checked in to the nearby hotel, one that let Negroes stay there as long as they paid in advance.

He went inside, past a desk and a yawning guard who waved him on, and found a guy in coveralls with a broom, which, Mantan had learned in two years in the business, was where you went to find out stuff.

"I'm looking for The Man with the Shoes," he said.

"You and everybody else," said the handyman. He squinted. "I seen you somewhere before."

"Not unless you pay to get in places I wouldn't," said Mantan.

"Bessie Smith?" said the workman. "I mean, you're not Bessie Smith. But why I think of her when I see you?"

Mantan smiled. "Toured with her and Ma Rainey last year. I tried to tell jokes, and people threw bricks and things at me till they came back on and sang. Theater Owners' Booking Agency. The T.O.B.A. circuit."

The guy smiled. "Tough On Black Asses, huh?"

"You got that right."

"Well, I thought you were pretty good. Caught you somewhere in the City. Went there for the jazz."

"Thank you—"

"Willie." The janitor stuck out his hand, shook Mantan's.

"Thank you, Willie. Mantan Brown." He looked around. "Can you tell me what the hoodoo's going on here?"

"Beats me. I done the *strangest* things I ever done this past week. I work here—at the studio itself, fetchin' and carryin' and ridin' a mop. Guy rented it two weeks ago—guy with the shoes is named Mr. Meister, a real yegg. He must be makin' a race movie—the waiting room, second down the hall to the left—looks like Connie's Club on Saturday night after all the slummers left. The guy directing the thing—Meister's just the watch chain—name's Slavo, Marcel Slavo. Nice guy, real deliberate and intense—somethin's wrong with him, looks like a jakeleg or blizzard-bunny to me—he's got some great scheme or somethin'. I been painting scenery for it. Don't make sense. You'd think they were making another *Intolerance,* but they only got cameras coming in Thursday and Friday, shooting time for a two-reeler. Other than that, Mr. Brown, I don't know a thing more than you do."

"Thanks."

The waiting room wasn't like Connie's, it was like a T.O.B.A. tent-show alumnus reunion. There was lots of yelling and hooting when he came in.

"Mantan!" "Why, Mr. Brown" "Looky who's here!"

As he shook hands he saw he was the only comedian there.

There was a pretty young woman, a high-yellow he hadn't seen before, sitting very quietly by herself. She had on a green wool dress and toque, and a weasel-trimmed wrap rested on the back of her chair.

"Somethin', huh?" asked Le Roi Chicken, a dancer from Harlem who'd been in revues with *both* Moran and Mack *and* Buck and Bubbles.

"Her name's Pauline Christian."

"Hey, Mr. Brown," said someone across the room. "I thought you was just a caution in *Mantan of the Apes!*"

Mantan smiled, pleased. They'd made the film in three days, mostly in the Authentic African Gardens of a white guy's plantation house in Sea Island, Georgia, during the mornings and afternoons before his tent-shows at night. Somebody had called somebody who'd called somebody else to get him the job. He hadn't seen the film yet, but from what he remembered of making it, it was probably pretty funny.

"I'm here for the five dollars a day just like all of you," he said.

"That's funny," said fifteen people in unison, "us all is getting *ten* dollars a day!"

While they were laughing, a door opened in the far corner. A tough white mug who looked like an icebox smoking a cigar came out, yelled for quiet, and read names off a list.

Mantan, Pauline Christian, and Lorenzo Fairweather were taken into an office.

"Welcome, welcome," said Mr. Meister, who was a shorter version of the guy who'd called off the names on the clipboard.

Marcel Slavo sat in a chair facing them. Willie had been right. Slavo had dark spots under his eyes and looked like he slept with his face on a waffle iron. He was pale as a slug, and smoking a Fatima in a holder.

"The others, the extras, will be fitted today, then sent home. They'll be back Thursday and Friday for the shooting. You three, plus Lafayette Monroe and Arkady Jackson, are the principals. Mr. Meister here—" Meister waved to them and Marcel continued "—has got money to shoot a two-reeler race picture. His friends would like to expand their movie investments. We'll go on to the script later, rehearse tomorrow and Wednesday, and shoot for two days. I know that's unusual, not the way you're all used to working, but this isn't the ordinary two-reeler. I want us all to be proud of it."

"And I—and my backers—want it in the can by Friday night," said Mr. Meister.

They laughed nervously.

"The two other principals will join us Wednesday. We can cover most of their shots Thursday afternoon," said Slavo.

He then talked with Lorenzo about the plays he'd been in, and with

Mantan about his act. "*Mantan of the Apes* was why I wanted you," he said. "And Pauline," he turned to her. "You've got great potential. I saw you in *Upholding the Race* last week. A small part, but you brought something to it. I think we can make a funny satire here, one people will remember." He seemed tired. He stopped a moment.

"And—?" said Meister.

"And I want to thank you. There's a movie out there right now. It's the apotheosis of screen art—"

"What?" asked Lorenzo.

"The bee's knees," said Mantan.

"Thank you, Mr. Brown. It's the epitome of moviemaking. It's in trouble because it was made in Germany; veterans' groups picketing outside, all that stuff everywhere it plays. There's never been anything like it, not in America, France, or Italy. And it's just a bunch of bohunks keeping people away from it. Well, it's art, and they can't stop it."

"And," said Meister conspiratorially, "they can't keep us from sending it up, making a comedy of it, and making some bucks."

"Now," said Slavo, all business. "I'd like you to make yourselves comfortable, while I read through what we've got for you. Some of the titles are just roughs, you'll get the idea though, so bear with me. We'll have a title writer go over it after we finish the shooting and cutting. Here's the scene: we open on a shot of cotton fields in Alabama, usual stuff, then we come in on a sign: *County Fair September 15-22*. Then we come down on a shot of the sideshow booths, the midway, big posters, et cetera."

And so it was that Mantan Brown found himself in the production of *The Medicine Cabinet of Dr. Killpatient*.

Mantan was on the set, watching them paint scenery.

Slavo was rehearsing Lafayette Monroe and Arkady Jackson, who'd come in that morning. They were still in their street clothes. Monroe must have been 7 feet 3 inches tall.

"Here we go," said Slavo, "try these."

What he'd given Lafayette were two halves of Ping-Pong balls with black dots drawn on them. The giant placed them over his eyes.

"Man, man," said Arkady.

Slavo was back ten feet, holding both arms and hands out, one inverted, forming a square with his thumbs and index fingers.

"Perfect!" he said. "Mantan?"

"Yes, Mr. Slavo?"

"Let's try the scene where you back around the corner and bump into him."

"Okay," said Brown.

They ran through it. Mantan backed into Lafayette, did a freeze, reached back, turned, did a double take, and was gone.

Arkady was rolling on the floor. The Ping-Pong balls popped off Lafayette's face as he exploded with laughter.

"Okay," said Slavo, catching his breath. "Okay. This time, Lafayette, just as he touches you, turn your head down a little and toward him. Slowly, but just so *you're* looking at him when he's looking at you."

"I can't see a thing, Mr. Slavo."

"There'll be holes in the pupils when we do it. And remember, a line of smoke's going to come up from the floor where Mr. Brown *was* when we get finished with the film."

"I'm afraid I'll bust out laughing," said Lafayette.

"Just think about money," said Slavo. "Let's go through it one more time. Only this time, Mantan . . ."

"Yes, sir?"

"This time, Mantan, bug your eyes out a little bit more."

The hair stood up on his neck.

"Yes sir, Mr. Slavo."

The circles under Slavo's eyes seemed to have darkened as the day wore on.

"I would have liked to have gone out to the West Coast with everyone else," he said, as they took a break during the run-throughs. "Then I realized this was a wide-open field, the race pictures. I make exactly the movies I want. They go out to 600 theaters in the North, and 850 in the South. They make money. Some go into state's rights distribution. I'm happy. Guys like Mr. Meister are happy—" He looked up to the catwalk overhead where Meister usually watched from "—the people who see the films are happy."

He put another cigarette in his holder. "I live like I want," he said. Then, "Let's get back to work, people."

"You tell her in this scene," said Slavo, "that as long as you're heeled, she has nothing to fear from the somnam—from what Lorenzo refers to as the Sleepy Guy."

He handed Mantan a slim straight razor.

Mantan looked at him. Pauline looked back and forth between them.

"Yes, Mr. Brown?" asked Slavo.

"Well, Mr. Slavo," he said. "This film's going out to every Negro theater in the U.S. of A., isn't it?"

"Yes."

"Well, you'll have everybody laughing *at* it, but not *with it.*"

"What do you mean?"

"This is the kind of razor cadets use to trim their mustaches before they go down to the dockyards to wait for the newest batch of Irish women for the sporting houses."

"Well, that's the incongruity, Mr. Brown."

"Willie? Willie?"

The workman appeared. "Willie, get $2.50 from Mr. Meister, and run down to the drugstore and get a Double Duck Number 2 for me to use."

"What the hell?" asked Meister, who'd been watching. "A tree's a tree. A rock's a rock. A razor's a razor. Use that one."

"It won't be right, Mr. Meister. Mainly, it won't be as funny as it *can* be."

"It's a tiny razor," said Meister. "It's funny, if you *think* it can defend both of you."

Slavo watched and waited.

"Have you seen the films of Mr. Mack Sennett?" asked Brown.

"Who hasn't? But he can't get work now either," said Meister.

"I mean his earlier stuff. Kops. Custard. Women in bathing suits."

"Of course."

"Well, Mr. Sennett once said, if you bend it, it's funny. If you break it, it isn't."

"Now a darkie is telling me about the Aristophanic roots of comedy!" said Meister, throwing up his hands. "What about this theory of Sennett's?"

"If I use the little razor," said Mantan, "it breaks."

Meister looked at him a moment, then reached in his pocket and pulled three big greenbacks off a roll and handed them to Willie. Willie left.

"I want to see this," said Meister. He crossed his arms, "Good thing you're not getting paid by the hour."

Willie was back in five minutes with a rectangular box. Inside was a cold stainless steel thing, mother-of-pearl handled with a gold thumb-stop, half the size of a meat cleaver. It could have been used to dry-shave the mane off one of Mack Sennett's lions in 15 seconds flat.

"Let's see you bend *that!*" said Meister.

They rehearsed the scene, Mantan and Pauline. When Brown flourished the razor, opening it with a quick look, a shift of his eyes each way, three guys who'd stopped painting scenery to watch fell down in the corner.

Meister left.

Slavo said, "For the next scene . . ."

It was easy to see Slavo wasn't getting whatever it was that was keeping him going.

The first morning of filming was a nightmare. Slavo was irritable. They shot sequentially for the most part (with a couple of major scenes held back for the next day). All the takes with the extras at the carnival were done early that morning, and some of them let go, with enough remaining to cover the inserts with the principals.

The set itself was disorienting. The painted shadows and reflections were so convincing Mantan found himself squinting when moving away from a painted wall because he expected bright light to be in his eyes there. There was no real light on the set except that which came in from the old overhead glass roof of the studio, and a few arc lights used for fill.

The walls were painted at odd angles; the merry-go-round was only two feet tall, with people standing around it. The Ferris Wheel was an ellipsoid of neon, with one car with people (two Negro midgets) in it, the others diminishingly smaller, then larger around the circumference. The tents looked like something out of a Jamaica ginger extract-addict's nightmare.

Then they filmed the scene of Dr. Killpatient at his sideshow, opening his giant medicine cabinet. The front was a mirror, like in a hotel bathroom. There was a crowd of extras standing in front of it, but what was reflected was a distant, windswept mountain (and in Alabama, too). Mantan watched them do the scene. As the cabinet opened, the mountain disappeared: the image revealed was of Mantan, Pauline, Lorenzo, and the extras.

"How'd you do that, Mr. Slavo?" asked one of the extras.

"Fort Lee magic," said Meister from his position on the catwalk above.

At last the morning was over. As they broke for lunch they heard loud voices coming from Meister's office. They all went to the drugstore across the street.

"I hear it's snow," said Arkady.

"Jake."

"Morphine."

"He's kicking the gong around," said another extra.

One guy who had read a lot of books said, "He's got a surfeit of the twentieth century."

"Whatever, this film's gonna scare the bejeezus out of Georgia, funny or not."

Mantan said nothing. He chewed at his sandwich slowly and drank his cup of coffee, looking out the window toward the cold façade of the studio. It looked just like any other warehouse building.

Slavo was a different man when they returned. He moved very slowly, taking his time setting things up.

"Okay . . . let's . . . do this right. And all the extras can go home early. Lafayette," he said to the black giant, who was putting in his Ping-Pong ball eyes. "Carry . . . Pauline across to left. Out of sight around the pyramid. Then, extras. Come on, jump around a lot. Shake your torches. Then off left. Simple. Easy. Places. Camera. Action! That's right, that's right. Keep moving, Lafe, slow but steady. Kick some more, Pauline. Good. Now. Show some disgust, people. You're indignant. He's got your choir soloist from the A.M.E. church. That's it. Take—"

"Stop it! Stop the camera thing. Cut!" yelled Meister from the catwalk.

"What?" yelled Slavo.

"You there! *You!*" yelled Meister. "Are you blind?"

An extra wearing sunglasses pointed to himself. "Me?"

"If you ain't blind, what're you doing with sunglasses on? It's night!"

"How the hell would anybody know?" asked the extra, looking around at the painted square moon in the sky. "This is the most fucked-up thing I ever been involved with in all my life."

"You can say that again," said someone else.

"You," said Meister to the first extra. "You're fired. Get out. You only get paid through lunch." He climbed down as the man started to leave, throwing his torch with the papier-mâché flames on the floor. "Give me your hat," said Meister. He took it from the man. He jammed it on his head and walked over with the rest of the extras, who had moved back off-camera. "I'll do the damn scene myself."

Slavo doubled up with laughter in his chair.

"What? What is it?" asked Meister.

"If . . . if they're going to notice a guy . . . with sunglasses," laughed Slavo, "they're . . . damn sure gonna notice a white man!"

Meister stood fuming.

"Here go," said Mantan, walking over to the producer. He took the hat from him, pulled it down over his eyes, took off his coat. He got in the middle of the extras and picked up an unused pitchfork. "Nobody'll notice one more darkie," he said.

"Let's do it, then," said Slavo. "Pauline? Lafayette?"

"Meister," said a voice behind them. Three white guys in dark suits and shirts stood there. How long they had been watching no one knew. "Meister, let's go talk," said one of them.

You could hear loud noises through the walls of Meister's office. Meister came out in the middle of a take, calling for Slavo.

"Goddammit to hell!" said Slavo. "Cut!" He charged into Meister's office. There was more yelling. Then it was quiet. Then only Meister was heard.

Lafayette Monroe took up most of the floor, sprawled out, drinking water from a quart jug. He wore a black body suit, and had one of the Ping-Pong balls out of his eye socket. Arkady had on his doctor's costume—frock coat, hair like a screech owl, big round glasses, gloves with dark lines drawn on the backs of them. A big wobbly crooked cane rested across his knees.

Pauline fanned herself with the hem of her long white nightgown.

"I smell trouble," said Lorenzo. "Big trouble."

The guys with the dark suits came out and went past them without a look.

Meister came out. He took his usual place, clambering up the ladder to the walkway above the set. He leaned on a light railing, saying nothing.

After a while, a shaken looking Marcel Slavo came out.

"Ladies and gentlemen," he said. "Let's finish this scene, then set up the next one. By that time, there'll be another gentleman here to finish up today, and to direct you tomorrow. I am off this film after the next scene . . . so let's make this take a good one okay?"

They finished the chase setup, and the pursuit, Slavo came and shook their hands, and hugged Pauline. "Thank you all," he said, and walked out the door.

Ten minutes later another guy came in, taking off his coat. He looked up at Meister, at the actors, and said, "Another coon pitcher, huh? Gimme five minutes with the script." He went into Meister's office.

Five minutes later he was out again "What a load of hooey," he said. "Okay," he said to Mantan and the other actors, "Who's who?"

When they were through the next afternoon, Meister peeled bills off a roll, gave each of the principals an extra five dollars, and said, "Keep in touch."

Mantan took his friend Freemore up to the place they told him Marcel Slavo lived.

They knocked three times before there was a muffled answer.

"Oh, Mr. Brown," said Slavo, as he opened the door. "Who's this?"

"This Joe Freemore. We're just heading out on the 'chitlin circuit' again."

"Well, I can't do anything for you," said Slavo. "I'm through. Haven't you heard? I'm all washed up."

"We wanted to show you our act."

"Why me?"

"Because you're an impartial audience," said Mantan.

Slavo went back in, sat in a chair at the table. Mantan saw that along with bootleg liquor bottles and ashtrays full of Fatima and Spud butts, the two razors from the movie lay on the table. Slavo followed his gaze.

"Souvenirs," he said. "Something to remind me of all my work. I remember what you said, Mr. Brown. It has been a great lesson to me."

"Comfortable, Mr. Slavo?" asked Freemore.

"Okay. Rollick me."

"Empty stage," said Mantan. "Joe and I meet."

"Why, hello!" said Joe.

"Golly, hi," said Mantan, pumping his hand. "I ain't seen you since—"

"—it was longer ago than that. You had just—"

"—that's right. And I hadn't been married for more than—"

"—seemed a lot longer than that. Say, did you hear about—"

"—you don't say! Why, I saw her not more than—"

"—it's the truth! And the cops say she looked—"

"—that bad, huh? Who'd have thought it of her? Why she used to look—"

"—speaking of her, did you hear that her husband—"

"—what? How could he have done that? He always—"

"—yeah, but not this time. I tell you he—"

"—that's impossible! Why, they told me he'd—"

"—that long, huh? Well, got to go. Give my best to—"

"—I sure will. Goodbye."

"Goodbye."

They turned to Slavo.

"They'll love it down in Mississippi," he said.

It was two weeks later, and the South Carolina weather was the crummiest, said the locals, in half a century. It had been raining—a steady, continuous, monotonous thrumming—for three days.

Mantan stopped under the hotel marquee, looking out toward a gray two-by-four excuse for a city park, where a couple of ducks and a goose were kicking up their feet and enjoying life to its fullest.

He went inside and borrowed a Columbia newspaper from the catatonic day manager. He went up the four flights to his semiluxury room, took off his sopping raincoat and threw it over the three-dollar Louis Quatorze knock-off chair, and spread the paper out on the bed.

He was reading the national news page when he came across the story from New Jersey.

The police said that, according to witnesses, during the whole time of the attack, the razor-wielding maniac had kept repeating, "Bend, d—n it, don't break! Bend, d—n it, don't break!"

The names of the victims were unknown to Mantan, but the attacker's name was Meister.

Twenty years later, while he was filming Mr. *Pilgrim Progresses*, a lady brought him a War Bond certificate, and a lobby card for him to autograph.

The card was from *The Medicine Cabinet of Dr Killpatient, Breezy Laff Riot*. There were no credits on it, but there on the card were Mantan, Pauline Christian, and Lorenzo Fairweather, and behind them the giant Lafayette Monroe in his medicine cabinet.

Mantan signed it with a great flourish with one of those huge pencils you get at county fairs when you knock down the Arkansas kitty.

He had never seen the film, never knew till now that it had been released.

As the lady walked away, he wondered if the film had been any good at all.

For Mr. Moreland, and for Icky Twerp.

Afterword to:

Occam's Ducks

1) Just because something's Politically Incorrect doesn't mean it isn't funny.
2) Nobody calls me Politically Correct and lives.

This story's about, among many other things, Black American actors of the films of the 1920s and later; guys like Mantan Moreland, Stepin Fetchit, G. Howe Black. They played in roles that were stereotyped, and beneath their talents, if not their dignity.

But strange and wonderful things could happen, especially with Mantan Moreland. As Birmingham Brown in the *Charlie Chan* movies, he suddenly started getting the best lines. The lines were stereotyped, but Moreland's delivery was right on the money. You didn't watch anyone else (*not* Keye Luke, *not* Warner Oland, *not* Sidney Toler). He was in a lot of movies with a lot of famous actors; once again, who were you watching?

While he was doing those, he was also in "race movies"—covered in the book *A Separate Cinema*—done by people like Oscar Micheaux, shown in all-black theaters in the northern U.S. and at blacks-only matinees in the American South in the '20s through the '40s. Produced on shoestrings, they could still get the best black talent around; they were *just like* Hollywood movies: they went from the truly appalling to the sublime. Moreland made several dozen (*The Professor Creeps, Mr. Washington Does His Deed*) that were takeoffs on Hollywood product.

Yes, there were all-black horror movies, like there were all-black musicals, all-black Westerns (*Harlem on the Prairie, The Bronze Buckaroo*), gangster films, religious movies, kid's movies. It *was* a separate cinema, and it's just now being mined, appreciated and restored.

So I was going to write about a black actor in a white-produced takeoff of *The Cabinet of Dr. Caligari* in the early Twenties. Moreland had been too young; *voila!* I came up with Mantan Brown. I knew the opening sequence would be pre-figurative. The story of the Griffith movie crew and *The Greatest Question* was real. So Mantan Brown's the steward on the yacht.

And the rest (besides watching *Caligari* ten or fifteen times and reading Budd's definitive book on the film, and of course *From Caligari to Hitler* by Kracauer, a book that's taken its lumps lately) was just figuring out how the hell to do it.

Once again, a dragged-out affair. I wrote it and read it at Sercon in Austin in January of 1992, wrote a second draft in Lake City, Colorado while fishing with Chad in August, sent it to Ellen Datlow, then rewrote some more in December 1992—eleven months is too long to be dicking with a short story, on and off.

I hope I did okay by guys like Mr. Moreland.

The second dedicatee of the story—Icky Twerp—was that same kind of ignored talent, the afternoon tv kid's show host, over KTVT in Ft. Worth in the 1950s. As Icky Twerp he hosted the Stooges, along with his apes, Ajax and Delphinium; knockabout skits, wild hair, bad suits and all, he *pedalled* the film projector and sparks came out of it. On Saturday nights he was Gorgon, the host of *Scream Theater*, and did some incredible stuff with videotape—then in its infancy—some of it before Steve Allen and Ernie Kovacs' use of it (since it looked *live*, he did stuff you couldn't believe). My memory may be failing, but I think he was also one of the voices on the *Mickey and Amanda* puppet show at noon. He even filled in for Cap'n Swabby when the captain had had too much spinach on the afternoon *Popeye Theater*.

His real name was Bill Camfield; if you want to see what he looked like, he played (I think) Wild Bill Hickock in *The Outlaws is Coming* (1964) in which all the Stooges' tv hosts from around the country played parts.

He died a few years ago; six or eight paragraphs about him on the AP wire. I'll miss him, too. They're *all* going. Tell them while you can what they've done for you.

When I got an advance copy of the *Omni* with the story in it, I opened it up, and my eyeballs fell out. It had a beautiful illustration by Gary Kelley.

I called up Neal Barrett Jr., who's been in this business since Pluto was a pup.

"Boy, you should see this, Neal," I said. "Not only is it a great illo, it's also exactly from the story *and* true to the spirit of it!"

There was silence on the line.

"You're lying, Howard," he said. "That *never* happens."

And he hung up on me.

Flatfeet!

1912

Captain Teeheezal turned his horse down toward the station house just as the Pacific Electric streetcar clanged to a stop at the intersection of Sunset and Ivar.

It was just 7 a.m. so only three people got off at the stop. Unless they worked at one of the new moving-picture factories a little further out in the valley, there was no reason for someone from the city to be in the town of Wilcox before the stores opened.

The motorman twisted his handle, there were sparks from the overhead wire, and the streetcar belled off down the narrow tracks. Teeheezal watched it recede, with the official sign *No Shooting Rabbits from the Rear Platform* over the back door.

"G'hup, Pear," he said to his horse. It paid no attention and walked at the same speed.

By and by he got to the police station. Patrolman Rube was out watering the zinnias that grew to each side of the porch. Teeheezal handed him the reins to his horse.

"What's up, Rube?"

"Not much, Cap'n," he said. "Shoulda been here yesterday. Sgt. Fatty brought by two steelhead and a coho salmon he caught, right where Pye Creek empties into the L.A. River. Big as your leg, all three of 'em. Took up the whole back of his wagon."

"I mean police business, Rube."

"Oh." The patrolman lifted his domed helmet and scratched. "Not that I know of."

"Well, anybody in the cells?"

"Uh, lessee . . ."

"I'll talk to the sergeant," said Teeheezal. "Make sure my horse stays in his stall."

"Sure thing, Captain." He led it around back.

The captain looked around at the quiet streets. In the small park across from the station, with its few benches and small artesian fountain, was the big sign *No Spooning by Order of Wilcox P.D.* Up toward the northeast the sun was coming full up over the hills.

Sgt. Hank wasn't at his big high desk. Teeheezal heard him banging around in the squad room to the left. The captain spun the blotter book around.

There was one entry:

Sat. 11:20 p.m. Jimson H. Friendless, actor, of Los Angeles City, d&d. Slept off, cell 2. Released Sunday 3 p.m. Arr. off. Patrolmen Buster and Chester.

Sgt. Hank came in. "Oh hello, chief."

"Where'd this offense take place?" He tapped the book.

"The Blondeau Tavern . . . uh, Station," said the sergeant.

"Oh." That was just inside his jurisdiction, but since the Wilcox village council had passed a local ordinance against the consumption and sale of alcohol, there had been few arrests.

"He probably got tanked somewhere in L.A. and got lost on the way home," said Sgt. Hank. "Say, you hear about them fish Sgt. Fatty brought in?"

"Yes, I did." He glared at Sgt. Hank.

"Oh. Okay. Oh, there's a postal card that came in the Saturday mail from Captain Angus for us all. I left it on your desk."

"Tell me if any big trouble happens," said Teeheezal. He went into the office and closed his door. Behind his desk was a big wicker rocking chair he'd had the village buy for him when he took the job early in the year. He sat down in it, took off his flat-billed cap, and put on his reading glasses.

Angus had been the captain before him for twenty-two years; he'd retired and left to see some of the world. (He'd been one of the two original constables when Colonel Wilcox laid out the planned residential village.) Teeheezal had never met the man.

He picked up the card—a view of Le Havre, France from the docks. Teeheezal turned it over. It had a Canadian postmark, and one half had the address: The Boys in Blue, Police HQ, Wilcox, Calif. U.S.A. The message read:

—Well, took a boat. You might have read about it. Had a snowball fight on deck while waiting to get into the lifeboats. The flares sure were pretty. We were much overloaded by the time we were picked up. (Last time I take a boat named for some of the minor Greek godlings.)

Will write again soon.

— Angus

PS: Pretty good dance band.

Teeheezal looked through the rest of the mail; wanted posters for guys three thousand miles away, something from the attorney general of California, a couple of flyers for political races that had nothing to do with the village of Wilcox.

The captain put his feet up on his desk, made sure they were nowhere near the kerosene lamp or the big red bellpull wired to the squad room, placed his glasses in their case, arranged his Farmer John tuft beard to one side, clasped his fingers across his chest, and began to snore.

The murder happened at the house of one of the curators, across the street from the museum.

Patrolman Buster woke the captain up at his home at four a.m. The Los Angeles County coroner was already there when Teeheezal arrived on his horse.

The door of the house had been broken down. The man had been strangled and then thrown back behind the bed where the body lay twisted with one foot out the open window sill.

"Found him just like that, the neighbors did," said Patrolman Buster. "Heard the ruckus, but by the time they got dressed and got here, whoever did it was gone."

Teeheezal glanced out the broken door. The front of the museum across the way was lit with electric lighting.

"Hmmmm," said the coroner, around the smoke from his El Cubano cigar. "They's dust all over this guy's pyjamas." He looked around. "Part of a print on the bedroom doorjamb, and a spot on the floor."

Patrolman Buster said "Hey! One on the front door. Looks like somebody popped it with a dirty towel."

The captain went back out on the front porch. He knelt down on the lawn, feeling with his hands.

He spoke to the crowd that had gathered out front. "Who's a neighbor here?" A man stepped out, waved. "He water his yard last night?"

"Yeah, just after he got off work."

Teeheezal went to the street and lay down.

"Buster, look here." The patrolman flopped down beside him. "There's some lighter dust on the gravel, see it?" Buster nodded his thin face. "Look over there, see?"

"Looks like mud, chief." They crawled to the right to get another angle, jumped up looking at the doorway of the museum.

"Let's get this place open," said the chief.

"I was just coming over; they called me about Fielding's death, when your ruffians came barging in," said the museum director, whose name was Carter Lord. "There was no need to rush me so." He had on suit pants but pyjama tops and a dressing gown.

"Shake a leg, pops," said Patrolman Buster.

There was a sign on the wall near the entrance: *The Treasures of Pharaoh Rut-en-tut-en April 20-June 13.*

The doors were steel; there were two locks Lord had to open. On the inside was a long push bar that operated them both.

"Don't touch anything, but tell me if something's out o' place," said Teeheezal.

Lord used a handkerchief to turn on the light switches.

He told them the layout of the place and the patrolmen took off in all directions.

There were display cases everywhere, and ostrich-looking fans, a bunch of gaudy boxes, things that looked like coffins. On the walls were paintings of people wearing diapers, standing sideways. At one end of the hall was a big upright wooden case. Patrolman Buster pointed out two dabs of mud just inside the door, a couple of feet apart. Then another a little further on, leading toward the back, then nothing.

Teeheezal looked around at all the shiny jewelry. "Rich guy?" he asked.

"Priceless," said Carter Lord. "Tomb goods, buried with him for the afterlife. The richest find yet in Egypt. We were very lucky to acquire it."

"How come you gettin' it?"

"We're a small, but a growing museum. It was our expedition—the best untampered tomb. Though there were skeletons in the outer corridors, and the outside seal had been broken, I'm told. Grave robbers had broken in but evidently got no further."

"How come?"

"Who knows?" asked Lord. "We're dealing with 4,500 years."

Patrolman Buster whistled.

Teeheezal walked to the back. Inside the upright case was the grey swaddled shape of a man, twisted, his arms across his chest, one eye closed, a deep open hole where the other had been. Miles of grey curling bandages went round and round and round him, making him look like a cartoon patient in a lost hospital.

"This is the guy?"

"Oh, heavens no," said Carter Lord. "The Pharaoh Rut-en-tut-en's mummy is on loan to the Field Museum in Chicago for study. This is probably some priest or minor noble who was buried for some reason with him. There were no markings on this case," he said, knocking on the plain wooden case. "The pharaoh was in that nested three-box sarcophagus over there."

Teeheezal leaned closer. He reached down and touched the left foot of the thing.

"Please don't touch that," said Carter Lord.

The patrolmen returned from their search of the building. "Nobody here but us *gendarmerie*," said Patrolman Rube.

"C'mere, Rube," said Teeheezal. "Reach down and touch this foot."

Rube looked into the box, jerked back. "Cripes! What an ugly! Which foot?"

"Both."

He did. "So?"

"One of them feel wet?"

Rube scratched his head. "I'm not sure."

"I asked you to *please* not touch that," said Carter Lord. "You're dealing with very fragile, irreplaceable things here."

"He's conducting a murder investigation here, bub," said Patrolman Mack.

"I understand that. But nothing here has committed murder, at least not for the last four thousand five hundred years. I'll have to ask that you desist."

Teeheezal looked at the face of the thing again. It looked back at him with a deep open hole where one eye had been, the other closed. Just—

The hair on Teeheezal's neck stood up. "Go get the emergency gun from the wagon," said the chief, not taking his eyes off the thing in the case.

"I'll have to *insist* that you leave *now!*" said Carter Lord.

Teeheezal reached over and pulled up a settee with oxhorn arms on it and sat down, facing the thing. He continued to stare at it. Somebody put the big heavy revolver in his hand.

"All you, go outside, except Rube. Rube, keep the door open so you can see me. Nobody do anything until I say so."

"That's the last straw!" said Carter Lord. "Who do I call to get you to cease and desist?"

"Take him where he can call the mayor, Buster."

Teeheezal stared and stared. The dead empty socket looked back at him. Nothing moved in the museum, for a long, long time. The revolver grew heavier and heavier. The chief's eyes watered. The empty socket stared back, the arms lay motionless across the twisted chest. Teeheezal stared.

"Rube!" he said after a longer time. He heard the patrolman jerk awake.

"Yeah, chief?"

"What do you think?"

"Well, I think about now, Captain, that they've got the mayor all agitated, and a coupla aldermen, and five, maybe ten minutes ago somebody's gonna have figured out that though the murder happened in Wilcox, right now you're sitting in Los Angeles."

Without taking his eyes from the thing, Teeheezal asked, "Are you funnin' me?"

"I never fun about murder, chief."

Three carloads of Los Angeles Police came around the corner on six wheels. They slammed to a stop, the noise of the hand-cranked sirens dying on the night. By now the crowd outside the place had grown to a couple of hundred.

What greeted the eyes of the Los Angeles Police was the Wilcox police wagon with its four horses in harness, most of the force, a crowd, and a small fire on the museum lawn across the street from the murder house.

Two legs were sticking sideways out of the fire. The wrappings flamed against the early morning light. Sparks rose up and swirled.

The chief of the Los Angeles Police Department walked up to where the captain poked at the fire with the butt end of a spear. Carter Lord and the Wilcox mayor, and a Los Angeles city councilman trailed behind the L.A. chief.

"Hello, Bob," said Teeheezal.

With a pop and a flash of cinders, the legs fell the rest of the way into the fire, and the wrappings roared up to nothingness.

"Teeheezal! What the hell do you think you're doing!? Going out of your jurisdiction, no notification. It looks like you're burning up Los Angeles City property here! Why didn't you call us?"

"Didn't have time, Bob," said Teeheezal. "I was in hot pursuit."

They all stood watching until the fire was out, then all climbed into their cars and wagons and drove away. The crowd dispersed, leaving Carter Lord in his dressing gown. With a sigh, he turned and went into the museum.

1913

If southern California had seasons, this would have been another late spring.

Teeheezal was at his desk, reading a letter from his niece Katje from back in Pennsylvania, where all his family but him had been for six generations.

There was a knock on his door. "What? What?" he yelled.

Patrolman Al stuck his head in. "Another card from Captain Angus. The sergeant said to give it to you."

He handed it to Teeheezal and left swiftly. Patrolman Al had once been a circus acrobat, and the circus had folded in Los Angeles City two years ago. He was a short thin wiry man, one of Teeheezal's few smooth-shaven patrolmen.

The card was a view of the Eiffel Tower, had a Paris postmark with the usual address on the back right side. On the left:

—Well, went to the Ballet last night. You would of thought someone spit on the French flag. Russians jumpin' around like Kansas City fools, Frogs punching each other out, women sticking umbrellas up guy's snouts. I been to a rodeo, a county fair, six picnics, and I have seen the Elephant, but this was pretty much the stupidest display of art appreciation I ever saw. Will write again soon.

— Angus

PS: *Ooh-lah-lah.*

"Hmmph!" said Teeheezal. He got up and went out into the desk area. Sergeant Hank had a stack of picture frames on his desk corner. He was over at the wall under the pictures of the mayor and the village aldermen. He had a hammer and was marking five spots for nails on the plaster with the stub of a carpenter's pencil.

"What's all this, then?" asked the captain.

"My pictures got in yesterday, chief," said Sgt. Hank. "I was going to put 'em up on this wall I have to stare at all day."

"Well, I can see how looking at the mayor's no fun," said Teeheezal. He picked up the top picture. It was a landscape. There was a guy chasing a deer in one corner, and some trees and teepees, and a bay, and a funny-shaped rock on a mountain in the distance.

He looked at the second. The hill with the strange rock was in it, but people had on sheets, and there were guys drawing circles and squares in the dirt and talking in front of little temples and herding sheep. It looked to be by the same artist.

"It's not just paintings," said Sgt. Hank, coming over to him. "It's a series by Thomas Cole, the guy who started what's referred to as the Hudson River School of painting way back in New York State, about eighty years ago. It's called *The Course of Empire*. Them's the first two— *The Savage State* and *The Pastoral or Arcadian State*. This next one's called *The Consummation of Empire*—see, there's this guy riding in a triumphal parade on an elephant, and there are these armies, all in this city like Rome or Carthage, it's been built here, and they're bringing stuff back from all over the world, and things are dandy."

Hank was more worked up than the chief had ever seen him. "But look at this next one, see, the jig is up. It's called *The Destruction of*

Empire. All them buildings are on fire, and there's a rainstorm, and people like Mongols are killing everybody in them big wide avenues, and busting up statues and looting the big temples, and bridges are falling down, and there's smoke everywhere."

Teeheezal saw the funny-shaped mountain was over in one corner of those two paintings.

"Then there's the last one, number five, *The Ruins of Empire*. Everything's quiet and still, all the buildings are broken, the woods are taking back everything, it's going back to the land. See, look there, there's pelicans nesting on top of that broken column, and the place is getting covered with ivy and briers and stuff. I ordered all these from a museum back in New York City," said Hank, proudly.

Teeheezal was still looking at the last one.

"And look," said Sgt. Hank, going back to the first one. "It's not just paintings, it's philosophical. See, here in the first one, it's just after dawn. Man's in his infancy. So's the day. Second one—pastoral, it's midmorning. Consummation—that's at noon. First three paintings all bright and clear. But destruction—that's in the afternoon, there's storms and lightning. Like nature's echoing what's going on with mankind, see? And the last one. Sun's almost set, but it's clear again, peaceful, like, you know, Nature takes its time . . ."

"Sgt. Hank," said Teeheezal. "When a guy gets arrested and comes in here drunk and disorderly, the last thing he wants to be bothered by is some philosophy."

"But, chief," said Sgt. Hank, "it's about the rise and fall of civilizations . . ."

"What the hell does running a police station have to do with civilization?" said Teeheezal. "You can hang one of 'em up. One at a time they look like nature views, and those don't bother anybody."

"All right, chief," said Sgt. Hank.

That day, it was the first one. When Teeheezal arrived for work, the next day, it was the second. And after that, the third, and on through the five pictures, one each day, then the sequence was repeated. Teeheezal never said a word. Neither did Hank.

1914

There had been murders three nights in a row in Los Angeles City when the day came for the Annual Wilcox Police vs. Firemen Baseball Picnic.

The patrolmen were all playing stripped down to their undershirts and uniform pants, while the firemen had on real flannel baseball outfits that said Hot Papas across the back. It was late in the afternoon, late in the game, the firemen ahead 17–12 in the eighth.

They were playing in the park next to the observatory. The patrol wagon was unhitched from its horses; the fire wagon stood steaming with its horses still in harness. Everyone in Wilcox knew not to bother the police or firemen this one day of the year.

Patrolman Al came to bat on his unicycle. He rolled into the batter's box. Patrolman Mack was held on second, and Patrolman Billy was hugging third. The pitcher wound up, took a long stretch and fired his goofball from behind his back with his glove hand while his right arm went through a vicious fastball motion.

Al connected with a meaty *crack*; the outfielders fell over themselves and then charged toward the Bronson place. Al wheeled down to first with blinding speed, swung wide ignoring the fake from the second baseman, turned between second and third, balancing himself in a stop while he watched the right fielder come up with the ball on the first bounce four hundred feet away.

He leaned almost to the ground, swung around, became a blur of pedals and pumping feet, passed third; the catcher got set, pounding his mitt, stretched out for the throw. The umpire leaned down, the ball bounced into the mitt, the catcher jerked around—

Al hung upside down, still seated on the unicycle, six feet in the air over the head of the catcher, motionless, sailing forward in a long somersault.

He came down on home plate with a thud and a bounce.

"Safe!" said the ump, sawing the air to each side.

The benches emptied as the catcher threw off his wire mask. Punches flew like they did after every close call.

Teeheezal and Sgt. Hank stayed on the bench eating a bag of peanuts. The people in the stands were yelling and laughing.

"Oh, almost forgot," said Sgt. Hank, digging in his pants pocket. "Here." He handed Teeheezal a postcard. It had an illegible postmark in a language with too many Zs. The front was an engraving of the statue of a hero whose name had six Ks in it.

—Well, was at a cafe. Bunch of seedy-looking students sitting at the table next to mine grumbling in Slavvy talk. This car come by filled

with plumed hats, made a wrong turn and started to back up. One of
the students jumped on the running board and let some air into the guy
in the back seat—'bout five shots I say. Would tell you more but I was
already lighting out for the territory. Place filled up with more police
than anywhere I ever seen but the B.P.O.P.C. convention in Chicago
back in '09. This was all big excitement last week but I'm sure it will
blow over. Will write more soon.

— Angus

PS: Even here, we got the news the Big Ditch is finally open.

It was the bottom of the eleventh and almost too dark to see when
the bleeding man staggered onto left field and fell down.

The man in the cloak threw off all six patrolmen. Rube used the
emergency pistol he'd gotten from the wagon just before the horses
went crazy and broke the harness, scattering all the picnic stuff
everywhere. He emptied the revolver into the tall dark man without
effect. The beady-eyed man swept Rube aside with one hand and came
toward Teeheezal.

The captain's foot slipped in all the stuff from the ball game.

The man in the dark cloak hissed and smiled crookedly, his eyes red
like a rat's.

Teeheezal reached down and picked up a Louisville Slugger. He
grabbed it by the sweet spot, smashed the handle against the ground,
and shoved the jagged end into the guy's chest.

"Merde!" said the man, and fell over.

Rube stood panting beside him. "I never missed, chief," he said.
"All six shots in the space of a half-dime."

"I saw," said Teeheezal, wondering at the lack of blood all over the
place.

"That was my favorite piece of lumber," said Patrolman Mack.

"We'll get you a new one," said the captain.

They had the undertaker keep the body in his basement, waiting for
somebody to claim it. After the investigation, they figured no one would,
and they were right. But the law was the law.

Sgt. Hank scratched his head and turned to the chief, as they were
looking at the man's effects.

"Why is it," he asked, "we're always having trouble with things in boxes?"

1915

Teeheezal got off the streetcar at the corner of what used to be Sunset and Ivar, but which the village council had now renamed, in honor of a motion picture studio out to the northwest, Sunset and Bison. Teeheezal figured some money had changed hands.

The P.E. Street Railway car bell jangled rapidly as it moved off toward Mount Lowe and the Cawston Ostrich Farms, and on down toward San Pedro.

In the park across from the station, Patrolmen Chester and Billy, almost indistinguishable behind their drooping walrus mustaches, were rousting out a couple, pointing to the *No Sparking* sign near the benches. He stood watching until the couple moved off down the street, while Billy and Chester, pleased with themselves, struck noble poses.

He went inside. The blotter on the desk was open:

Tues. 2:14 a.m. Two men, Alonzo Partain and D. Falcher Greaves, no known addresses, moving picture acting extras, arrested d&d and on suspicion of criminal intent, in front of pawn shop at Gower and Sunset. Dressed in uniforms of the G.A.R. and the Confederate States and carrying muskets. Griffith studio notified. Released on bond to Jones, business manager, 4:30 a.m. Ptlmn. Mack. R.D.O.T.

The last phrase officially meant Released until Day Of Trial, but was stationhouse for Rub-Down with Oak Towel, meaning Patrolman Mack, who was 6 feet 11 inches and 350 pounds, had had to use considerable force dealing with them.

"Mack have trouble?" he asked Sgt. Hank.

"Not that Fatty said. In fact, he said when Mack carried them in, they were sleeping like babies."

"What's this Griffith thing?"

"Movie company out in Edendale, doing a War Between the States picture. Mack figured they were waiting till the hock shop opened to pawn their rifles and swords. This guy Jones was ready to blow his top, said they sneaked off the location late yesterday afternoon."

Teeheezal picked up the newspaper from the corner of the sergeant's desk. He scanned the headlines and decks. "What do you think of that?" he asked. "Guy building a whole new swanky residential area, naming it for his wife?"

"Ain't that something?" said Sgt. Hank. "Say, there's an ad for the new Little Tramp flicker, bigger than the film it's playing with. That man's a caution! He's the funniest guy I ever seen in my life. I hear he's a Limey. Got a mustache like an afterthought."

"I don't think anybody's been really funny since Flora Finch and John Bunny," said Teeheezal. "This Brit'll have to go some to beat *John Bunny Commits Suicide.*"

"Well, you should give him a try," said Sgt. Hank. "Oh, forgot yesterday. Got another from Captain Angus. Here go." He handed it to Teeheezal.

It had a view of Lisbon, Portugal as seen from some mackerel-slapper church tower, the usual address, and on the other half:

—Well I had another boat sink out from under me. This time it was a kraut torpedo, and we was on a neutral ship. Had trouble getting into the lifeboats because of all the crates of howitzer shells on deck. Was pulled down by the suck when she went under. Saw airplane bombs and such coming out the holes in the sides while I was under water. Last time I take a boat called after the Roman name for a third-rate country. Will write again soon.

— Angus

PS: How about the Willard-Johnson fight?

The windows suddenly rattled. Then came dull booms from far away. "What's that?"

"Probably the Griffith people. They're filming the battle of Chickamauga or something. Out in the country, way past the Ince Ranch, even."

"What they using, nitro?"

"Beats me. But there's nothing we can do about it. They got a county permit."

"Sometimes," said Teeheezal, "I think motion picture companies is running the town of Wilcox. And the whole U.S. of A. for that matter."

1916

Jesus Christ, smoking a cigar, drove by in a Model T.

Then the San Pedro trolleycar went by, full of Assyrians, with their spears and shields sticking out the windows. Teeheezal stood on the corner, hands on hips, watching them go by.

Over behind the corner of Prospect and Talmadge the walls of Babylon rose up, with statues of bird-headed guys and dancing elephants everywhere, and big moveable towers all around it. There were scaffolds and girders everywhere, people climbing up and down like ants. A huge banner stretched across the eight-block lot: *D.W. Griffith Production— The Mother and the Law.*

He walked back to the station-house. Outside, the patrolmen were waxing the shining new black box-like truck with Police Patrol painted on the sides. It had brass hand-cranked sirens outside each front door, and brass handholds along each side above the runningboards. They'd only had it for three days, and had yet to use it for a real emergency, though they'd joy-rode it a couple of times, sirens screaming, with the whole force hanging on or inside it, terrifying the fewer and fewer horses on the streets. Their own draught-horses had been put out to pasture at Sgt. Fatty's farm, and the stable out back converted into a garage.

The village fathers had also wired the station-house for electricity, and installed a second phone in Teeheezal's office, along with an electric alarm bell for the squad room on his desk.

The town was growing. It was in the air. Even some moving pictures now said Made in Wilcox, U.S.A. at the end of them.

The blotter, after a busy weekend, was blank.

The postcard was on his desk. It had an English postmark, and was a view of the River Liffey.

—Well, with the world the way it is, I thought the Old Sod would be a quiet place for the holiday. Had meant to write you boys a real letter, so went to the Main Post Office. Thought I'd have the place to myself. Boy was I wrong about that. Last time I look for peace and quiet on Easter Sunday. Will write more later.

— Angus

PS: This will play heck with Daylight Summer Time.

Teeheezal was asleep when the whole force burst into his office and Sgt. Hank started unlocking the rack with the riot guns and rifles.

"What the ding-dong?" yelled Teeheezal, getting up off the floor.

"They say Pancho Villa's coming!" yelled a patrolman. "He knocked over a coupla banks in New Mexico!"

Teeheezal held up his hand. They all stopped moving. He sat back down in his chair and put his feet back up on his desk.

"Call me when he gets to Long Beach," he said.

Sgt. Hank locked the rack back up, then they all tiptoed out of the office.

—Look out! Get 'im! Get 'im! Watch it!!—

The hair-covered man tore the cell bars away and was gone into the moonlit night.

"Read everything you can, Hank," said Teeheezal. "Nothing else has worked."

"You sure you know what to do?" asked the captain.

"I know exactly *what* to do," said Patrolman Al. "I just don't *like* it. Are you sure Sgt. Hank is right?"

"Well, no. But if you got a better idea, tell me."

Al swallowed hard. He was on his big unicycle, the one with the chain drive. There was a woman's scream from across the park.

"Make sure he's after *you*," said Teeheezal. "See you at the place. And Al . . ."

"Say 'break a leg', Captain."

"Uh . . . break a leg, Al."

Al was gone. They jumped in the police patrol truck and roared off.

They saw them coming through the moonlight, something on a wheel and a loping shape.

Al was nearly horizontal as he passed, eyes wide, down the ramp at the undertaker's, and across the cellar room. Patrolman Buster closed his eyes and jerked the vault door open at the second before Al would have smashed into it. Al flew in, chain whizzing, and something with hot meat breath brushed Buster.

Patrolman Al went up the wall and did a flip. The thing crashed into the wall under him. As Al went out, he jerked the broken baseball bat out of the guy it had been in for two years.

There was a hiss and a snarl behind him as he went out the door that Buster, eyes still closed, slammed to and triple-locked, then Mack and Billy dropped the giant steel bar in place.

Al stopped, then he and the unicycle fainted.

There were crashes and thumps for two hours, then whimpering sounds and squeals for a while.

They went in and beat what was left with big bars of silver, and put the broken Louisville Slugger back in what was left of the hole.

As they were warming their hands at the dying embers of the double fire outside the undertaker's that night, it began to snow. Before it was over, it snowed five inches.

1917

The captain walked by the *No Smooching* sign in the park on his way to talk to a local store owner about the third break-in in a month. The first two times the man had complained about the lack of police concern, first to Teeheezal, then the mayor.

Last night it had happened again, while Patrolmen Al and Billy had been watching the place.

He was on his way to tell the store owner it was an inside job, and to stare the man down. If the break-ins stopped, it had been the owner himself.

He passed by a hashhouse with a sign outside that said "Bratwurst and Sauerkraut 15¢". As he watched, the cook, wearing his hat and a knee-length apron, pulled the sign from the easel and replaced it with one that said "Victory Cabbage and Sausage 15¢".

There was a noise from the alleyway ahead, a bunch of voices yelling "get 'im, get 'im" then out of the alley ran something Teeheezal at first thought was a rat or a rabbit. But it didn't move like either of them, though it was moving as fast as it could.

A group of men and women burst out onto the street with rocks, and chunks of wood sailing in front of them, thirty feet behind it. It dodged, then more people came from the other side of the street, and the thing turned to run away downtown. The crowd caught up with it. There was a single yelp, then the thudding sounds of bricks hitting something soft. Twenty people stood over it, their arms moving. Then they stopped and cleared off the street and into the alleyways on either side without a word from anyone.

Teeheezal walked up to the pile of wood and stones with the rivulet of blood coming out from under it.

The captain knew the people to whom the dachshund had belonged, so he put it in a borrowed tow sack, and took that and put it on their porch with a note. *Sorry. Cpt. T.*

When he got within sight of the station-house, Patrolman Chester came running out. "Captain! Captain!" he yelled.

"I know," said Teeheezal. "We're at war with Germany."

A month later another card arrived. It had a view of the Flatiron Building in New York City, a Newark, New Jersey postmark, and the usual address. On the left back it said:

—Well, went to the first Sunday baseball game at the Polo Grounds. New York's Finest would have made you proud. They stood at attention at the national anthem then waited for the first pitch before they arrested McGraw and Mathewson for the Blue Law violation. You can imagine what happened next. My credo is—when it comes to a choice between religion and baseball, baseball wins every time. Last time I go to a ball game until they find some way to play it at night. Ha ha. Will write more later.

—Angus

PS: Sorry about Buffalo Bill.

1918

If every rumor were true, the Huns would be in the White House by now. Teeheezal had just seen a government motion picture (before the regular one) about how to spot the Kaiser in case he was in the neighborhood spreading panic stories or putting cholera germs in your reservoir.

Now, last night, one had spread through the whole California coast about a U-boat landing. Everybody was sure it had happened at San Pedro, or Long Beach, or maybe it was in Santa Barbara, or along the Sur River, or somewhere. And somebody's cousin or uncle or friend had seen it happen, but when the Army got there there wasn't a trace.

The blotter had fourteen calls noted. One of them reminded the Wilcox police that the president himself was coming to Denver, Colorado, for a speech—coincidence, or what?

"I'm tired of war and the rumors of war," said Teeheezal.

"Well, people out here feel pretty helpless, watching what's going on ten thousand miles away. They got to contribute to the war effort *somehow*," said walrus-mustached Patrolman Billy.

Innocently enough, Patrolmen Mack and Rube decided to swing down by the railroad yards on their way in from patrol. It wasn't on their beat that night, but Sgt. Fatty had told them he'd seen some fat rabbits down there last week, and, tomorrow being their days off, they were going to check it over before buying new slingshots.

The patrol wagon careened by, men hanging on for dear life, picked up Teeheezal from his front yard, and roared off toward the railroad tracks.

The three German sailors went down in a typhoon of shotgun fire and hardly slowed them down at all.

What they did have trouble with was the giant lowland gorilla in the spiked *pickelhaube* helmet, and the eight foot high iron automaton with the letter Q stenciled across its chest.

The Federal men were all over the place. In the demolished railyard were two huge boxes marked for delivery to the Brown Palace in Denver.

"Good work, Captain Teeheezal," said the Secret Service man. "How'd you get the lowdown on this?"

"Ask the two patrolmen," he said.

At the same time, Mack and Rube said "Dogged, unrelenting police procedures."

The postcard came later than usual that year, after the Armistice.

It was a plain card, one side for the address, the other for the message.

—*Well here in Rekjavik things are really hopping. Today they became an independent nation, and the firewater's flowing like the geysers. It's going to be a three-day blind drunk for all I can figure. Tell Sgt. Fatty the fish are all as long as your leg here. Pretty neat country; not as cold as the name. Last time I come to a place where nobody's at work for a week. Will write more later.*

— Angus

PS: Read they're giving women over 30 in Britain the vote — can we be far behind? Ha ha.

PPS: I seem to have a touch of the 'flu.

1919

Sgt. Hank didn't look up from the big thick book in his hand when

Teeheezal came out of his office and walked over and poured himself a cup of steaming coffee. Say whatever else about the Peace mess in Europe, it was good to be off rationing again. Teeheezal's nephew had actually brought home some butter and steaks from a regular grocery store and butcher's last week.

"What's Wilson stepping in today?"

No answer.

"Hey!"

"Huh?! Oh, gosh chief. Was all wrapped up in this book. What'd you say?"

"Asking about the president. Seen the paper?"

"It's here somewhere," said Sgt. Hank. "Sorry, chief, but this is about the greatest book I ever read."

"Damn thick square thing," said Teeheezal. He looked closely at a page. "Hey, that's a kraut book!"

"Austria. Well, yeah, it's by a German, but not like any German you ever thought of."

Teeheezal tried to read it, from what he remembered of when he went to school in Pennsylvania fifty years ago. It was full of two-dollar words, the sentences were a mile long, and the verb was way down at the bottom of the page.

"This don't make a goddam bit of sense," he said. "This guy must be a college perfesser."

"It's got a cumulative effect," said Sgt. Hank. "It's about the rise of cultures and civilizations, and how Third Century B.C. China's just like France under Napoleon, and how all civilizations grow and get strong, and wither and die. Just like a plant or an animal, like they're alive themselves. And how when the civilization gets around to being an empire it's already too late, and they all end up with Caesars and Emperors and suchlike. Gosh, chief, you can't imagine. I've read it twice already, and every time I get more and more out of it . . ."

"Where'd you get a book like that?"

"My cousin's a reporter at the Peace Commission conference. Somebody told him about it, and he got one sent to me, thought it'd be something I'd like. I hear it's already out of print, and the guy's rewriting it."

"What else does this prof. say?"

"Well, gee. A lot. Like I said, that all civilizations are more alike than not. That everything ends up in winter, like, after a spring and summer and fall." He pointed to the Cole picture on the wall—today it was *The Pastoral State*. "Like, like the pictures. Only a lot deeper. He says for instance, that Europe's time is over—"

"It don't take a goddammed genius to know that," said Teeheezal.

"No—you don't understand. He started writing this in 1911, it says. He already knew it was heading for the big blooie. He says that Europe's turn's over, being top dog. Now it's the turn of America . . . and . . . and Russia."

Teeheezal stared at the sergeant.

"We just fought a fuckin' war to get rid of ideas like that," he said. "How much is a book like that worth, you think?"

"Why, it's priceless, chief. There aren't any more of them. And it's full of great ideas!"

Teeheezal reached in his pocket and took out a twenty-dollar gold piece (six weeks of Sgt. Hank's pay) and put it on the sergeant's desk.

He picked up the big book by one corner of the cover, walked over, lifted the stovelid with the handle, and tossed the book in.

"We just settled Germany's hash," said Teeheezal. "It comes to it, we'll settle Russia's too."

He picked up the sports section and went into his office and closed the door.

Sgt. Hank sat with his mouth open. He looked back and forth from the gold piece to the stove to the picture to Teeheezal's door.

He was still doing that when Patrolmen Rube and Buster brought in someone on a charge of drunk and disorderly.

1920

Captain Teeheezal turned his Model T across the oncoming traffic at the corner of Conklin and Arbuckle. He ignored the horns and sound of brakes and pulled into his parking place in front of the station-house.

A shadow swept across the hood of his car, then another. He looked up and out. Two condors flew against the pink southwest sky where the orange ball of the sun was ready to set.

Sgt. Fatty was just coming into view down the street, carrying his big supper basket, ready to take over the night shift.

Captain Teeheezal had been at a meeting with the new mayor about all the changes that were coming when Wilcox was incorporated as a city.

Sgt. Hank came running out, waving a telegram. "This just came for you."

Teeheezal tore open the Western Union envelope.

TO: ALL POLICE DEPARTMENTS, ALL CITIES,
          UNITED STATES OF AMERICA
FROM: OFFICE OF THE ATTORNEY GENERAL

1. VOLSTEAD ACT (PROHIBITION) IS NOW LAW STOP ALL POLICE DEPARTMENTS EXPECTED TO ENFORCE COMPLIANCE STOP

2. ROUND UP ALL THE REDS STOP

PALMER

Teeheezal and the sergeant raced to punch the big red button on the sergeant's desk near the three phones. Bells went off in the squad room in the tower atop the station. Sgt. Fatty's lunch basket was on the sidewalk out front when they got back outside. He reappeared from around back, driving the black box of a truck marked Police Patrol, driving with one hand and cranking the hand siren with the other, until Sgt. Hank jumped in beside him and began working the siren on the passenger side.

Patrolmen came from everywhere, the squad room, the garage, running down the streets, their nightsticks in their hands—Al, Mack, Buster, Chester, Billy and Rube—and jumped onto the back of the truck, some missing, grabbing the back fender and being dragged until they righted themselves and climbed up with their fellows.

Teeheezal stood on the running board, nearly falling off as they hit the curb at the park across the street, where the benches had a *No Petting* sign above them.

"Head for the dago part of town," said Teeheezal, taking his belt and holster through the window from Sgt. Hank. "Here," he said to the sergeant, knocking his hand away from the siren crank. "Lemme do that!"

The world was a high screaming whine, and a blur of speed and nightsticks in motion when there was a job to be done.

Afterword to:

Flatfeet!

The genesis of this one was easy.

I was reading about the Palmer Raids of 1920 and realized the guys doing them would be the Keystone Cops, or someone very much like them.

And I knew they were also where Griffith filmed *Birth of a Nation* and *Intolerance* (it would have been neater, more resonant, if the order had been reversed, but what the hell, you can't have everything).

So we are into World-Form and Morphosis-of-Culture land yet again.

I first ran into Oswald Spengler in an article by Fritz Leiber in *Amra* when I was in high school. (Leiber and Harry Fischer had created three European brothers Hamilcar, Odoacer and Hasdrubal-something who supposedly refuted everything Spengler had said, back in the 1930s.) I immediately got the two-volume Atkinson translation out of the library. I opened it to volume 1, page 1. My eyes grew heavy . . . heavy. I fell immediately to sleep.

For years I slogged my way through Spengler's *Decline of the West* in odd hours, and I could *always* go to sleep by opening it anywhere, while I was lying down.

But I made it, kids. You can't imagine the impact the books had on late '20s America: there were answers to Spengler, answers to his answers, etc. "Must the West Decline?" was on everybody's lips. (The answer's yes, from here in 1996, but we haven't realized it yet.)

I've used Spengler before. My 1976 story "*Der Untergang des Abendlandesmenschen*" means "the down-going of the men of the sunset-lands" or "decline of the cowboy" and it too, takes place in the late '20s, has a Spenglerian base not apparent from its Cowboys & Nazis vs. Vampires storyline.

So now I have a story in which Spengler is underneath some silent film slapstick cops. What can I do to show this? Well, there's the book. There's the Thomas Cole paintings (the definitive Thomas Cole book came out, of course, a few months *after* I finished this story, *after* I needed it). There's the movie stuff. There's wandering Angus and his postcards.

There's the monsters. Okay, let's apply a Spenglerian underpinning to the monsters.

First one's a mummy, from Egypt, way back at the beginning, and in Africa. Then a vampire: a medieval European monster. A werewolf, a product of the Renaissance in its final form; the rebirth of Classical learning with a hairy face. And the lowland gorilla and the Automaton (*The Master Mystery* with Harry Houdini, 1918) products of, respectively, colonialism and technology. *Voila!* See how easy this writing stuff is?

This is probably the most round, firm and fully-packed story I've ever done, for what goes on and how it's written and what happens and why. I wrote it in three days, read it the third afternoon, rewrote it and sent it to Gardner Dozois, who bought it (in the form of a postcard from Angus) a week later.

Yow! This is the way writing should be.

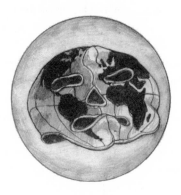

El Castillo de la Perseverancia

1.

Every day, Rhonda had passed the bright pink wall on the Avenida Guerrero opposite the Bella Vista Hotel on the way to her art classes.

Today it was neither bright nor altogether pink. Someone had sprayed a dark blue cloudlike smudge across three meters of it, and in the cloud, had painted in neon green, in Spanish:

> *The World which has slumbered so long,*
> *now begins to awaken . . .*

A few other passersby noticed it, made *tssking* noises and continued on. One man, wearing two hats, a derby topped by a planters' hat, stopped, hands on hips, staring. He slowly shook his head.

"Next thing you know, the *alcalde* will ask for new taxes to clean such messes," he said, not to her, or to anyone.

Rhonda went on toward the Cortes Palace. She remembered how confusing the streets were to her when she had first come here six months ago. When she found that the College of Fine Arts was next to Hernan Cortes' old summer home, she realized she could find her way to classes from anywhere in the town except from across the barrancas, or from out past the Morelos State Penitentiary, places she'd only been a couple of times sketching for her classes.

She neared the old *zocalo* and tried to imagine what it had been like here five hundred years ago; probably too many guys in jaguar skins and parrot feathers running around.

There was a furniture and appliance store ahead. A man was in the front window setting up a display. She neared it. He was arranging dozens of alarm clocks—quartzes, electrics, windups—and clock radio phones on small tilted shelves, from one side of the large window to the other, reaching back behind him through a small doorway that opened back into the store. Small hands passed the timepieces out to him.

He looked up and saw Rhonda watching him, and smiled at her over his dapper mustache. He was dressed in a natty suit, *muy guapa*, the locals would say. He said something back through the small door; the thick glass muffling his words. A rectangle of card-board came out. The man laid it down, lay his head on his steepled horizontal hands, feigning sleep. Then he picked up one of the clocks, shook it around like it was coming apart, and made big circles with his thumbs and index fingers around his eyes, mouth agape.

Then he turned the rectangle around. In Spanish, the sign said:

> *¡The whole world, which wants to sleep so long,*
> *can now wake itself up!*

A chill went through Rhonda, a true horripilation through her whole upper body and down her right leg.

The man had a puzzled look on his face. He had placed the sign in its holder among the clocks, indicating his wares for sale with spread hands.

She slowly shook her head no.

The man looked crestfallen, then straightened himself, shot his cuffs, and crawled back through his little door.

As Rhonda turned to continue on to class, a 1965 blue and white Ford Galaxie convertible came by her, its top down.

In the car were three masked and cloaked wrestlers.

2.

The three men walked into the office of the registrar in the collegia menor.

"*¿En que puedo serville?*" asked the woman at the desk without looking up.

"*Si*," said the older of the three men. "I am Señor Nadie. These are my compañeros, El Ravo Tepextehualtepec, and El Hijo de la Selva, whom I was fortunate enough to pass on the street on my way here in my car, and offered a ride, as we were all coming here to inquire about classes."

The woman had looked up. The older man was dressed in tights, boots and a black cape, but had a bare chest, with salt and pepper hair on it. His mask, which like those of the others covered his whole head, had a question mark on the face of it. The second was in a head-to-foot body suit, with red shorts and boots, a yellow cloak, and on the chest and mask was a yellow lightning bolt. The third was naked but for a loincloth and jungle boots. His mask was woodland camo.

"You have your B.U.P.'s?" asked the woman.

"Certainly," said El Ravo Tepextehualtepec, whom all his fans called El Ravo Tepe, to differentiate him from all the other El Ravos in the sport.

"Day or night classes?" she asked.

"Day, of course," said El Hijo de la Selva. "Night is when we wrestle."

3. Hecho en Mexico

Outside, near his pickup, his dog barked twice.

"Hush, Hecho," he said.

He put on the face mask and the disposable gloves over his plastic coveralls, cranked up the compressor and began spraying primer paint all over the taped and mudded dry-wall.

All around were the sounds of hammering and nailguns. Two weeks ago this part of Yucatan was a newly-drained swamp. Now it was three rows of apartment blocks on the outskirts of a town that had not been there a year before, worker's rooms for the byproducts of the tourist trade.

At least now they gave you gloves and coveralls and masks. When he'd started as a painter's helper two years ago, at the age of seventeen, you went to work and sprayed the stuff all week and threw away your clothes on *viernes*. You got the stuff off your body with paint thinner and Go-Jo Cleaner.

He could hear Hecho begin to whine even over the *brrrupping* noise of the compressor. "Hush!" he yelled out, muffled. He turned off the compressor.

There was a long whine, and the sound of shaking in the pickup bed.

He looked out. The rope with which he tied his dog in the pickup was frayed and hung over the side. He saw his dog running, a half-meter of rope dangling from its collar. It climbed a pile of lumber scraps at the end of the site.

"Come back here!" he said. As he cupped his hands to yell, he tore the coveralls open on the latchplate on the doorjamb.

Hecho lay down on the lumber pile, head between his paws. He had never done that before. *Loco perro.*

He turned to go back to the inside room, passing the stacks of medicine cabinet mirrors at the front door. Why they had been stacked there, when half the apartments weren't even weathered-in yet, he had no idea.

He pulled down his facemask and pulled off the gloves, which were stuck now to the torn plastic coveralls by the primer paint, so he let them dangle. He'd have to get another pair when he put on new coveralls anyway.

The dog yowled and ran away.

He stopped. In the mirror, the torn plastic flapped like another skin. The gloves hung like newly-shed hands from the ends of his arms. His facemask with a big smear of grey across it looked like another loose mouth and jaw next to his own.

He was turning to admire the effect when something put him on like a cheap suit.

4.

A slow Wednesday night at the Arena Tomalin:

After the prelims, El Hijo de la Selva fought Dinosaurito in a three-fall event. He won the first fall, lost the second, and won the third.

Then, to louder applause from the sparse crowd, El Ravo Tepe took on El Buitré Marvelloso. He won the first fall, lost the second, won the third and the match.

Two masked women wrestlers allowed all but the most iron-kidneyed a chance to visit the *taza de retrete.*

The main event: Señor Nadie contra El Pocilga Desordenado, a Tabascan who had failed at sumo in Japan, and who had come back and sat on a series of lesser *luchadores* until he gained the chance to go against the top-rated masked wrestler.

Señor Nadie won the first fall with a combination of wristlocks and outside-bar-stepover-toeholds. El Pocilga won the second by falling onto Señor Nadie as soon as the round started. At the end of the third fall, Señor Nadie left the ring victorious while the maintenance crew tried to get El Pocilga out of the snarled net that had been the ringropes and turnbuckles. Two spectators had been hit by the flying ringposts and were treated for cuts and bruises.

Such was wrestling in Quanahuac.

5. Sin Horquilla

He was at the company picnic in the park outside Ciudad Juarez to which he had taken his wife and children every year for the past twelve years. Today he was playing washer toss with three other older men while all around him younger people and their families played hundred-to-a-side soccer. The park was filled with screams of joy and pain, discord and harmony, like any other Sociedad Anonima outing.

Suddenly, the El Pato® sauce he'd been sampling since nine in the morning caught up with him.

"¡*Condenar!*" he said. Sweat broke out on his mustached upper lip. He took off for the line of old outhouses at the far edge of the park.

"That's the fastest I've seen him move in many years," said one of his co-workers.

He slowed a little when he realized he would make it. A woman came out of the one he was headed for, slamming the heavy wooden door on its tired screen door spring. The local priest, there to bless the chalupas at the big sit-down outdoor dinner that night, came out of another.

"Excuse me, padre," he said, crossing himself. As he reached for the worn brass doorhandle, the horseshoe nailed above the doorway fell down with a clang. He hesitated, then went in. When he was through, he would find a rock to nail the iron thing back up with. The door closed behind him.

The priest experienced a horripilation that stopped and turned him. He looked around. He fixed his collar and shook his shirt cuffs where they stuck out from his cassock.

There was a sound like giant rubbery wings behind him.

Something hit the ceiling of the third outhouse from the inside. There was a thrashing around, and a smash against the walls. Then another series of thumps up against the inside of the slanted corrugated tin roof that buckled it.

A sound of low mumbling came from the outhouse, then a third thrashing, then silence.

The priest started towards it. He wondered if the man had suffered a heart attack or a seizure of some kind.

"Are you all right?" he asked, reaching for the doorhandle, looking around to see if he could see the company doctor.

He swung the door open. The man's head lolled, the whites of his eyes showing. Then they came down and snapped into focus on the priest.

"In Christ's name . . ." said the priest.

"Fuck your God," said the man, and headed for the line of cars parked across from the soccer field.

6.

Rhonda walked by the wall again on her way to meet Federico, the Italian student in her life-drawing class.

The wall had been painted over the week before—there was a pink swath, done with a roller, through most of the design. In another week the enamel would bleed through the pink latex, and the words would show again.

Federico was to meet her at the Cine, just off the Avenida Morelos. They were going to see *Los Manos de Orlak* con Peter Lorre, and *El Maldicíon de la Momia* con Lon Chaney menor. The Cine Morelos seemed to stay in business by showing films that had been on American television for fifty years.

She realized she'd gone one block too far on the Avenida Guerrero, and turned to her left. She saw one of the diagonal streets leading down the block behind the Bella Vista Hotel and headed toward it.

She passed an upscale cantina—one of the tourist traps, no doubt—and heard music coming out. Lounge music must sound the same in every country.

A smooth baritone came out of the speakers—she pictured the tuxedoed smoothie to whom it belonged. He did not have a mustache, and never would.

Then she heard his words:

> *My world, so asleep in its bed,*
> *woke to the morning of your love.*

She stopped, hand on the doorframe, and looked inside.

The singer was old, bleary-eyed, and looked as if he'd come out second in his youth in a clawhammer fight. He was dressed like Leo Carillo, who had played Pancho in the old *Cisco Kid* television show, hat and all, or like a Latino Andy Devine. He saw Rhonda and smiled at her over his salt-and-pepper walrus mustache.

She turned and went down the street toward the Cine Morelos.

Far off in the distance the two volcanoes loomed in the last of the blue-purple light.

7.

The air was cool and smelled good outside the dressing rooms behind the Arena Tomalin.

There were already two cigarette glows in the dark against the far wall of the little courtyard reserved for the wrestlers.

The man who had just come out lit one of his own with a lighter from the left pocket of his dressing gown.

"Ay," he said. "Some night, eh?"

"We were talking of the same thing. Not at all like last week."

"During a night like this," said the man who had just come out, "I ask myself, what would Santo have done in the same situation."

"Ah, Santo," said one of the others.

"Or Blue Demon," said the other.

"They do not make them like Santo anymore. Such grace and sureness, both in the ring and out."

"Like when he fought the Frankenstein monster in the Wax Museum."

"Or the Martians, like in *Santo Contra la Invasion de los Marcianos!*"

"Or when he teamed with Blue Demon to fight the Nazis in Atlantis!"

"The Vampire Women? What about those?"

"Which Vampire Women? *The Vampire Women* was *un roncador grande*. I spent days watching it one afternoon," said one of the men who had been there first.

"No, no. Not the *Vampire Women* movie, that was bad. The *Santo en la Venganza de los Mujeres Vampiros*."

"Oh, si. Putting Santo in any movie improves it."

"Have you seen the Crying Woman movies. Or *Mummies of Guanajuatos?*"

"Of course. Or the Aztec Mummy films. Ah, that Popoca. To think he was in love five hundred years with the dead princess. The pains he went through . . ."

"And *La Nave de los Monstruos!* Uk, Zak and Utir! Espectro of the Planet Death! Tor the Robot. That was a movie!"

"To think how it must be," said one of them. "To wrestle cleanly, to be famous, to play yourself in movies of your own adventures . . ."

They all sighed.

"What Santo probably would have done on such a messed-up wrestling night as this," said the youngest, "is to have tried to forget about it, and go home and get a good night's sleep."

"As I am," said the second.

"And me," said the third.

Their three cigarettes became flying red dots in the night, bouncing sparks in the concrete courtyard.

The door to the dressing rooms opened, they went in, and it closed.

8. Soy Un Hombre Mas Pobre . . .

The limo dropped him outside his Mexico City office, at the corner of Salvador and Piño Suarez.

He went inside, nodding to the guard, took his elevator to the private entry to his office, went inside and put his sharkskin attaché on the corner of his desk. There were three pieces of paper in his in-box that he had to sign sometime during the day. There was a package on the credenza all the way across the office.

A light blinked on his phone. He picked it up. "*¡Bueno, y que?*" he said. It was the president of the American company he worked for. He listened. "*En seguida. Entonces. Si. No. Si, si. Buenos dias.*" He hung up.

He got the package from the antique dealer and unwrapped it, using his mammoth ivory scrimshaw letter opener.

Inside was the Cantiflas chocolate mug, the carnival glass pitcher with the 1968 Olympics commemorative design etched into it, and a book, a recognition guide to European mushrooms. They were not for him, but gifts for executives of other companies who had an interest in them. He looked at them a moment, wondering at the things people spent their time acquiring. He started to call his secretary and reached for the key on his computer. He bumped the book off onto the stainproof pile carpet.

It flipped open to the chapter on morels, and an old 1000-peso note fell out. Once it had been worth $120.00 U.S. After the fourth devaluation, it was worthless. He bent to pick it up.

He realized it was *all* about money. Everything. Entirely. From beginning to end, every second of it, even from before till after.

There was a surflike pounding in the air. He looked up and knew what he would see, and sure enough, the four hundred billion coins, dubloons, sesterces, pieces of eight, yen, marks, francs and pine-tree shillings washed over him in a cleansing, baptismal wave.

Now that he understood, he laughed. It was simple, so utterly simple.

9.

In three different provinces that week, three new *luchadores enmascarados* appeared on Amateur King of the Hill match nights. One wore a red horned mask, one a mask that was the mask of a human head and face with a zipper through it, one wore the mask of a globe of the earth. The speed with which they dispatched all comers was the only topic of the conversation of those who saw them.

Who were those guys? Where had they come from?

10.

She poured non-dairy creamer into her coffee and watched it soak up all the brown color. Nothing that dissolves instantly can be good for you, she thought. When she had started classes six months ago, there were still pots of cream or milk at the end of the student cafeteria serving line.

It was mid-afternoon, a Tuesday, so her first break for lunch, the choice being 10 a.m. or then. There were few people there, the occasional professor, a group of provincial eighteen-year-olds like a flock of birds, solitaries and couples.

She usually sat in the corner, as far away from the serving line as she could, so she wouldn't be bothered. Most local guys were pretty much jerks about women. So were most American guys; it was just that the local guys were more honest about it.

As she'd entered, she'd seen that the tables where she'd like to sit had people at them, but now as she turned away from the creamer, she saw they'd all emptied out. There were china cups and plates on the dark brown serving trays scattered around, napkins with lipstick on them, paper cups. As she neared the farthest table, she saw there was a paperback book lying, creased and dogeared, near one of the trays.

She looked up to see if anyone was moving away. No one.

She sat, took a drink of coffee, opened her microwave burrito, and looked at the book. A collection of dramas. But not, as she turned the pages, by Rudolfo Usigli or Lopé de Vega, but a collection of medieval English Mystery and Morality plays, with transliterated Middle English on one page, and Spanish on the other. It was by a couple of Italians.

A double-dogear marked a play called *The Castle of Perseverance*. She turned back to the introduction, read part of it. It was evidently a play like *Everyman*, which she had seen in high school, with personified evils and goods and a (to the modern mind) yokel of a protagonist, like Goofy, only dumb. In this case he was called Mankind.

She put the book with hers, finished her burrito and the caffeined chemical drink, and headed for her 3 p.m. painting class.

11.

He adjusted his mask and let himself into the apartment with a key.

There was no one there. He went to the music system and turned it on. A preset radio station came on, volume at six. He turned it down. The song was ? and the Mysterians' "96 Tears". When it was nearly over it faded and up came "Sleepwalk" by Santo and Johnny. It was the same all over Mexico; stations from the Estados Unidos leaked in all over the FM band. He wondered how powerful their stations were.

He loosened his shirt and found himself a Tres Equis in the refrigerador. He was halfway through it when he heard a key in the lock and the woman came in.

"Oh," she said. "You're already here. Sorry." She had a shopping bag and a grocery sack with her.

"Uf!" she said, putting the grocery sack on the counter, and opening the refrigerador. "The traffic! The crowding! I thought I would swoon!" She closed the door, the empty sack flew into the garbage. "They are tearing up Calle las Casas again." She walked into the bedroom. Through the open door he saw her pass back and forth, more or less clothing alternately covering and revealing different parts of her.

"Then I ran into the son of that French film director, the one who worked in Brazil so many years. The father, I mean. I still don't know what *el hijo* does for a living." She stayed out of sight. There was the sound of running water.

He took another swallow of beer.

She passed by naked; a second later she went by covered from neck to ankles, then came back by hopping through some garment on one foot.

"He tried to catch me up on some gossip which you would not be interested in. It made very little sense, even to me," she said.

He slowly moved the beer around in the bottom of the can with a slight swirling motion of his hand.

She stood in the bedroom doorway. She wore white silk hose and red high heels. The single other garment was a red and black lace cupless push-up bustier that ended at the navel, and from which the garter clips hung. She had on a thick woven gold-link necklace. Her glistening black hair stood out from around the Creature From the Black Lagoon mask she now wore.

"Come here, you big lug," she said, crooking her finger.

He put the beer can down beside the chair, stood as if in a dream, and began to walk.

12.

—Caramba! What a fight! Now El Diablo Peligroso has Lobo Griso in the *cangrejo Monterrey!* The Grey Wolf is begging for mercy! Now the referee puts the question. *¿Que? ¡Grito Tio!* Yes, yes, Señors y Señores; El Diablo Peligroso remains undefeated since appearing on the scene less than a month ago!—

—the inside-bar-stepover-toehold. Now Vestido Zooto works on—wait! Wait! Yes. *¡Cielo!* Carne Xipe has broken loose! He's under—now out! Wait. Yes, yes, now he has Vestido Zooto in the *¡alacran de pecho!* Yes, Yes! The pectoral scorpion has done its work. Carne Xipe wins again. They are taking Zooto out of the ring in agony. His arms hang useless at his sides—

—The crowd boos. Not much has happened. El Balon Gordo reaches out—what happened? Oh, look, look! El Mundo Grosero has El Balon in his famous hold, *el sueño de Japon*. El Balon is groggy. He's reaching for—El Mundo is using only one hand—he's, he's looking at his watch! What a gesture! Late for supper, eh, Mundo? There goes El Balon. He's on his knees, he's falling. He's down. Goodness gracious! Mundo is already leaving the ring! Now the referee is counting *him!*—he's put one foot back in the ring—he's in. *Now* he's the winner. The crowd is on its feet—listen to them. They are booing and cheering at the same time! Never have I seen this! Never—

"Your correspondent has asked himself again and again; where did these *luchadores* come from? How could they rise so fast in the world of wrestling? What are their goals? They are all three undefeated. The fans both love them and hate them; they want to see them like the fabled Juggernaut, unstoppable. And they want to see them stopped, dead cold. And there are only three who could possibly do it: the three shining companions—they know who they are—sure, professional, persevering, unpresuming. The only question is: when and where will the fight be? The whole wrestling world; no, all Mexico asks. We await our answer."

Pin-Down Martinez
Estrellos de Luchadores

13.

Rhonda sat up in bed, chilled and panting. She'd had a dream that made no sense that she could remember; it had only irritated her that it was taking so long and nothing was happening. Then she'd jerked awake, thinking she was cold.

Instead the room was stifling. She found her glasses on the bedside table, went to the window of her rented room and opened it.

More hot air came in. She undid her pajama top buttons, stood at the window. The clock said 0110.

Around the edges of the four-storey building behind the rooming house she saw soft flashes. She leaned out the left window.

Lightning played off clouds above the distant twin volcanoes. She could only see the shape of Iztacchihuatl, but saw residual flashes, which must be beyond Popocatépetl, and further south. Maybe the storm was coming this way, though most of their weather came from the west, off the Pacific.

There was no thunder; the storm was thirty kilometers away. In a minute or two came the faintest stirring of a breeze, so slight she did not know from which direction. The air coming into the room was slightly cooler. She stayed there, elbows resting on the window sill. The clock said 0211.

She turned on the light and wrote her aunt, who'd sent her a blanket two weeks before, a thank-you aerogramme. Then she turned off the light and went back to sleep.

She was surprised to find, when she left for class the next morning, that it had rained during the night, and the streets were dark and glistening under a cerulean sky with not a hint of cadmium white in it.

14.

"I want flesh," said Carne Xipe, moving around the office ceaselessly. "I want them to worship flesh, the flesh, food, meat. As when the pyramids—battle, blood sacrifice! Sacrifice—" He rubbed the mask that covered his head, the mask of a head with a zipper through it.

"Of course you do," said Mundo Grosero, tapping a cigarette on the face of his watch.

"Bah!" said Diablo Peligroso. "Flesh is no good unless there is the worship of the power behind it. Inversion. Their religion turned upside down, backwards. Renunciation. Flesh is just one way. No God! Evil. Ha ha. Let them know they are tempted, and there is nothing, *nothing* at the other end. Call on their God, hear an empty echo. I am the call. I am the empty echo. I want them to call out and only hear themselves calling out." His red horned mask, and the eyes in it, were filled with pain.

"Of course you do," said Mundo Grosero.

Carne Xipe and El Diablo Peligroso looked at him.

"And what do you want for them?" asked El Diablo.

"That's easy," said El Mundo Grosero, flicking out his Safari lighter so that the flame stood up to the end of his cigarette. A smile turned up through the Southern Western Hemisphere of his mask.

"I want to make them all just like *yanquis.*"

15

"You have to fight them," said Señor Sanabria, the head of the wrestling *federacion*.

"To paraphrase a boxer," said Señor Nadie, "we don't *have* to do anything but be Latino and die."

Señor Sanabria looked back and forth from El Ravo Tepe to El Hijo. "Help me," he said.

"I hate to say it," said El Ravo Tepe, "but the big question-mark guy is right. We know nothing of these gents. We don't know their aims, whether they are honorable."

"You've fought plenty of people," said Sanabria, "with, shall we say, *espiritus groseros* before. Especially you, Señor Nadie. Remember El Gorilla Acapulcano? El Gigante Gordo?"

"Those were merely dirty wrestlers," said Señor Nadie.

"Si," said El Hijo, the youngest. "Or so I've heard."

"Then it's not the money?" asked the president.

"Of course not!" said El Hijo de la Selva. He looked at the other two. "Or do I speak out of turn?"

"I'd do it for five old centavos—" They all laughed. "—actually, ten," said Señor Nadie, ". . . if I were sure of two things. Myself. And them."

"That goes for me, too," said El Ravo Tepe.

"Also," said El Hijo.

"Then," said Señor Sanabria, "I must bring up an indelicate inducement." He reached in his desk, pulled out some xeroxed pages of typed copy.

"It's from Pin-Down Martinez, isn't it?" asked Señor Nadie. "He still uses that outmoded Underwood Standard at the wrestling magazine office."

"Only it's not for the *Estrellos*," said Sanabria. "It's a guest editorial for the Saturday morning newspaper. He sent a copy over this morning." He offered it to Señor Nadie.

"Tell me."

"He says if you three do not take the challenge, he will believe for once and for all those scurrilous rumors are true, that wrestling matches are fixed."

El Ravo was on his feet. El Hijo de la Selva was looking for something to throw, and somewhere to throw it.

Señor Nadie held up his hand.

"*¿Compañeros?*"

16.

¡GIGANTIC SPECTACLE!
ARENA TOMALIN
¡BATTLE OF THE AGES!

*

LUCHA LIBRÉ

*

FREE-FOR-ALL WRESTLING
STYLO TEJAS DEATH-MATCH
con Barbed Wire

*

Los Compañeros de los Arenas:
SEÑOR NADIE
EL RAVO TEPEXTEHUALTEPEC

y

EL HIJO DE LA SELVA

contra

El MUNDO Grosero
El CARNE Xipe

y

El DIABLO Peligroso

MIERCOLES 2 NOVIEMBRE en punto de 9
ARENA TOMALIN

¡Vds. Ahi o Vds un Trasnochadé!

17.

Rhonda was coming down with a cold or sore throat or the flu. She ached all over, but after her last class, she took the book she had found in the cafeteria to the college Lost and Found. She had been meaning to do it for a week or two, but had remembered it that morning, before she became really miserable.

"I found this book," she said to the student behind the desk.

"*¡Ay, caramba!*" he said. "It must be made of gold." He looked it over, and at the piece of paper in his hand. "Lucky you," he said, handing it over to her.

"Reward," it said. "Lost book. Anthology of plays. *Plays of Mystery and Morality* ed. Malcondotti and Prolisse. En Español with English text on facing page. Call Nahuatl 4-1009. Reward."

She picked up the phone on the desk and called someone who wasn't the one with the offer of the reward, but said that he would be back soon. She gave him her mailing address, and told him to pick up the book at the lost and found.

She put the phone back on the cradle. "The person calling for the book is named José Humanidadas," she said to the student on the desk. "He says please make a note of that and not give it to anyone else."

"*Effectamente*," he said, reaching for a pen and paper.

Two days later, she received an envelope with no return address. Inside were two tickets to a wrestling match at the Arena Tomalin, and a piece of paper that said "Thanks for finding it."

By then, her cold had already raged and was on the ebb tide, she was miserable, and had been taking cough suppressant with codeine for eighteen hours.

18.

First Federico was going with her, then he wasn't, then he was.

Rhonda started for the Arena Tomalin, which was used for every kind of sporting event in this town. As she turned the corner and saw the huge lines, she stopped. Never before in her life had she been to a wrestling match or considered going to one.

She'd had another big dose of cough medicine just before she left the *pension*, and had gotten a little unsteady on her feet.

She sat on the low wall across from the arena. She saw that tv trucks were parked off to one side, their satellite antennae pointed at the same spot in the sky. Why would anyone come to a wrestling match if it were on tv?

To her left, on another building, was a bright blue cloud spray, and in the middle of it, in neon green, the slogan:

> *That world, which has slumbered so long,*
> *Now begins to awaken.*

She stared at it. It was the only one she had seen besides that first one across from the Hotel Bella Vista. She got up and moved towards the long lines of people at the doors of the Arena.

"Immediate seating for blue reserved seat tickets through the blue door by the ticket booth," said an usher with a megaphone to the crowd. "Immediate reserved seating through the blue door."

She looked down. Her tickets were blue.

She left a note and a ticket for Federico at the window and followed another usher to a seat in the third row. She looked around. Television cameras were on platforms built around the domed ceiling of the sportatorium, and reporters with minicams walked back and forth in front of the ring.

There were four long aisles into the place. People rushed to and fro. "¡Dulce de algodon!" yelled a man with a tray in front of him in which fluffy pink head-sized balls were stuck. "¡Dulce de algodon!" Rhonda noticed she was four seats over from the aisle, which probably meant she would be handing food and money back and across each way all night. Or however long it took.

In a few minutes, the announcer came out. The audience applauded and cheered. He began to speak, and they were with him until the word "preliminaries" came out.

The crowd was on its feet, booing and whistling. The booing stopped when two clowns, dressed as masked wrestlers came down the eastern and western aisles. Their masks had large red noses on the front of them, their tights were baggy, and they had on boots with meter-long toes.

They went through all the motions. Just as they prepared to grapple for the first time, a huge bank of the arena lights sputtered out, then all the lights around the ceiling, except for those on the side of the ring with Rhonda.

Giant shadows of the two wrestling clowns sprang up onto the far wall of the place. They were ten meters high. Rhonda watched them, instead of the clowns, as did other spectators. The titanic figures swirled and swooped. The crowd began laughing and applauding. The clowns redoubled their efforts.

Soon both the noses were gone—one clown bounced the other one's like a jack-ball off the canvas mat. The second pulled an athletic supporter out of his shorts, put the other one's nose in it, whirled it around and around his head and let go like a slingshot, hitting the other right between the eyeslits. He fell to the canvas with a thud, stiff-legged.

The crowd roared with laughter. To Rhonda, who had been watching the big shadows, it didn't seem that funny.

They had fixed the lights.

Other people with reserved seats had begun to file in around her—she had never thought wrestling, like opera, was something you could be fashionably late to. The people had talked during the entire clown act, and now were talking through the match between the two clean-cut non-masked wrestlers in the one-fall, ten-minute time limit match.

Some people further back were on their feet, yelling encouragement. Some people could get excited about almost anything.

She looked around. Still no Federico.

That match over, the crowd grew restless as technical people put up the two and a half meter high cyclone fence with two strands of barbed wire on top, and two cages, at diagonal corners of the square.

Rhonda nodded in the warm air. The cough medicine was still working on her. The next thing she knew, there was a fanfare on the speakers, jolting her awake.

"Señors and Señores," said the announcer, his voice echoing and rising. "Let's get ready to *escaramuza*!" The crowd went crazy.

"The Challengers:

From Ciudad Juarez, El Diablo Peligroso!"

The north door of the Arena flew open with Spielberg light effects, and coming down the aisle was a man in red tights with a horned, masked head.

"From Mexico City, El Mundo Grosero!"

The west door opened, the lights blinded everybody, and a wrestler with blue and green tights, and a mask of the globe of the earth came down that aisle.

"From the Yucatan, El Carne Xipe!"

From the south, amid the lights, came a man with a flesh-colored cape, flesh-colored body suit with red gashes in it and-at first Rhonda thought he had no mask on, but as he passed, she saw that his mask was the mask of a normal-looking head, with a zipper through it, all the way from the base of the neck, over the top and down to the chin.

The three wrestlers got to the ring at the same time and got into the little cage in their corner.

"Ladies and Gentlemen," yelled the announcer. "The Champions. The Compañeros of the Ring: Señor Nadie, El Ravo Tepextehualtepec and El Hijo de la Selva!!!"

The roar that went up was earsplitting. The three men bounded up the eastern aisle, waving to the crowd, and went into their cage, where the maintenance people waited.

"A Texas-style barbed-wire Death Match, no time limit, for the true championship team of all Mexico. Once the contestants are in, the match begins. It ends only when one team, or member of a team, remains conscious or in the ring. For this, there is no referee," said the announcer. "Officials of the Mexican Union of All-Professional Wrestling are explaining to each team the conditions of the match . . ."

"What do you mean?" asked El Ravo Tepe. "No unmasking? The official said it was legal. What fun is it to fight another *enmascarado* if you can't take off his mask?"

"Would you like it done to you?" asked Señor Nadie.

"Has never happened. And never will," said El Ravo.

"I am of two minds," said El Hijo. "I would not like it done to me. In many ways it cheapens the sport. But then, there are some people who deserve unmasking. They are not worthy of the mask. Humiliation is the only thing they understand. I have done it once; the guy asked for it. But I didn't like it."

"The true *enmascarado* has no need of such displays," said Señor Nadie. "Would that we all had the spirit and wisdom of a Santo or a Demonio Azul. Then would we know when an opponent is truly defeated, rather than just unconscious. We could all, in a normal match, quit before the count, and still know we had won. Bullfighting must be a lot like that, only in the end, someone or something dies, and there must be blood on the sand."

The two others were quiet in the cage, then El Hijo spoke.

"I know one thing. Those *Pavos* we fight will have no compunction about taking off our masks."

"Heads inside or not," said El Ravo Tepe.

Rhonda listened to the conversations around her.

"—a de J.C." said the man in the front row to someone else.

A candy hawker came by. Rhonda passed some jujubes and money across from right to left and left to right.

"Aw, go ahead," said another man to the woman beside him. "It won't hurt." He held up a candied apple. "Caramel. Look." He bit into it. "Yummmm."

"I'm on a diet," she said. "My doctor told me not to."

The guy with the fruit for sale stood nervously licking his lips.

"No," she said, finally.

"Aw, phooey," said the man. "Give me another one, though." He took the candied fruit on the stick and bit into it, turning toward the ring. He sat with one in each hand.

"¡*Dulce. Dulce de algodon!*" said another concessionaire, beside her on the aisle. She noticed the small badge on his hat. Hummingbird Foods, Southern Division, in the shape of a smiling cloisonné hummer.

". . . so he burned up the meat," said a man with his hat on to the priest beside him dressed in street clothes. He bit into a potato-and-egg burrito. "Look, all he did was get some of the recipe a little wrong. No reason to be upset, just get some more meat and do it right."

"¡*Achicharados!*" yelled another foodseller. "¡*Achicharados!* Hot dripping *achicharados!*"

"I hope we get to see some real holds," said a girl who had not yet had her *quinceaños* to the boy beside her as she clutched a copy of *Estrellos de Luchadores to* her.

"¡*Bomba zumbida!*" said the boy. "¡*Una bomba atomics!*"

"Sure, we'll give you the horse," said a man in a business suit to another dressed as a rancher, "just put up all your property as collateral."

". . . John Wayne," said a woman. "When he died, everything changed. I said, things will never ever be the same with the Duke dead, I assure you that. Why, the communists . . ."

An old man sighed a row back. "The Japanese. *Los Alemanes.* ¡*Ay de me!*"

"¡*Achicharados!*" yelled the barker.

A beerseller came by. Someone past Rhonda stopped him. He passed over a bottle of beer, Rhonda passed the money back, and the change. The person next to her tapped her on the shoulder. He held up an *abrebotella* which was attached by an elastic cord to an Orvis pin-reel on the Hummingbird Foods man's white jacket. She pulled it over to the man with the beer bottle. He opened the cap. Foam went everywhere, and he let go of the bottle opener. It *zeeted* back and thumped the beerseller in the chest.

"¡*Mal educado!*" said the vendor, glaring and moving on.

The house lights went down. The bell rang.

The wrestlers charged from their cages into the ring. The technical people knocked the cages down in a trice, and one locked each door with a Club®.

By then, no one was watching the maintenance men.

Rhonda tried to keep up with what was going on. Everyone was screaming. The devil-suit wrestler had the Tarzan-guy in some kind of stranglehold. The guy with the globe for a head had the whole head of the guy with the question mark in one big hand. The guy with a face for a mask had both his hands into the chest of the guy with the lightning bolts.

Then it all changed, and everybody had a different hold on everybody else. Punches flew. Feet pounded. Somebody smashed against the cyclone fence. The barbed wire whined. There were screams inside and outside the ring. Sinews cracked. She heard the sound of breathing, from the crowd, the wrestlers, herself. She saw drops of sweat on the canvas, and imagined how hot it was out there.

Then the lights went out again, everywhere but her side of the arena, and the giant shadows sprang up. The three guys who'd come in together looked around a second, which gave their opponents time to jump on their heads again.

"¡*Caracoles!*" he said. He was an old man now, and the tv was turned up loud so he could hear it.

He watched what was happening.

"I am truly needed," he said to himself. He reached for his cane, pulled himself up, reached the balance point, went backwards into the chair again.

Then he swung up and stood, pushing with his cane to keep from going too far forwards.

"¡*Ay de me!*" He started toward the closet in the back room.

He had not wrestled in more than thirty years. He had not even played himself in the movies for twenty-five. He had watched a series of younger, stronger men wrestle under his name, and people who could actually act play him in the films. When they'd had the huge going-away party for him when he left the sport, it was an actor up there getting all the silver watches and memberships in country clubs.

He tried to keep an eye on the tv from the back room. He opened the closet door with a key. He looked over the rows of silver masks and tights, the cloaks and capes. When he had put them aside, and moved to this retirement community, no one had known.

He reached for one of his special masks. He was more than two hundred kilometers away. He would have to call his Air Force general friend, get a jet, parachute into the Arena Tomalin through the skylight, just as he had done in the old days.

His cane caught on a pair of tights and he fell forward, smashing his head against the back of the closet. He came up bleeding, silver sequins and rhinestones stuck on his gashed forehead. He pressed a pair of tights against the cut, moved back to the living room and his chair.

"¡Uf," he said. "*No tengo energia como lo!*"

He sat in his chair, bloody tights wadded against his balding head, tears running down his face.

On the tv, Carne Xipe had El Hijo de la Selva in the Deltoid Grinder hold.

"I don't understand," yelled El Hijo to Señor Nadie. "We keep knocking them down but they won't—Ouch! Yahh!" There was a pop of sinews as El Diablo Peligroso grabbed him three or four places.

"We must keep on, amigos," said Señor Nadie. He grabbed El Mundo Grosero where it would do the most good, going from an inside to an outside-stepover-bar-toehold, forgetting for a second that the object was not a fall, but to remove him from the ring.

From somewhere, Carne Xipe stuck a finger in the eyeslit of his mask and poked. Señor Nadie screamed and caught the hand as he fell. He was dragged toward the side of the ring by two pairs of hands.

Then he saw El Ravo's boots out of his good eye, and the hands let go, and Señor Nadie came up, throwing punches and kidney chops, eye watering.

The big shadow of the devil and the world crossed the lightning.

Then the forest eclipsed the world, and the question mark sailed through the air and took out the masked unmasked shadow.

With grunts from below, the shadows loomed up and up the far walls. Somebody screamed, louder than ever, and there was the sound of breaking bone.

They stood panting, El Hijo de la Selva holding his useless left hand. Even his mask was twisted with pain.

The three challengers closed in on them, their strength seemingly renewed. Carne Xipe had his arms out to the sides, ready to reapply the Pectoral Scorpion. El Diablo Peligroso moved sideways back and forth, waiting for his chance to get into the Monterrey Crab. El Mundo Grosero had his right arm out, head high, wanting one of the champions to walk into the Japanese sleephold.

Closer and closer they came.

"We must persevere," said Señor Nadie, barely able to keep his breath going. "We must fight the best fight of our lives, cleanly and—"

A woman was screaming above all the other noise in the darkened arena. "¡Desvestidos los mascars!" she shrieked.

The wrestlers did not know to whom she was yelling.

Then in English: "Take off their masks!"

The noise in the sportatorium went way down.

"Rip off their masks, you namby-pamby jerks!" she yelled through the silence. The champions looked at each other, then charged in.

Rhonda looked around her. For a second, everyone in the Arena Tomalin looked back. Then their heads turned away as the wrestlers collided.

She sat back down.

El Hijo de La Selva pulled with his good hand at the barely moving head of Carne Xipe. The mask of the mask of a face came loose, like pulling off a second skin. El Hijo jerked back—underneath was the same face as on the mask. Then he pulled the mask completely off, and the body quit struggling.

There was a river beyond the darkness, leading toward a place that was light. A dog stood on the bank of the river, barking, jumping back and forth. He stepped into the water, and the dog ran in a splashing circle around him, then began to swim, looking back over its shoulder, barking encouragement.

He swam toward the light, following the dog, familiar yet not the same as before.

Then they were on the other side in the light.

El Ravo Tepextehualtepec swung El Diablo Peligroso around and around by the horns, faster and faster, keeping a turning point on the Club® in the enemy corner. The mask began to loosen as El Diablo pulled a couple of g's. Then the mask came over the chin, ripping cartilage from his nose, blood flying, and he sailed through the air into the corner post like a sack of cement.

The nun pointed to the block of granite as big as Mount Everest. And he saw far up it the tiny hummingbird brushing the edge of the block with its wings.

A small polished groove encircled the block.

He sighed. He was at a kind of peace. He was getting exactly what he deserved.

Señor Nadie sat on the heaving chest of El Mundo Grosero. There was nothing left for El Mundo to do, and not much to do it with. Señor Nadie heard the cheering as El Ravo and El Hijo finished their work.

He leaned down very close to the Indian Ocean where the mouth was; it twisted away, revealing the Australian and Pacific ear.

Señor Nadie grabbed the whole Eastern Hemisphere with his large hand. He leaned down close to the ear and pulled.

"Caducidad," he said as he did.

He rushed northwest through the air, swooped over mountains, came down close to the fields, zoomed faster, went past a town out to a shack in the Salinas Valley, went down to the ground, through the door, across the room, and up between a woman's legs.

And came right back out again.

"A girl," said the midwife.

They were going to name her Elena Esperanza por América Rodriguez when it came time for the christening, and they were going to raise her to have it better than they had, and get a good education, and become a doctor or a teacher or an astronaut.

Wait, he wanted to say, there has been some mistake. I'm not a girl, I'm a grown man. I'm not being born to a poor illegal family in California,

I'm a rich man living in Mexico City. I'm not even really a wrestler, I'm an arbitrageur, an executive. I have more platinum cards than other people my age have hemorrhoids. I am feared in my field. I can destroy people's lives, close down whole towns with a memo. There has been some mistake. I will make a few phone calls and clear all this up. *That* was what he meant to say.

What he said was:

"WAAAAAAAAAHHHHHH!"

19.

Rhonda went by the painted-over wall on her way to classes. She came even with the furniture and appliance store in the early morning, and saw the little dapper man was finishing a new display, this time of those tiny model beds that would be perfect in a three-year-old's palace.

He saw her, brightened, indicated his wares, reached back through the small door and took out a placard and put it on the easel:

> *Now the world, awake so long,*
> *Can find easeful slumber.*

She smiled. He smiled, then climbed through the door and was gone.

Rhonda walked on, and again the blue and white Ford Galaxie went by. Only this time, the wrestlers had on their question mark, lightning bolt and camouflage masks, but were wearing jeans and T-shirts, except the older one driving, who wore a bush jacket over his T-shirt. They turned out of sight down toward the *collegia menor*.

Señor Nadie was on his way to his woodworking class. El Ravo Tepe was taking electronics. And El Hijo de la Selva was enrolled in gardening.

For Fred Duarte and Karen Meschke, and Miguel Ramos: John D. Berry who came up with exactly the right word at exactly the right time, and Pat Cadigan who knew it had to be a junior college.

Afterword to:

El Castillo de la Perseverancia

You would think after 26 years at it, writing would get easier.

Not if you're any good at all, he said modestly; it gets harder and harder, because you should be making yourself do what you haven't done before.

Like trying to do *this* one.

I was going to be one of the three writer guests-of-honor at the 21st World Fantasy Convention in Baltimore in October of 1995, "Honoring short fantasy fiction" ("and three guys who can't make a living at it" I said). Me, Terry Bisson, Lucius Shepard. Stephen Brown of SF *Eye* fame was doing the program book, and we each had to write a novella or novelette for it (we could sell them for *real money* somewhere else later).

Fine and dandy, except that I had to go on the odyssey I talked about in the introduction: a) take 14 boxes of books, papers, etc. to the Texas A&M University Special Collections Library; b) go see *all* my relatives in Mississippi and Arkansas; c) drive 2,418 miles with everything else I owned and find a place to live on a steelhead river; d) teach the first week of Clarion West in Seattle; and e) appear at Westercon in Portland three days after finishing my Clarion gig.

"a)" is in April. By the time I'll be at "e)" it'll be the 6th of July.

I also sent Stephen a list of about six novella/novelette ideas I had in mind: see if there was some theme, say, or resonance, from the things the three of us were going to do.

The *very next day* after I sent the list, I wrote him another letter. I knew which novelette I was going to do.

Because on the day I'd sent him the list, one of those pieces of phlegm the American body politic coughs up every so often got up in the House of Representatives and introduced a bill to make English not just the First Language, or the Official Language, but the *Only Language* of the United States of America.

(Is it just me, or is the irony lost on these people who don't want anything but English spoken—"just like Our Lord Jesus Christ did", to quote a '20s Texas governor, and a woman too—that the people who want to do this have their headquarters in *Pueblo, Colorado*?)

So I knew in that instant I was going to write the masked wrestler story.

When I got to Washington State with a bad CV joint squealing like a banshee, I went to Eileen Gunn, John D. Berry and Rhonda Boothe's house. I was pretty happy and about as tired as I'd ever been.

Then I threw myself into my six-week-plan of finding a place (Oso), cleaning it up (three days), trying to fish like hell while I could before Clarion West (reading the submission stories all the while). Two things happened: Eileen gave me one of those old ledger books, the kind Bob Cratchitt used to use, to write in, and I talked to Rhonda about her years as a foreign student in Italy.

Well, *tempus*, you know, *fugits*, as it always does. I had a Santo movie with me—one of the bad later color ones I found in Texas at a K-Mart—and *Robot vs the Aztec Mummy*; I was reading lots of mystery and morality plays from the 1300s; and remembering my days at the North Side Coliseum in Ft. Worth, watching Pepper Gomez take on Duke Kehanemuka with his Stomach Claw.

By and by I'm working on the story, a paragraph here, a paragraph there, a whole page one day, in the big ledger, all through the first week of Clarion West. (Trying to do anything, while being a Clarion instructor, except being available 18 hours a day to give the class everything you've got, is a *mistake*.) I got two pages in the three days between Clarion and Westercon, maybe a page at the convention.

By this time, Stephen Brown is sweating those real big bricks, because he's dealing with three guys who *always* come through, even at the last possible minute. At the con I get word Lucius is sending his in that day, and that Terry's has been in a week.

Pressure's on The Kid.

I roared home from Portland and finished the first draft at 8:30 p.m. on the 6th of July 1995. I started typing and typed till 3 p.m. on the 7th. I roared off to the nearest town (Arlington) and Express-mailed a copy to Stephen Brown and then another to Gardner Dozois, regular mail (so I could eat).

Proofs came back from Stephen on the 12th—out the same day—and when Gardner (who was also doing Clarion that year) showed up, he said he was taking the story.

Aside from pissing off a U.S. Rep., I wanted to say a few things writing this story.

And once again, I'm the avatar of the Zeitgeist. I'm so far ahead of the curve, as Marechal Ney said, "What is behind me is of no concern to me". Gardner sat in on the Wrasslin' and SF panel at El Paso *this* July: he'd just gotten *another* SF Wrasslin' story, and was probably going to publish it and "El Castillo . . ." in the same issue of *Asimov's*, like he did when he got the two Fidel Castro baseball stories the same week a couple years back. As Gardner pointed out, *he's* been mistaken for Haystacks Calhoun before . . .

It just does not get any easier, but when you're through, you can walk proud by any mirror in the place . . .

Scientifiction

One of her knobs itched.

Lala reached inside her vest and scratched it with the hand not holding the spear.

Something made a sound to her left. She unbuttoned her jacket's elbow flaps so she could hear better; turned back and forth. Nothing else.

She stood at the guard post on the cliff outside the Settlement overlooking the water. The sun lay as it always had, low on the horizon, big and dull in color, speckled with black, giving off much below-red along its rim. Out of the black dots, occasional other colors flared through, sometimes in long slow curtains that faded as they rose.

The water was flat. There was a thin cold wind which barely rippled its surface. A thick crust of salt, reddish-brown in the dim light, lay along its edges.

The sound came again. This time she saw one of the roaches down to the left, along the shore. She shifted her spear. Then she saw it was one of the smaller, solitary purple-colored ones, not one of the ones who ran in the great packs.

The roach had come down to the ocean along the beach to the left of the Settlement. The beach itself was bare except for the salt-boulders at the waterline.

Out in the curve of the flat sound two small outcrops of rock stuck out. The farthest out was covered, like the beach, with salt-rocks, but the closer had a sparse growth of lichens on the landward side.

The purple roach hesitated, feeling the air with its antennae. Then it began to run toward the island, and only broke through the surface tension halfway out, dropping down into it, but not sinking because of the salinity of the water. It wallowed on toward the rock outcropping, its legs working awkwardly, rising and falling, sending ripples out across the flat water of the sound.

A fin broke by the far island, delta-shaped. Then another down the curve of the sound, out from the salt-beach.

The roach stopped, half-sunk in the ocean, not moving.

A third fin, and tail, came up and went down just off the lichen-covered rocks.

The cockroach turned around, more ripples spreading out from it, and began crawling its way back toward the beach.

The fins showed again, swung into line.

The roach worked harder, picking up speed.

Three furrows of water, humped moving tunnels, came toward it from three sides.

The roach slosh-wallowed furiously.

There was a smash and slap of water, two more slaps and a crunch. Spray went up, obscuring that part of the bay. Then it settled; two or three swirls drifted away. One leg, still working, floated to the surface, making feeble ripples. Something dark took the leg under, fin breaking water, then was gone.

Then the sea was flat again under the red-speckled sun that took up a fifth of the sky.

Footsteps on the ramp.

Atta came down from the Settlement, spear in hand. She rubbed antennules with Lala. "You're relieved of guard duty, Lala," she said. "Anything happening?"

"Not much," said Lala. She turned to go up the ramp, then stopped. "Ever notice how there are fewer and fewer of those solitary roaches all the time?"

"It's the Roach-Packs," said Atta, spitting. "Because of them, there's fewer and fewer of everything out in the Cold World." She pulled her coat tighter around her.

Lala went up the ramp and back through the wall into the Settlement.

She made herself some lichen soup on the Fuel-stove. Then she went into resting-phase, and then stirred herself and groomed, taking care especially of the knob on her right side halfway between her arm and leg. Its twin on the left was not giving her any trouble at all.

Then she went down the runs and corridors to visit the workshop of Doer Tola—who was usually busy, but interested in everything—to tell her what she'd seen on watch.

The Doer greeted her with her antennules in the outer workshop. She listened to Lala's story, then said, "I just found something you should see. Come with me."

They went into the inner room, lit by the glow of a Fuel-furnace and several Fuel-lamps. Occasionally one of the lamps gave off one of the long sparks that went right through your body without burning.

A roach was tied down on a low table, its legs hanging over the sides. It was half their size, and Lala could tell by its grey-brown color it was from a pack. It moved weakly, death some short time away.

"One of the ones not killed on their last raid," said Doer Tola. She went to the Fuel-furnace and drew up the door, then blocked the lamps with covers of the grey metal. Lala could still see dimly in the below-red.

Doer Tola brought a covered Fuel-lantern near the roach. "Watch," she said.

She uncovered a small portion of the lantern. The first light falling along its side made the roach's legs move very fast, even in its weakened state.

She repeated the movement. Again the wounded roach moved.

"I'm convinced they have something along their sides that makes them move when the light changes quickly."

The roach let out a feeble sound.

"Don't you see?" she asked Lala. "The light never changes. At least, not from the sun. And it looks like it's trying to move *away* from the light. What could be the use of that? The Settlement's the only source of light besides the sun and stars, and the light should not change *that* much . . . it has me puzzled. I suppose I'll have to take one of these things apart and find out. Probably not this one, though; it's too full of holes."

The roach moved weakly and a low whining sound came from it.

"And I'm sure this one's voice organs were damaged," she said. She groomed one of her antennules with her right forearms. "The more we find out about them, the better we can understand them—maybe even control them."

"That would be nice," said Lala.

There was a jump of brightness that both of them felt; even the roach struggled. They looked around. A long spark came through the wall from the landward side.

They heard a rattle of voices. Then the sound of feet in the corridors, then at the entry to the workshop.

"Doer Tola! Doer Tola!" yelled a voice. Someone rushed in as Tola uncovered the lantern.

"Doer Tola! Doer Tola!" said the excited worker. "Something—something—"

"Calm down, calm down," said Tola, rubbing her antennules toward the worker's head. "What is it?"

"We—we don't know. But—we think it's a new Sparky!"

"You've never seen a Sparky," said the Doer. "Hardly anyone has." But she was getting excited too; both Lala and the worker could smell it.

"It's big! It's bright, brighter than anything, brighter than the Sun!" said the worker.

"Where?"

"Come on!" said the worker (her name was Ilna). "This way, Doer, this way!"

They stood on the very top of the Settlement, on the jumbled pile of straight rocks that leaned up. The sun was behind them, the sky darkening to halfway overhead from it, then brightness—brightness in the upper registers; a fountain of higher light came up from the low place behind the Settlement. It shot up into the air many times taller than the nearest real hill, thin and wavery at its top, brighter and thicker at the bottom.

Long sparks came from it, some of them through the ground in front. Others went up, out into the sky, dulling the stars. It got bigger as they watched.

The whole populace was on the Settlement buildings, excited, talking—the air was as thick with smells as after a raid from a roving pack.

"Well, well," said Doer Tola. "I never thought I would see one. It has to be a Sparky; there's nothing else it could be."

There was a hum all around them. The Leader and Doer Sima came up, watched a short while. The Leader was very nervous, putting out as much indecision as the Sparky put out light.

Sima and Tola rubbed antennules and talked excitedly with each other.

"Well," said the Leader (there was just so long she could watch before she went back to being Leader). "What are we to do?"

"Oooh!" said the crowd. A big long spark curved up out over the Settlement and went into the sea. More showered into the low hills around them.

"Doer Sima will take a party out to see how big it is, and what it's doing," said Tola. "They'll have to go get Fuel-miner's suits, if it really is a Sparky."

"What else *could* it be?" asked the Leader.

"Nothing else is possible," said Doer Sima. "But we must find out first its size."

"And I'll inventory all the Fuel-miners equipment, see how much more we'll need," said Tola. "The lichen-harvesters should be working— we're all probably going to be at this a while."

"Just make sure you deal quickly with this thing," said the Leader. "I've heard *stories*."

"We've all heard tales," said Doer Sima. "What we need are hard, usable facts."

"You should go talk to Grandfather Bugg," said Lala.

They all turned to look at her, the Leader showing surprise. "Lala, isn't it? Why should we?"

"He's seen a Sparky before. He told me once."

"You and Doer Tola can go see the old relict if you want," said the Leader. "I'll be about readying the Settlement for whatever actions we need to take, whatever plan the Doers decide on."

"My people," she said, turning to the crowd. "Watch for a while if you like, unless it becomes violent; this *is* a true wonder. But soon we will be busy, very busy indeed. I suggest that you get rest-phased, for, once we know where we stand, we will not stop. The very life of the Settlement might depend on it . . ." With a wave, she was away.

Some began to go back down into the corridors and buildings, but kept looking backwards, stopped, watched. The Sparky grew higher and higher; more and more beams and sprays came out of it.

It was, as Ilna had said, brighter than the sun. For, to Lala's surprise, she looked down at the ground and found that her shadow was on the wrong side.

Not many came here.

It was down one of the unmarked, unused old corridors, where the Settlers had first lived and begun to fill this place of wonders. Lala and her mother had lived here too, when she was very young, resting-phase and resting-phase ago.

A worker came by on some business or other. No one else was near, unlike the other corridors in the Settlement, where someone was always about.

A strange smell filled the air.

"That's him, I suppose," said Doer Tola.

"No, I think it's the Old Smell. The one from the early days. Maybe even from the Cold World," said Lala.

"That's very probably a myth," said the Doer. "Anyway, unlikely."

"I'm surprised you and Doer Sima haven't been here, studying."

"Believe me," said the Doer. "The Leader keeps us hopping, and there's plenty more and plenty more to find out. But this *is* interesting . . ." She had stopped to look at digging marks on the wall.

"Doer Tola. The Sparky?"

"What? Oh, yes." They went down a long dark corridor, the smell increasing. "Well, it's him *too*," said Lala. Then:

"Grandfather? Grandfather Bugg?"

"Heh? Huh? Who's that come to see old Grandfather Bugg?"

"Lala. And Doer Tola!"

"Doer . . . Doer . . . Oh, yeah, yeah. Must be big doin's! Come on in, the door's open. Hee hee hee."

The room was very dark; there wasn't even a Fuel-lamp open. They let their eyes adjust.

"Over here," he said. "I ain't so good on colors anymore, but I'm still okay in the below-red, and me an' above-purple's just like *that*."

He was more time-diminished, older than even Lala remembered. His chest was sunken in, his legs were spindly (one of them was missing from the second-knee down). His abdomen was very swollen and hung out from his clothing. He had a *thing*; in the old days he had kept it covered.

"What's it, Lala? Been a long time since I seen you. Seems like just a little time ago you was with your mama—"

Doer Tola made a noise.

"Grandfather Bugg," said Lala. "There's a new Sparky!"

"You're excretin' me," he said.

"No," said Doer Tola. "Lala said you'd seen one before."

"Seen two," he said.

"Two?"

"Once when I was litty-bitty. Somebody had to hold me up I was so young. All I actually 'member of that one, it was bright. But they talked about it a long while after. That was the really bad one where bad stuff happened after'erds."

"What things?" asked the Doer.

"Well, can't remember what they's most upset about. I's litty-bitty, didn't understand. Some big things movin' round, big troubles. But the bad lasted a long time *after* that Sparky. I saw that myself, growin' up."

"Like what?"

"Well, like, like kids being hatched with *six* legs, you know, another set of arms or legs in the middle. Right out of the knobs. Some wasn't born at all. Or all wrong. They told me as I's growin' it took a real long time to put that Sparky out. Kept trying to come back."

"You never told me about that one," said Lala. "You only told me about the one when you were grown."

"Well that one was real bad, but bad right at the first. Lost a lotta people in that one. Came up right in the middle of the Settlement, just past where the Meetin' Hall is now. Took too much time to get people out, decide what to do, get the work organized. You can tell how bad it was if they needed *me* to help," he said.

"The Meeting Hall?" asked Doer Tola.

"Well, yep, just past where it was built. Where's this 'un?"

"Outside. Eastward. It's very big, very bright."

"You ain't seen bright till you stared right into the middle of one of 'em like I did," said Grandfather Bugg. "I have to see this. Imagine, three Sparkies in one lifetime!"

"There'll be time," said Doer Tola. "No matter how fast we can organize. Unless . . . unless it gets so bad and hot we have to leave. What do you remember about putting it out?"

"Well, what was you *gonna* do if I wasn't around?"

"Organize the Fuel-miners. Get Fuel-miners' suits for the workers. Make covering slabs out of the Fuel-miners' suit-metal."

"That dull grey heavy stuff?"

"Yes."

"Go on."

"Well, cover the Sparky with the metal. Two sheets, if need be."

"That's good, that's good. But that's what they did with the one when I was a baby; that's why it kept comin' back. You need some of that black stuff, what you call it . . ."

"The shiny black stuff?"

"Naw, naw, that crumbly black stuff—oh, excrete, what you call it? That stuff the miners is always havin' to dig through to get to the Fuel!"

"We call it the crumbly black stuff," said Doer Tola.

"That's *it*. *That* crumbly black stuff! You got to pile it on real good, all around, all over the dull grey metal slab. Before you put the slab on, too. Otherwise it'll come back, sure as shootin'!"

"You're positive about that?"

"You think I spent who knows how long shovellin' that stuff into the Sparky not to know what I'm talkin' about?"

"We always assumed that crumbly black stuff was just an indicator you'd find fuel there."

"You're the Doer! You tell *me!*" said Grandfather Bugg. The air was filled with irritation and the Old Smell. "I just know it works. *Somebody* back then was smart enough to figger it out. Don't y'all talk to each other?"

"Not as such," said Doer Tola. "I don't guess it could hurt. Thank you. Time is of the essence. Lala?"

"Shortly," she said. The Doer left.

Grandfather Bugg fidgeted, annoyed.

"I'm sorry I haven't been to see you. I have been busy, both working and guarding, whatever needs done."

"I'm sure you are," said Grandfather Bugg. "They was a time people came to see me when they didn't need me, on a sudden. Like you used to."

"I thought you could tell us a lot."

"Evidently, I *can*."

"No, not just this. I know you're not that old, but you used to say it used to be all different. That we probably came from the Cold World."

"Well, maybe we did, and maybe we didn't. I never was sure. I know that they was a time though, when guys like me was needed and respected (not that I ever was, but my great-great-great-great Grandfather Bugg still did it). They was a time when I would have been needed; I coulda help make you 10,000 sisters, and they would of all been *you!*"

"How was that possible?"

"I don't know. Never did. That's what my great-great-great-great Grandfather Bugg told *me.*"

"I should go now," said Lala.

"Don't forget. I want to see that Sparky, and soon. Fore it burns us all up!"

"I'll send some people for you."

"Excrete!" he said. "One or two's enough."

"Alright."

"You do that," he said. He looked her up and down. "Anybody tell you you got a fine young shape, from what I can tell in the below-red?"

"Oh, Grandfather Bugg!" she said. She left.

Then they began to work, and they worked and worked and worked.

They had to move everything out behind the Settlement near the Sparky's raging lights—everything from the workshops and the mines. They beat out two great sheets of dull gray Miners' suit-metal, the size Doer Sima indicated they would need. Sometimes Lala helped the workers and miners at the hammers, sometimes she ran lichen up to everybody from the farms down below, sometimes she stood guard.

The lights of the Sparky had at first kept the pack-roaches away, then had drawn them near, but not too near. So the guard-watch had to be sharp, both on the Settlement and the workers out behind it.

The Sparky's flames went higher; it was more violent in the above-purple, so bright they disappeared into the higher-vision halfway up the column. Great long twisting flares roiled through it. The ground itself began to heat up, burning at the base of the Sparky. It grew larger, and they had to beat the sheets out to cover more area.

Others brought up heaps of the crumbly black stuff, piling it higher and higher, as close to the Sparky as deemed safe.

The heat grew. The whole Settlement was bathed in glowing light; huge moving shadows of the workers and miners danced on its walls as they came and went.

At last they were ready. Some workers had been detailed to build a ramped incline toward the Sparky. They, and everyone who had to work out there, had been fitted with Fuel-miners' suits, or simpler ones.

They cut down on the heat from the Sparky but they were clumsy; body heat soon made the insides clammy. The eyepieces fogged constantly.

The ones working on the ramp could only do it a very short time before having to rest. But the ramp extended closer, higher, so the first plate could be pushed on its way. They had to stop, finally. The heat, sparks and light were overpowering up that close.

The whole Settlement was readied, suits all around even for the guards. They brought Grandfather Bugg, in a chair, to the top of the highest part of the Settlement, so he could watch.

They lined up the first great plate on the ramp.

The Leader stood in her Fuel-miner's suit along with the rest.

Doer Sima signalled. A long line of workers threw boulders of the crumbly black stuff from one to another, the last two throwing them toward the sputtering blaze of the Sparky.

There were mostly Fuel-miners on the front edge of the great dull grey slab. Lala found herself on the front corner nearest the Sparky.

It roared above them. She was walking backwards, feeling the heat and the light on the back of her Miners' suit; she watched its reflection stretching up behind her in the dull grey slab, the fanned flaming light blotting out stars and sky—everything but itself.

Then someone stumbled, two fell on the far back end. The slab jerked from her grip as the front line of Miners ran to the sides. The metal edge came back forward, hit her. She tripped, swung around, lost footing on the edge of the ramp, scrambled; as she came up the slab swung into her again and she fell twisting backwards. And fell headfirst into the Sparky.

There was an intense instant of light and pain. A spark bigger than her head went through her.

Still she fell, long after she should have hit the ground and been killed. Then the air crushed down on her, forcing itself into her spiracles.

Bright. Too bright. That color between yellow and blue. Too blue, too.

Lala hit the soft yielding ground. *Green*. That was the color. The ground was green, covered with something soft.

Shapes. Shapes all around.

Thick thick air. Smells and tastes came to her antennules in a haze she could not distinguish. She was stunned in all her senses, wondered why she was not burning.

The sky was *blue*. The sun was not where it should be. It was *high* in the sky, off to the upper right. It was a *full* round circle. It was far too small and very very bright.

She balanced on her wobbly legs. She turned her head and the helmet of the Fuel-miner's suit.

Far up behind her in the air was a flicker, a shimmer where the Sparky must be, from where she'd fallen. But it was barely there. As she watched a long spark appeared, came out, but it moved slowly, as slowly as she could walk, and went up into the air.

It was as she turned to follow its path that she saw another thing.

There was a thing coming through the air. It was like a slim roach, only black and yellow; it had clear things above its back that went up and down in pattern: up bend down bend up bend down bend. It came toward her much more slowly than even the spark moved. She could see the shimmer from the small bright sun on the clear things on its back. She could see it looking at her.

It was so *small*.

She saw that there were other, larger things beyond the thing with clear wings on its back that hung in the air before her.

The air was too thick, the sky too blue, the ground a green blur. It was all too sudden, too overpowering. She began to fall to her leg-joints, saw the green ground coming up toward her.

Those other large things had been moving, moving all the time, very very slowly. Her depth perception was not working right, with all the colors. They must be ten or twelve times as large as she. Larger than anything living should be.

There were three of them. One had appeared slowly from the left, she reasoned, out of a grey space she saw now was the edge of a building *all straight and level*, not jumbled up like the Settlement. She had not seen the first two at their biggest because they were bent forward pushing something.

The something was round on the ends and long in the middle. They pushed it very slowly and it moved very slowly forward.

Then she saw that one of the three things was looking at her very slowly. It and the two others were covered with something very loosely; her below-red was not working much but there were shapes inside (the sun and *everything* was giving off below-red). Something like her own Fuel-miner's suit. It had a bulky head and two large shiny round places like eyes, only set too far forward and close together for good vision.

It slowly reached out and slowly touched one of the two bent-over ones slowly moving the round thing.

The one it touched turned and watched her slowly.

The other kept rolling the thing, then pushed it to one side and rolled it a little faster, and then slowly turned back to the two others.

Indistinct loud noises came to Lala through the sleeves of her suit. More indistinct noises.

Then the third one turned to look at her slowly.

Slowly the middle one started toward her.

She jerked upright, and took two steps backward.

The one coming at her stopped slowly, waited, started slowly again. The other two slowly looked around the first and then looked toward each other and then looked back. It took them a long time.

The big thing advanced on her. Soon she would have to do something.

She looked back at the shimmer from the Sparky. It hung high in the air, higher than she could get to. There was nothing to climb on to get there. The shimmer was feeble, flickering, barely visible with so much light from the sun, the sky, the green ground.

The thing got very close very slowly and very largely. She had never seen anything that big move before, no matter how slowly. The other two had started toward her, one to one side, one to the other.

She ran to the left.

The one closest looked left and right slowly as it came on.

Then she ran to the right.

The one on the right jerked back slowly away from her when she stopped.

The one in the middle looked slowly around and saw her, his back to the glowing Sparky.

The one on the far side left the ground. Could they, like the black and yellow thing, hold themselves up in the air? But no. It leaned up then down while it was in the air and parts of it touched the green ground again.

Loud indistinct sounds came from it and the other two.

An arm-like thing came out for her from the right. There were five extensions on the end of it. They were curving inward. They would miss her.

Then Lala ran. She ran toward the one on the ground. She jumped up near the top end, pushing off it. She grabbed the one in the middle somewhere far up. Where she grabbed gave; she swung slowly back and forth. Arm-things came down toward her slowly.

She saw, as she pushed off from it into the air, into the eye-place on the thing, and through it she had a glimpse of an eye. It was *round*, like the eye-place outside it. There seemed to be cilia around it. It grew slowly wide.

Then she was gone, on the leap, out toward the Sparky, into the white, into the hot pain, the sharp streaks of piercing heavy light.

And onto the ground.

Onto the shimmering white and dull blue ground. Beside one of the crumbly black pieces. The heavy air was gone. She could breathe again.

"Lala!" someone yelled, and a rope flopped near her; she grabbed it, losing her helmet, and they pulled her up the slope.

Anxious faces, the smell of concern. Behind her the Sparky, sending raging heavy blue light into the air.

She lost the conscious use of her body for some little while. It all went away.

It all came back. Someone had put another helmet on her.

She turned from where she lay.

Everyone was there. They were not working. They were all standing stock-still, even the guards on the outside. They were all looking into the heart of the Sparky.

A dark place was forming in its midst, high up. It was just a smudge, a shape, but unmoving while the rest of the Sparky was sputtering, shimmering jets of fire and light.

The populace—workers, guards, Fuel-miners, the Doers, the Leader— were fascinated.

Lala turned her head back. Another dark place formed beside the first, more indistinct.

"Work!" yelled Lala. "Quick! Work! Work!"

The crowd jerked at her words. Then the Leader and the Doers started yelling "Work! Work!" The smell of activity filled the thin air, even over the reek of the Sparky.

The Fuel-miners regripped the grey metal slab, staggering under the load. Workers in patchwork suits threw chunks of the black stuff into the roaring base of the unnatural furnace. The line stretched back to the tumbled mass of fragments, workers heaving one to the next, passing the chunks along the line, throwing them at the raging light before them.

They slid the grey metal slab out, closer, closer, pulling it over the jumble of black fragments growing around them.

Lala pushed on the back edge, doing what she could. The light in front of her was too bright to look at.

She looked up above, into the fan of the Sparky. There were three, four—no, something else began to appear—five dark places in the middle of it.

"Now!" screamed Doer Tola.

The Fuel-miners heaved, pushed, ran forward.

"More black stuff!" yelled the Leader.

The long slab of grey metal slid out onto the base of the Sparky. A jumble of black boulders bounced atop it.

The Sparky wavered, shook; long streaks of light came out of it through the ground before them.

The dark thing in the air in its middle was now five things going into one thing, getting wider. They could see it moving now.

"The other slab!" yelled Doer Sima.

"More black! More slab!" screamed the Leader.

The Sparky flared bright again.

The workers were a blur, speeding up; the pile of black boulders went down quickly as they threw it atop the first metal slab on the Sparky.

The Fuel-miners struggled with the second slab. It was heavier and thicker.

"Everybody! Guards! Everybody!" yelled the Leader.

They dropped their spears and ran in to help.

Doer Tola said to the worker-line at the black-pile: "No matter what happens, keep piling it on till it's all gone. Then get more!" Then she ran down to the dull metal slab.

"I said 'Everybody'!" screamed the Leader, looking around. There were those throwing the black stuff, and those pushing the slab, and her. She ran down to the back edge of the slab and pushed.

"Push, push!" yelled voices. The black crumbly boulders had covered so much of the ramp their footing slipped.

Above them the Sparky stood up, slinging off light. In its center the five dark things, the thing they joined, the thing behind it, hung over them. There had never been anything so large. And it grew. Another dark place formed near the base of the Sparky, off to their right.

The slab went up, over the highest black boulder, down, stuck. They lifted, pushed, heaved.

Lala saw the Sparky's reflection, the dark shape in the metal before her. She pulled. The Leader, two workers away with a look of grim determination, shifted her grip. Heave. Push.

Lala's head went into the slab. Her helmet twisted. She couldn't see.

The light went down.

Lala turned her helmet back. Everybody gave one more shove.

She saw the light from the Sparky had halved, then the sparks arched out shorter. The dark shape above them and the one level with the ground to the right moved then, still slow, but a violent shuddering, wrenching it slowly back and forth.

There was a sound beginning, low and slow and far away, and it was building in volume.

They ran. All of them, up and out and away. The workers dropped their black crumbly burdens, backed toward the Settlement.

The dark thing in the air moved slowly from one side to the other as the sound grew and grew, up from the bottom where they could hear it, louder and louder, their tympani aching already, and it went louder, higher—

The dark thing dropped to the ground, spewing steam, and bounced once. The one over to the right flipped into the air, spun, turned, lay still and smoking.

The Sparky went down to a spewing glow, no worse than one of the Fuel-pocket fires the miners dealt with all the time.

The sky came back, dark. Their eyes adjusted to the light from the dark red sun on the other side of the Settlement. The dim stars hung in the east, beyond the glowing remnants of the Sparky.

The Fuel-miners and workers ran out, avoiding the smoking dark things—which gave off a bad smell, as when the lichen was cooked too long—and shovelled more black stuff on the slabs.

"Hee-hee-hee!" came the thin voice of Grandfather Bugg from the highest part of the Settlement. "Couldn't have done it better myself! Wouldn't have missed it for the world!"

"Well done, my people," said the Leader, readjusting her Fuel-miner's suit. "That's what hard work gets you."

Doers Tola and Sima had their antennules together. Lala heard them making preparations to fight the Sparkies in advance so they wouldn't have to go through all this if it happened again.

Then she realized how tired and hurt she was, and how much she ached. She walked toward the Settlement.

As she was passing through the gate, Grandfather Bugg bent forward from his chair and said "Say, little Missie. Lookin' good today. *Tckh-tckh-tckh!*"

She stood on the same high building later, looking at the east, at the dark sky and stars. Her shadow stretched before her as it should.

It seemed as if all those things had happened in a resting-phase.

She looked at the site of the Sparky, now a huge pile of black crumbly boulders. Barely a flicker of light came out, no more than from the walls of any room.

Her side still hurt from the battering she had taken, and her left eye had lost most of its focus.

The places where the dark things had lain for a time were empty, except for the charred remnant of the coverings. Doer Tola had some of them in her workshop to examine.

Lala reached under her jacket and scratched her right side knob.

From somewhere far back out in the Cold World came the howling of the roach-pack.

Afterword to:

Scientifiction

What went into this story?

The unwritten *Bucky Bug* comic book (which was nothing *remotely* like this). The last section of Wells' *The Time Machine*. Bryan Ferry's version of "These Foolish Things", which is not about a lost love, as most people sing it, but about an absent lover, the way Mr. Ferry convinces you. Listening to dogs howl while I was out catching an 18" Dolly Varden yesterday in the rain. A need to push the old writing envelope a little further ("Is he a man, is he a cannonball" to quote R.A. Lafferty from another context). A couple of books on insects, and some thinking about nuclear wastes. The Academy-Award winning animated cartoon from 1938, *Peace on Earth* (rent it now). A lot of books with talking sappy animals living in tin-can-and-overshoes towns. (Notice how many of these need Man to have been there to throw away Stuff? Who thinks we're not useful?) Any poem that starts, "A bunch of the bugs were chirping it up at the Hemiptera Saloon . . ." Beatrix Potter, to whom I came, fortunately for me, at the age of 38. (She was going to be in my unwritten Jack-the-Ripper story, "The Tale of the Fierce Bad Gentleman", the opening line of which was "It was so close and stifling in the Reverend's study that Beatrix had a terrible desire to remove her gloves.") The Pulitzer Prize cartoon of the young European and the death's-head prostitute. "And so on," as Professor Marvell says, "and so forth."

I wanted, in the words of W.M. Frohock, to make you swallow a 6-lb ham, tin can and all, and only later say "ouch".

And, of course, a self-imposed deadline before I had to go back and be Best Man at the wedding of Robert Taylor and Judy McDowell. I made the gig, but not the deadline.

It took a Mighty Effort to keep from calling this "Your Chitin Heart", which I think has already been used by Frank Herbert or somebody . . .

In my great dream, do I know what I'm doing?

You'll have to watch me every minute to find out.

See you long 'bout the Millennium.

Bibliography: or after 26 years they give you a cold potato . . .

Books: hc—hardcover   tp—trade paperback   pb—mass market paperback

I. Novels

The Texas-Israeli War: 1999
with Jake (Buddy) Saunders
Ballantine, 1974 pb, five U.S. Printings through 1986. French, Italian, Spanish editions through the years, my favourite of which is titled *Israel Frappé a Dallas.*

Them Bones
Ace SF Specials (edited by Terry Carr) Ace, 1984, pb
Also: Mark V. Ziesing, 1989 hc (and limited in box with
            A Dozen Tough Jobs)
            Legend (Century Hutchison) UK hc, tp and pb
            Histoire D'Os ediciones Decouverte Paris 1986 pb and tp
            Heyne Verlag German paid half an advance on it but
            never published it, 1986
            Scheletari nel Mississippi Arnoldo Mondadori Editore,
            Italy 1985
            Vain Vanhat Luut, Helsinki 1992

Forthcoming:
I, John Mandeville (26 years and still counting . . .)
The Moon World
Moving Waters (a fishing novel . . .)

II. Novellas

A Dozen Tough Jobs
Mark V. Ziesing, 1989 hc (and limited in box with *Them Bones*)
Also: in *Night of the Cooters*, Legend, UK, 1991 tp
            in *Strange Monsters of the Recent Past*, Ace 1991 pb

You Could Go Home Again
Cheap Street, 1993 hc (edition of 111 copies)
Also: Omni Online Neon/Visions, 1995

III. Collections

Howard Who?
Doubleday, 1986 hc
Contents: Introduction by George R. R. Martin. "The Ugly Chickens", "*Der Untergang des Abendlandesmenschen*", "Ike at the Mike", "Dr. Hudson's Secret Gorilla", ". . . the World, as we Know't", "Green Brother", "Mary Margaret Road-Grader", "Save A Place in the Lifeboat for Me", "Horror, We Got", "Man-Mountain Gentian", "God's Hooks", "Heirs of the Perisphere".

All About Strange Monsters of the Recent Past: Neat Stories by Howard Waldrop
Ursus Imprints, 1987, hc. Cover by Don Punchatz, illustrations by Tim Kirk, Terry Lee, Nancy Niles, Hank Janus, Thomas Blackshear II, A Mason, Robert Haas.
Contents: Introduction by Gardner Dozois. "All About Strange Monsters of the Recent Past", "Helpless, Helpless", "Fair Game", "What Makes Heironymous Run?", "The Lions Are Asleep This Night", "Flying Saucer Rock and Roll", "He-we-Await" (original to this collection). Afterword: "The Left-Handed Muse" by Lewis Shiner.

Strange Things in Close-Up: The Nearly Complete Howard Waldrop
Legend (Century Hutchison) UK, 1989 tp. Contents of *Howard Who?* and *All About Strange Monsters Of The Recent Past* (minus the Dozois introduction) in one volume.

Strange Monsters of the Recent Past
Ace, 1991 pb. Contents of *All About Strange Monsters Of The Recent Past* minus the art, with the addition of *A Dozen Tough Jobs.*

Night of the Cooters: More Neat Stories by Howard Waldrop	Ursus Imprints/Mark V. Ziesing, 1990 (actually, 1991) hc (and limited box & with cooter). Cover by Don Punchatz; illustrations by Terry Lee, Janet Aulisio, Don Maitz, Karen Barnes, Roger Stine, Arnie Fenner and Jim Fanning. Contents: Introduction by Chad Oliver. "Night of the Cooters", "French Scenes", "Passing of the Western", "Adventure of the Grinder's Whistle", "Thirty Minutes Over Broadway!", "The Annotated Jetboy", "Hoover's Men", "Do Ya, Do Ya Wanna Dance?", "Wild, Wild Horses", "Fin de Cyclé" (original to this collection). Also: Ace, 1993 pb, with Punchatz cover, minus art
Night of the Cooters: More Neat Stuff	Legend (Random Century UK), 1991 tp, contents as hardcover, minus Chad's introduction, plus *A Dozen Tough Jobs* and afterword.

IV. Short Fiction

(If this appears weird, and the dates skip around, that's because they're in the order in which they were *written*. I have a few things to say about some of them. *HW* means they were collected in *Howard Who?*, AASM means *All About Strange Monsters of the Recent Past*, NOTC, *Night of the Cooters*. A couple of dozen of them were up for Hugos, Nebulas or World Fantasy Awards, but I'm not that vain . . . What isn't included is the hundred or so stories never published or in some kind of limbo, or retired to the Old Stories Home . . .)

"Lunchbox"	*Analog*, May 1972
"All About Strange Monsters of the Recent Past" AASM	*Shayol* #4, volume 1, no.4, April 1981 (Was supposed to be in a couple of David Gerrold anthologies from he early to late '70s — they bit *el dusto*.)
"Apprenticeship"	*Modern Stories* #1, ed. Lewis Shiner, April 1983
"My Sweet Lady Jo"	*Universe* 4, ed. Terry Carr, Random House 1974. SFBC 1974. Popular Library, pb 1975
"Mono No Aware"	*Haunt of Horror* #2, August 1973
"Custer's Last Jump"	with Steven Utley, *Universe* 6, ed. Terry Carr, Random House, 1976 (Carr and Silverberg traded this one back and forth for four years while they kept changing publishers; Carr won.) Also: *Best SF of the Year: 6th Annual Collection*, ed. Gardner Dozois, Dutton, 1977 *Best SF of the Year* #6, ed. Terry Carr, Holt 1977, Ballantine pb. *Der Gross Uhr*, Werner Jenschke, Heyne Verlag 1977 *Science Fiction A-Z*, ed. Asimov, Greenberg, Waugh, Houghton-Mifflin 1981 *Alternate Histories*, ed. Martin H Greenberg, Garland 1986 *Space Dogfights*, ed. Martin H Greenberg and Charles Waugh, Ace 1992 *Custer's Last Jump*, Ticonderoga Publications, 1996 (edition of 200 copies)
"Even the Children Know"	(o.t. "Where I Lodge a Little While . . .") with Steven Utley, *Famous Monsters of Filmland* #102, August 1973
"Men of Greywater Station"	with George R.R. Martin, *Amazing*, March 1976 Reprinted in George's second collection, *Songs of Stars and Shadows*, Pocket, 1977 and ever since, pb.
"Up Uranus!" (by 'F.D. Wyatt')	with Steven Utley and George Proctor, *Adam*, vol. 19 #1, June 1974

"Time and Variance"	with Buddy (Jake) Saunders and Steven Utley, *Vertex*, vol. 2 #3, June 1974
"Crab"	(o.t. "Rex and Regina") with Steven Utley, *Eternity SF*, May 1975
"Sic Transit . . ."	(o.t. "Willow Beeman") with Steven Utley, *Stellar #2*, ed. Judy Lynn del Rey, Ballantine 1976

(The above 4 stories were written on the *nocte mirablu* May 1-2, 1973. All our then-wives were at a baby shower. First Utley, Proctor and I wrote "Up Uranus!". Then Buddy, Steve and I wrote "Time and Variance"; then Steven and I wrote "Crab". The shower over, Proctor and Buddy went home. Steve and I sat down and got our Lafferty story out of our system. You tell kids things like that nowadays, and they won't believe you. My portion of the take for each was $5.00, $17.50, $26.66 and $70.00.)

"A Voice and Bitter Weeping"	with Buddy (Jake) Saunders, *Galaxy*, June 1973 (The first three chapters of what became *The Texas-Israeli War: 1999*, minus my part of the writing . . .) Also: *Best of Galaxy 2*, Award Books, 1974
"Unsleeping Beauty and the Beast"	*Lone Star Universe*, ed. Steven Utley & George Proctor, Heidelberg Press, Austin, 1976 (This was originally sold to *Galaxy*, who held it for two years without publishing or paying for it: I took it back.)
"Sun Up"	with A.A. (Al) Jackson IV, *Faster Than Light*, ed. Jack Dann & George Zebrowski, Harper & Row, 1976, pb Ace 1982
"Mary Margaret Road-Grader" HW	*Orbit 18*, ed. Damon Knight, Harper & Row 1976 Also: *Best SF of the Year: 6th Annual Collection*, ed. Gardner Dozois, Dutton, 1977
"Black as the Pit, From Pole to Pole"	with Steven Utley, *New Dimensions 7*, ed. Robert Silverberg, Harper & Row 1977 Also: *Year's Finest Fantasy*, ed. Terry Car, Berkley Putnam 1978 *Best SF of the Year: 7th Annual Collection*, ed. Gardner Dozois, Dutton, 1978
"Save A Place in the Lifeboat for Me" HW	*Nickelodeon #2*, September 1976
"Adventures of the Grinder's Whistle" (by 'Sir Edward Malone') NOTC	*Chacal #2*, September 1976
"Dr. Hudson's Secret Gorilla" HW	*Shayol #1*, November 1977 Also: *Rivals of King Kong*, ed. Michel Parry, Corgi UK 1977 (French, Turkish, German, Japanese editions since)
"*Der Untergang des Abendlandeschmenschen*" HW	*Chacal #1*, 1976 Also: *Mammoth Book of Vampires*, ed. Stephen Jones, Carrol & Graf, 1992 tp Comic-book adaptation, *System Shock*, forthcoming.
"Billy Big-Eyes"	The *Berkley Showcase*, ed. Victoria Schochet & John Silbersack, Berkley 1980 pb (Originally sold to *Biogenesis*, ed. George Zebrowski, Unity Press, 1978—the publisher went under.)
"C'thulablanca and other lost screen-plays: Moamrath in Hollywood"	*MidAmericon Program Book*, ed. Tom Reamy, 1976 Also: *Shaggy B.E.M. Stories: an anthology of Science Fiction Paraodies*, ed. Michael Resnick, Nolacon II, 1988.
"Horror, We Got" HW	*Shayol #3*, Summer 1979

"The Ugly Chickens" HW	*Universe 10*, ed. Terry Carr, Doubleday 1980 Also: *Dream's Edge*, ed. Terry Carr, Sierra Club 1980 *1981 Annual Year's Best SF*, ed. Donald Wollheim, DAW, 1981 *Best SF of the Year #10*, ed. Terry Carr, Pocket, 1981 *Best SF of the Year: 10th Annual Collection*, ed. Gardner Dozois, Dutton, 1981 *Nebula Award Stories, 16* ed. Jerry Pournelle, Holt 1981 *Best of Universe*, ed. Terry Carr, Doubleday 1982 *Hayakawa's SF Magazine* *Vokrug Sveta Magazine*, Moscow, June 1989 *Hayakawa's Best SF of the Eighties*, 1992 *The Legend Book of Science Fiction*, ed. Gardner Dozois, UK 1992
"Green Brother" HW	*Shayol #5*, April 1982 Also: *Dinosaurs!* ed. Dann & Dozois, Ace 1990 *Hayakawa's SF Magazine*, August 1993 *Weird Business*, graphic story hardback ed Joe Lansdale, Rick Klaw, Ben Ostrander, Mojo Press 1995—adaptation by Steven Utley, art by John Lucas.
"In the Shubbi Arms"	with Steven Utley, *Galaxy*, August 1980 (the last issue—we killed it.)
". . . the World, As We Know't" HW	*Shayol #6*, December 1982 Also: *The Norton Book of Science Fiction* ed. Ursula K Le Guin & Brian Attebery, Norton, 1993
"Flying Saucer Rock and Roll" AASM	*Omni*, January 1985 Also: *The Year's Best SF: Third Annual Collection*, ed. Gardner Dozois, Bluejay 1987 *13 Phantastichen Rockstories*, Fantasy Prods. Germany (never appeared) *Omni SF 7*, Zebra 1990 pb (Originally sold to Marta Randall's *New Dimensions 13*, 1980—Pocket Books pulled it *after* review copies went out.)
"Ike at the Mike" HW	*Omni*, June 1982 Also: *Best of Omni SF #1*, ed. Ellen Datlow, Zebra 1984 *13 Phantastichen Rockstories*, Fantasy Prods. Germany (never appeared) One-act play adaptation, Minicon 1991, by the Johnsons (I charged them $10 and gave my agent a buck.) *Elvis Rising*, ed. Kay Sloan & Constance Pierece, Avon 1993 tp *Mondo Elvis*, ed. Richard Peabody & Lucinda Ebersole, St. Martins Press 1994 tp
"God's Hooks" HW	*Universe 12*, ed. Terry Carr Doubleday 1982, hc, Zebra 1983 pb Also: *Bestiary!*, ed. Dann & Dozois, Ace 1986 *The One That Got Away*, ed. Greenberg & Waugh, Bonanza Books 1989 *Modern Classics of Fantasy*, ed. Gardner Dozois, St Martins 1996
"Man-Mountain Gentian" HW	*Omni*, September 1983 Also: *The Year's Best SF: First Annual Collection*, ed. Gardner Dozois, Bluejay 1984 *Omni Book of Science Fiction #5*, ed. Ellen Datlow, Zebra 1987 *Hayakawa's SF Magazine* (trans. Yoshio Kobayashi), April 1990
"Heirs of the Perisphere" HW	*Playboy*, July 1985 Also: *Nebula Awards 21*, ed. George Zebrowski, HBJ 1987 *SF Yearbook*, Moewig Verlag, Germany 1988

"Helpless, Helpless" AASM	*Light Years and Dark*, ed. Michael Bishop, Berkley 1984 tp
"What Makes Heironymous Run?" AASM	*Shayol #7*, (volume 3, no.1), 1985 (I killed it, too.)

"Fair Game"
AASM
	Afterlives, ed. Pamela Sargent & Ian Watson, Vintage, 1986
	tp. French, German, Italian editions.
	Also: *The Year's Best SF: 4th Annual Collection*, ed. Gardner
	          Dozois, St Martins 1987
	          Univers 1988, Editions Jai Lu Paris 1988, as "L'homme
	          sauvage"
	          Paragons, ed. Robin Wilson, St Martins

"The Lions Are Asleep This Night"
AASM
	Omni, August 1986
	Also: *1987 Annual World's Best SF*, ed. Donald Wollheim,
	          DAW 1987
	          Future Earths: Under African Skies, eds. M. Resnick &
	          G. Dozois, DAW 1993

"Night of the Cooters"
NOTC
	Omni, April 1987
	Also: *Year's Best SF: 5th Annual Collection*, ed. Dozois St
	          Martins 1988
	          Dramatization, audio cassette, radio play, Shockwave
	          Theater, Minneapolis MN, April 17, 1992 (adapt.
	          by Jerry Stearns)
	          Invaders! ed. Jack Dann & Gardner Dozois, Ace 1994
	          War of the Worlds: Global Dispatches, ed. K. Anderson,
	          Bantam Spectra 1996 hc

"Thirty Minutes Over Broadway!" NOTC	*Wild Cards 1* ed. George RR Martin, Bantam 1987 pb, SFBC hc, editions all over the world. Also: *Orbit Science Fiction Yearbook*, ed, David Garnett, Orbit 1987

"He-we-Await"
AASM
	original to *All About Strange Monsters Of The Recent Past*
	Also: *Asimov's SF Magazine*, Mid-December 1987
	          Year's Best Horror Stories (audio cassette) Decirum Prods
	          ed. Card & Greenberg (paid for, never produced) 1988.
	          Transcendental Tales from Asimov's, ed. Gardner Dozois,
	          Donning/Starblaze 1989

"French Scenes"
NOTC
	Synergy 2 ed. George Zebrowski HBJ 1988
	Also: *Orbit Science Fiction Yearbook #2*, ed. David
	          Garnett UK 1989
	          The Gonzo Tapes (me reading) Scorpio Prods. 1992

"Wild, Wild Horses" NOTC	*Omni*, June 1988 Also: *Horses!* ed. Jack Dann & Gardner Dozois, Ace 1994

"Do Ya, Do Ya Wanna Dance?"
NOTC
	Asimov's SF Magazine, August 1988
	Also: *The Year's Best SF: 6th Annual Collection*, ed. Gardner
	          Dozois, St Martins 1989
	          Asimov's SF Lite, ed. Gardner Dozois, Ace 1993

"Hoover's Men" NOTC	*Omni*, October 1988 Also: *Omni Visions I*, ed. Ellen Datlow, Omni Books 1993
"Passing of the Western" NOTC	*Razored Saddles*, ed. Joe Lansdale & Pat Lobrutto, Dark Harvest 1989 hc (& ltd), Avon pb 1990 Also: *The Gonzo Tapes* (me reading) Scorpio Prods. 1992
"Fin de Cyclé" NOTC	original to *Night Of The Cooters* Also: *Asimov's SF Magazine*, Mid-December 1991

"Why Did?"	*Omni*, April 1994
	(This was originally sold in 1989; I replaced it with "The Effects of Alienation" and pulled WD?, rewrote it and resold it in 1993—Thanks, Ellen.)

"The Effects of Alienation"	*Omni*, October 1992

"Occam's Ducks"	*Omni*, February 1995

"The Sawing Boys"	*Black Thorn, White Rose*, ed. Ellen Datlow & Terri Windling, William Morrow 1994 hc, Avon 1995 pb
	Also: *Year's Best SF: 12th Annual Collection*, ed. Gardner Dozois, St Martins 1995

"Household Words; Or, The Powers-That-Be"	*Amazing*, Winter 1994 (after 68 years, I killed it)
	Also: *Christmas Magic* ed. David Hartwell, Tor 1994 pb

"Flatfeet!"	*Asimov's*, February 1996

"El Castillo De La Perseverancia"	*Baltimore World Fantasy Convention Book*, October 1995
	Also: *Asimov's* (forthcoming)

"The Heart of Whitenesse"	*New Worlds*, White Wolf, August 1997

"Scientifiction"	original to *Going Home Again*, Eidolon Publications, 1997

"Mr. Goober's Show"	*Omni Online*, Spring 1998—the last issue (sorry, Ellen)

V. Selected non-fiction (mostly on writing)

"Tom, Tom!"	*San Diego Lightfoot Sue and Other Stories* by Tom Reamy, Earthlight Press, 1980, hc (& ltd) (not in the Berkley pb)

"Ideas That Will Kill Your Grandmother"	(Introduction) in *The Monadic Universe*, George Zebrowski, Ace, 1985 pb

"The Annotated Jetboy" NOTC	*Mile-High Futures*. November 1986
	Also: *Orbit Science Fiction Yearbook*, ed. David Garnett, Orbit 1987

"Walk a Kilometer in My Mocassins"	(afterword) *Them Bones*, Ziesing 1989 hc

"Take My Tough Job. Please."	(afterword) *A Dozen Tough Jobs*, in the Legend (UK) *Night of the Cooters* tp

"Iceberg, Goldberg, it's all the same to me"	(on my style in the writing of "Fair Game"), *Paragons*, ed. Robin Wilson, St Martins, April 1996

"Going Home Again"	(afterword to "You Could Go Home Again")

(This leaves out a couple of hundred book and movie reviews, articles, con bios, interviews of various geeks, and blowing off my bazoo. It's been 26 years.)

VI. Interviews

"Howard Waldrop"	Int. Darly Lane, William Vernon, David Carson. *The Sound of Wonder: Interviews from the SF Radio Show*. Vol 1. Oryx Press, Phoenix 1985

"Sittin' Around Drinkin' With Howard"	Int. Lawrence Person, Dwight Brown, Richard Simental. *Nova Express*, Vol 1. #3 1988

"Eye to Eye with Lewis Shiner & Howard Waldrop"	Int. Lew and Howard, *SF Eye* Vol. 1 #5 July 1989